DARK ALLIANCE

KINDRED SOULS

THE CHILDREN OF THE GODS
BOOK SIXTY-EIGHT

I. T. LUCAS

Published by Evening Star Press

EveningStarPress.com

ISBN-13: 978-1-957139-43-2

1

JADE

Jade strode into the infirmary and surveyed the cots that had been arranged in two neat rows in the center of the room. Several had been vacated, but many were still occupied.

Immortal Guardians watched over the injured, and for some reason, one of them was sitting on a chair next to her second-in-command's cot and was holding her hand. With his back turned to her, she couldn't see his face, but given the breadth of his shoulders, he wasn't a Kra-ell. The males of her species were much stronger than the immortals, but they were built slimmer.

Besides, no Kra-ell male would have shown Kagra such disrespect.

Mothers held their children's hands when they were small and frightened, but Kagra was a grown female and a warrior, and according to the liberators' doctor, she wasn't dying.

Liberators.

That still remained to be seen.

So far, the god who called himself Tom had done what he'd promised and more, freeing her people without a single unintended casualty, but Jade didn't trust gods, and that included the scions of the progressives who'd fought alongside the Kra-ell in the big rebellion back on the home planet.

Even when their intentions were noble, the gods' patronizing attitude toward the Kra-ell was offensive, and their ingrained belief in their own superiority was infuriating.

Jade had no choice but to accept Tom's help, and she still needed him to catch Igor so she could finally avenge her sons and the other males of her tribe. But once that was done, she wouldn't let the god or his immortal companions rule over her and her people.

Given that Tom was a powerful compeller on a par with Igor, that might not be easy to do, but she'd be damned if she lived another day enslaved to a male or a female, for that matter.

If Jade ever served anyone again, it would be by choice, and she would only serve a worthy Kra-ell ruler like the queen and her children, who Jade had sworn to protect.

Well, she'd only sworn to protect the queen, and she was no longer in the queen's service, but once a vow was made it never expired, and it didn't matter that she wasn't supposed to even know that the royal twins had been onboard the ship heading to Earth.

She'd failed to protect them just as she'd failed to protect her people, but there was no guilt associated with that failure because there had been nothing she could have done to prevent their ship's destruction, and without the mother ship, there was no way for her to locate the other escape pods.

In all likelihood, the twins and most of the other settlers hadn't survived.

Walking over to Kagra's cot, Jade grabbed a stool on the way and placed it next to the immortal's chair. "Does my second-in-command require a dedicated guard?"

It would have been better to conduct this conversation while she was looming over him, but the effect would have been lost if she had wobbled on her feet.

How long had she been awake?

It felt like she hadn't slept for days.

Given the copious quantity of Valstar's blood Jade had gorged on, she should have felt energized, but his blood must have been contaminated by the drug she'd put in his drink, and she could feel its effects. It was only by the Mother's grace that she'd functioned as well as she had and killed four of her sons' murderers. Kagra had dispatched two more, but she'd nearly lost her own life in the process.

Nevertheless, Jade wasn't going to get any sleep until Igor showed up. It was already eleven o'clock in the morning, and she was starting to get worried.

The immortal tilted his head and smiled. "I'm not here to guard your second. I'm checking on the female whose life I saved." He let go of Kagra's hand and offered his hand to Jade. "I'm Phinas."

So he was the one she'd heard about. The Guardian who'd leaped from fifty feet away and smashed his exoskeleton-reinforced fist into Gorven's head, killing him on impact.

From what Jade had been told, it was no small feat to perform such acrobatics with the tremendously heavy suit on.

The immortal was an impressive warrior.

"I'm Jade." Shaking what he'd offered, she dipped her head in respect. "Thank you for saving Kagra. I owe you a life-debt."

He held on to her hand. "You don't owe me anything because I didn't do it for you. But just out of curiosity, what does a life-debt mean?"

She liked his reply. But even though he hadn't saved Kagra for her, she still owed him a life-debt, and once it was offered, it had to be paid. "It means that I will defend you with my life if needed, and anything you ask of me is yours."

He arched a brow with a sly smile lifting one corner of his full lips. "Anything?"

Males.

No matter what species they were, they had only one thing on their minds. Although with how exhausted and dirty Jade was, the evidence of what she'd done crusting over her leathers, Phinas must be either teasing or just not very discriminating about the females he flirted with.

Then again, warriors pumped up from the battle were more lustful than usual.

To answer his question, though, anything meant anything.

Jade held his gaze. "That's what I said."

"What if I ask for your firstborn?"

She winced. "Too late for that. Both my first and second born sons are dead, slaughtered by Igor and his cronies."

The smile died on his lips, and he inclined his head. "My apologies. I didn't know."

"I thought that the Guardians had been briefed about the history of my tribe. Tom knew about my sons even before he got here, and so did Marcel, Sofia's boyfriend."

"I'm not a Guardian," Phinas said.

Was he a medic? That would explain why he was checking up on Kagra. Military medical staff received the same training as warriors, but if he were a medic, the doctor would have introduced him to her. Maybe he was in charge of munitions, or a tech?

"I was told that the one who'd saved Kagra's life wore an exoskeleton suit. Did the techs and medics get to wear them too?"

He smiled. "I'm not a tech or a medic. I'm first and fore- most a warrior, but I'm not a Guardian because I'm not part of the Guardian force. I'm part of a group of volunteers." He glanced at one of the Guardians standing watch over the injured. "What do you call me and my men?"

"Kalugal's men," the Guardian said.

"Who is Kalugal?" Jade asked.

When Phinas glanced at the Guardian again, the guy shook his head.

"I'm sorry." Phinas smiled apologetically. "I'm not at liberty to discuss the clan's inner politics with you. You will have to ask Yamanu or Bhathian. They are in charge of this operation."

"I thought Tom was in charge."

Phinas shrugged. "I can't comment on that either. All I can tell you is that Tom is not a Guardian."

"That makes sense." He was a god, but the other Kra-ell in the infirmary didn't know that. She couldn't say it out loud. "He wouldn't be part of the military arm of the clan. That would be left to the descendants."

"That's correct." Phinas flashed her a charming smile. "It's a pleasure to talk to a female who is a warrior herself and knows how those things work."

"I assume that your females are not fighters."

He shook his head. "That's another thing I cannot comment on. All I can say is that I haven't had the pleasure of chatting with a female fighter before." He turned his gaze to Kagra. "Watching her fight was awe-inspiring. I have been trained to fight with swords and daggers, and I recognize skill when I see it. She's incredible."

Pride filled Jade's chest. "Kagra is exceptional. That's why I chose her as my second-in-command. When she wakes up, she will be upset about letting herself get gutted."

Jade turned around to look for the doctor the Guardians had brought along. She found him on the other side of the large room, checking on one of the injured hybrids.

When he felt her gaze and lifted his head, she asked, "Why is Kagra sleeping so much? You said that she's healing well."

He smiled sheepishly. "I gave her sedatives so she'd sleep."

"I thought you were only giving her painkillers."

He put his hand in his coat pocket. "I gave her both. Sleeping will help her heal faster."

PHINAS

*P*hinas took the opportunity of Jade talking with Merlin to adjust himself and cross his legs.

From the moment he'd laid eyes on her, he'd been sporting a hard-on that he'd been desperately trying to hide. Despite being exhausted, dirty, and covered in dry blood splotches, the female was so damn hot that she made him as randy as a buck in heat.

It wasn't his style.

Phinas was coolheaded and reserved, and he'd never let females get under his skin.

Perhaps the spike in his libido had been caused by the testosterone still coursing through his blood after the battle, or maybe it was the fault of those damn tight leather pants and sheer mesh shirt of hers, or maybe the turn-on was the sword sheathed in a fancy scabbard and hung low on her hips, her swagger as she'd walked into the infirmary, the palpable power radiating from her, or all of the above.

Regardless of the trigger, though, the result was the same. He'd had trouble stringing two coherent thoughts together, as evidenced by his unfortunate blunder.

He'd heard that the males of Jade's tribe had been slaughtered by her captors, and he should have realized that she could have had a son or sons among them. But that was what happened when his mind was occupied by thoughts of stripping her naked.

He would leave the sword belt and boots on, though.

Jade was tall and slim, and her face was beautiful despite her huge eyes and hard expression. She had no breasts to speak of, but her ass was round and firm, just the way he liked it. However, the disturbing truth was that he was more turned on by her inner power than by her enticing feminine assets, and the fact that she was a ruthless killer only added to her dangerous allure.

That was strange as hell for him and entirely out of character.

Despite having been raised in Navuh's camp among males who believed that women were created to please and serve them and breed, Phinas wasn't a misogynist.

He'd never been one, but he was old, and in days past, women and men had very different roles in society.

Female warriors did not exist in his world, but he'd always believed that being mothers and caretakers was no less important, probably more so, but like other males of the time, he believed that motherhood was a female's ultimate calling and that women weren't suited for jobs that men performed.

Warriors took lives. Women created life and nurtured it.

After he'd been recruited by Kalugal and escaped Navuh's camp, Phinas had traveled to the US, where at the time women had been regarded with a little more respect, but not by much.

It had taken many more years for Western society to realize what had taken him mere weeks.

As soon as Phinas had been able to interact with women

who were free to express themselves, he'd realized that they were as smart and as capable as men, just not as physically strong and aggressive, and that was fine. Not every male was born to be a fighter, either.

That being said, he was a dominant male by nature, and he'd never thought he would be attracted to someone like Jade. A female who could hand him his ass.

"Are you going to sit here all day?" Jade asked him. "Aren't you needed somewhere else?"

He arched a brow. "Does it bother you that I'm watching over Kagra?"

What he'd really wanted to ask was whether she was jealous of the attention he was giving her injured second.

"Kagra has the doctor to watch over her." Jade hung her head and let out a breath. "I'm so damn tired, but that's not an excuse. You're not one of my subjects, and what you do with your time is none of my business."

"You're not one of my subjects either, but my advice to you is to get some sleep."

"I can't. There is still so much to do, and Kagra is out, so I have no one to assist me. But even if she was fine, I still wouldn't go to sleep. I'm waiting for Igor's capture so I can finally kill him."

As a vicious expression twisted her lips, her fangs made an appearance, and her eyes blazed with red light, but even that wasn't enough to diminish his attraction to her.

On the contrary, he wanted her even more.

"You won't be much good to anyone when you fall flat on your face. You need to sleep for at least a couple of hours to recharge." He waved his hand at the empty cot next to Kagra's. "You can lie down right over here, and I'll wake you up the moment Igor is captured."

"I also need to talk to my daughter." She looked at the cot longingly. "But maybe I should rest for a few minutes before

I do that." She pushed to her feet and walked to the other cot.

"How old is she?"

"Drova is sixteen." Jade unbuckled her sword belt. "She's a fine female with a lot of potential, but we don't get along, and I'm about to kill her father, which isn't going to help make things better between us." She put the sword under the cot and lay down with her boots on.

He had a feeling that Jade wouldn't have shared that information if she wasn't so tired, which made her less guarded.

It probably wasn't a secret that Igor was the father of her daughter, but it wasn't the kind of thing a woman told a stranger she'd just met.

The murderer of her sons had forced her to breed with him.

Jade must be forged from titanium alloy.

"Is she close to her father?" Phinas asked.

Jade snorted. "No one is close to Igor. He's a sociopath. But he's still her father." She closed her eyes. "Maybe I should kill him first and talk to her later?"

She turned on her side, giving him a great view of her gorgeous ass. "I'm just going to rest for a few minutes."

"You should rest for longer than that. I'll watch over you," he said with such conviction that she turned around and looked at him.

"Thank you. But that won't be necessary." Jade waved her hand at the Guardians. "I'm sure they can protect me if needed."

He doubted she would rely on them to defend her. Her sword was right there under her cot, reachable in a split second.

"I'm not going anywhere." He crossed his arms over his chest.

"Suit yourself." She turned around again.

Phinas wanted to learn more about Jade, to find out what kind of hellfire had forged such a tough female, but it would have to wait until after she'd exacted revenge for the slaughter of the males of her tribe and the subjugation of its females.

KIAN

he last person Kian had expected to walk into the war room at one o'clock in the morning was his mother.

He pushed to his feet, walked over to her, and leaned to kiss her cheek. "Did you have trouble sleeping, Mother?"

A goddess only needed a few hours of sleep, but his mother was an early riser, and she enjoyed walking outside when the sun was just cresting the horizon. Her eyes were too sensitive for the harsh Southern California sun, even in the winter, and she liked being able to forgo the goggle-like sunglasses that she needed to wear other times when getting out of the house.

"I brought you coffee and pastries from the vending machines." She motioned for her butler to come in.

"Good evening, Master Kian." The Odu put the tray with the coffees and the wrapped pastries on the conference table, bowed, and headed out the door.

Kian pulled out a chair for her. "You still haven't told me why you are up and about so late."

She shrugged one delicate shoulder. "I could not sleep,

and I did not want to call you in case you were in the midst of directing the battle, and I didn't want to call the house and wake Syssi up either. So I came to see if you were still here and whether the evil Igor was captured." She smiled. "If I had known that you were all alone in here, I would have come to keep you company earlier."

She could've texted him, but she just hadn't wanted to give him a chance to tell her not to come.

After he'd told her about Jade's promise to Toven, Annani probably couldn't contain her curiosity. She wanted to hear what Jade had told Toven about the gods, the Kra-ell, and their home planet.

Kian took one of the paper cups and removed the lid. "Turner and Onegus went home to shower and change and catch a couple of hours of sleep, but they are coming back."

"You should have done the same."

"Until Igor is caught, someone needs to be in the war room at all times. Roni is in the lab, monitoring Igor's bank accounts, and I'm getting updates from the compound."

"How is Toven doing?" she asked.

"He and Mia worked all night to free everyone from Igor's compulsion, and last I heard, they were asleep on the couch in the common room in the human section. William removed everyone's collars, and he's resting as well. The Guardians are taking turns watching the purebloods and the hybrids, and Merlin is taking care of the injured. Did I cover everyone?"

"You didn't mention Marcel and Sofia."

Kian smiled. His mother was well-informed, and she had everyone cataloged in her brain. He could throw at her the name of any clan member, and she would know everything about them, down to their favorite foods and where they had visited on their last vacation.

Remembering that many details about so many people

was a truly remarkable ability, but what was even more remarkable was how much she cared about each member of her clan.

"They are also in the human quarters, helping calm people down."

"How is Jade?"

"The last I heard, she took a nap on one of the cots in the infirmary. Her second-in-command was badly injured. Merlin patched her up, and she's going to be fine."

He'd already told her that there were no casualties on their side and that on the Kra-ell side, only Igor's inner circle cronies had been killed by Jade and Kagra, and several pure-bloods and hybrids were injured.

Annani smoothed the folds of her gown, readjusting it over her knees. "You know what I really want to know. You were too busy before, but this seems like a quiet time, and you can spare a few minutes to tell me what Jade shared with Toven about the gods."

Kian winced. "You're not going to like what I tell you."

"I want to hear it anyway."

"The gods weren't nice people, and those who they sent to Earth were rebels, banished here for their part in a rebellion."

Annani nodded solemnly. "I had a feeling it was something like that. Otherwise, they would not have been abandoned on Earth with no ability to return home or even communicate with their families."

"There is one part that you're going to love, though. You are most likely the granddaughter of the gods' king. Some of the rebels were his own children, and he sent them to Earth along with the others. Given that Ahn, Ekin, and Athor were all leaders of the gods' local community, each in their respective field of authority, they were no doubt royalty."

Annani smiled. "I had a feeling about that as well. My

father wore the mantle of leadership with such inborn grace and dignity, but he never called himself king. Nevertheless, my mother insisted that I behave like a princess." She smoothed her skirt again even though it didn't need it. "What was the rebellion about?"

"The Kra-ell. Turns out that the Kra-ell were the gods' first attempt at creating a hybrid creature to serve them. But the old gods were not as progressive as your father and his siblings. They treated the Kra-ell like slaves. The young gods did not approve of the way the Kra-ell were being treated or rather mistreated. First, they demanded better conditions for the Kra-ell, and when that was achieved, they demanded equal rights and access to education, but the king and his council refused." Kian paused to unwrap a pastry. "Jade said that hundreds of generations passed between the stages of the Kra-ell emancipation, so it wasn't like those demands were made one right after the other."

"What happened during the rebellion?" Annani asked.

"The Kra-ell were stronger physically, which was probably by design because they were meant to be laborers, and back then, the gods didn't include susceptibility to mind manipulation in their genetic enhancements, so they couldn't defend themselves by seizing the Kra-ell minds. The gods had superior weapons, and their underground cities were fortified, but the Kra-ell had the numbers. The king mobilized the Odus, who were originally designed to be house servants, and they were converted to be defenders of the gods against the Kra-ell. But even with the Odus, the gods couldn't win, and the casualties on both sides were staggering. The king of the gods and the queen of the Kra-ell negotiated a peace treaty, and part of it was the decommissioning of the Odus." He leaned back and took a sip from his coffee. "In my opinion, the only reason for the king of the gods to agree to decommission the Odus was fear of them being used against him in another rebellion. Otherwise, it makes no sense for the gods to give up their best defensive weapon."

Annani tilted her head. "It might not be their best weapon anymore. Once the rebellion was over, they probably developed something better than the Odus and made sure that it could not fall into the wrong hands, or what they considered rebel hands."

"I agree."

They were probably both right. Kian wasn't much of a politician, but he knew how they operated, especially those who had been in power for too long and had no intentions of losing their seat to another. After the king decommissioned the Odus, most likely with a lot of fanfare and publicity for the consumption of his public, he must have started developing an alternative in secret. There was no way he'd left himself exposed to the possibility of another rebellion.

The next time someone dared to oppose him, he would have had a brutal and efficient response at the ready, one that was entirely under his control.

In fact, with the genetic manipulation mastery of the gods, he'd probably ordered another species to be altered for that purpose—creatures who were as strong as the Kra-ell but susceptible to mind manipulation and easy to destroy.

Was Kian letting his imagination run away from him?

Maybe.

But as it'd been proven time and again, reality was stranger than fiction.

"Was that the full version or a summary of what Jade had told Toven?" Annani asked. "So many questions remain unanswered."

"It was a summary, but Jade's full version was far from complete either. There are many things she probably doesn't know, and her spin is obviously tilted in the Kra-ell's favor. After Igor is apprehended and Jade takes charge of her community, we will ask her to tell us more."

TOVEN

"*I*'m worried." Toven ran his fingers through his hair. "Igor should have called by now."

It was almost two o'clock in the afternoon, and it was becoming clear that Igor was onto them. There was still a chance that he was on his way, maybe flying back from Moscow or some other distant location, but the fact that he hadn't tried to call Valstar or anyone else was telling.

That was why Toven had called the meeting. He, William, and the head guardians had assembled in the human quarters' common room, with Kian, Onegus, and Turner participating in the meeting via the tablet propped on the coffee table.

The humans stayed away, giving them the privacy they needed, and Yamanu had encased them in a bubble of silence to make sure no one could listen in on them.

Bhathian nodded. "What really bothers me is that when we turned the compound's communications back on, there weren't any missed calls from him in the logs."

As all eyes turned to William, he rubbed a finger over the bridge of his nose as if he was pushing his glasses up, except he wasn't wearing any. "I don't know what to tell you. I double checked all the transmissions, and everything is working fine. At six o'clock in the morning, we switched on the recorded footage and set it to transmit normal Monday morning activity. He shouldn't have noticed anything amiss unless he spent hours watching and noticed that it was going on a loop."

"Did he try to detonate the explosives?" Kian asked.

William shook his head. "He didn't. Neither did he attempt to detonate the collars. I checked."

"What now?" Toven asked. "Until Igor is caught, we have to keep the purebloods and the hybrids on lockdown. How much longer do we wait?"

"We can't wait," Turner said. "It's true that Igor has only one pureblood and two hybrids with him, but he could use his compulsion power to bring the Russian Army to storm the compound or even their air force to bomb the place, although I doubt he would go that far. I assume that he wants his people back alive."

"I'm not so sure," Kian said. "If he had the entire place rigged, he has no qualms about bombing the compound and killing everyone."

Turner shook his head. "He can't do that. I think the rigging was meant as a last-stand kind of thing, and he didn't intend to implement it unless all hope was lost. According to what Jade told us, it seems that Igor doesn't know where to find more of the surviving Kra-ell, and without his people, he has nothing. He needs the females to keep breeding more Kra-ell, and he even needs some of the males to provide the necessary genetic variety. He would do anything to get his people back, or at least some of them."

Yamanu stretched his long legs in front of him. "I still don't get how he figured out what was going on here. Even if he noticed something was off with what the hidden cameras were transmitting, he couldn't have guessed that a stronger compeller took over his people, because he couldn't possibly have known about Toven. Igor would have assumed that he could just walk back in and compel everyone to his will."

"I'm not sure about that," Toven said. "Jade knew that the gods' king exiled several of his children to Earth, and the king was a powerful compeller. It's not such a huge leap to assume that some of them or their descendants possess the ability. The fact that they couldn't find us didn't mean that we were gone."

"It's also possible that there are strong compellers among the other survivors," Turner said. "Jade didn't mention it, but then she didn't tell us much at all. It's also possible that once Igor suspected something, he gained access to satellite footage of the area. The explosions in the middle of the night would have registered clearly despite the heavy foliage. Yamanu's enormous silencing bubble hid the blasts from the humans in the area, but it could not have hidden them from satellites and other monitoring equipment. If the Russians measure seismic activity in the area, the explosions would have registered on that equipment as well."

"Where is Jade?" Kian asked. "Perhaps she has some ideas."

"Asleep," Bhathian said. "She went to visit her second-in-command in the infirmary and fell asleep on one of the cots. Phinas is watching over her."

"You should wake her up," Turner said. "And you should also interrogate Valstar again. He probably knows Igor better than Jade does."

"I should do that." Toven pushed to his feet. "When I first interrogated him, I asked questions that pertained to catching Igor upon his return. The guy is used to living under a powerful compeller, so he knows all the tricks of how to avoid answering questions unless they are very precisely phrased, and I might not have asked the right ones."

"Are you going to take Mia to him?" Kian asked.

"She's asleep, and I don't need her now that Valstar is no longer under Igor's compulsion." Toven chuckled. "I'm glad that we didn't allow Jade to kill him. He might know a lot of things that she doesn't, and it would be interesting to compare their versions of history."

"By the way," Bhathian said. "Did Igor try to call Safe Haven? He must have suspected that there was a connection."

"All incoming calls are filtered through the translating software," Onegus said. "Even if he tried to get to Emmett, he wouldn't have been able to get any information out of him. Besides, it's the middle of the night there. All he would have gotten was the answering machine."

"True," Turner said. "Leon is on high alert. He will let us know if Igor tries to contact Emmett or Sofia."

JADE

*J*ade knew she was dreaming, but it didn't make her anguish any less torturous. For over two decades, she'd been plagued by the nightmare of her people being murdered while she and the other females watched, helpless to do anything to stop the slaughter.

Igor had frozen everyone with one command, making it easy for his cronies to plow through the males of her tribe as if they were stalks of grain. The horror in their eyes was as fresh in her mind today as it had been back then. Unable to move a muscle, the males watched their sons and brothers die moments before their own end had come.

Something had broken inside her that day, and ever since, the only thing keeping her from falling apart was rage and the need for revenge.

Her males hadn't fallen in battle or died in a duel. They had been denied an honorable death and therefore hadn't earned a place in the fields of the brave.

Igor had not only robbed them of their corporeal lives, but he had also destroyed their eternity on the other side of the veil. Back home, only the worst of criminals had been executed without being given the option to fight to win their freedom or die honorably, but the only crime her males had ever committed was having been born male.

Had the Mother shown them mercy and allowed them to enter the fields of the brave? They would have fought if they could. Was it fair to deny them access through no fault of their own?

"Please," Jade begged the deity of her people for the thousandth time. "Please."

"Jade." A hand shook her shoulder. "Wake up."

She bolted up, nearly toppling over the side of the flimsy cot. Nevertheless, her hand shot up to grip the throat of the male standing over her.

"Whoa." He caught her wrist and applied pressure. "It's me, Phinas. Let go."

It took a split second for the memory of him to resurface, and as it did, she released him immediately. "Never do that again," she hissed through elongated fangs.

"Noted." He rubbed his neck. "Were you having a nightmare?"

There was no shame in having nightmares about the slaughter of her people. Being tough didn't mean being heartless or indifferent. "Yes." She reached for the sword under the cot. "How long was I asleep?"

"Almost three hours," Kagra said from behind Phinas.

Jade swallowed a vile curse. "Was Igor caught?"

"No." Phinas moved aside. "I have a feeling he's onto us."

Jade's fangs throbbed with the thirst for Igor's blood. "If he doesn't show up, I will hunt him to the ends of the earth and any other world he might escape to." She buckled the sword belt around her hips. "I will bleed him to death very slowly and very painfully."

Phinas grinned. "I shouldn't say what I'm about to, but I can't help it. You're even hotter when you're vicious."

Males.

Phinas had no sense of self-preservation. She'd had him by the throat only moments ago, and he'd felt the power of her grip. She could've snapped his neck with ease.

The guy was either stupidly reckless or just as stupidly brave.

Nevertheless, his impudence was refreshing.

No one had ever dared speak to her like that, not even Igor.

Except with Igor, it wasn't because he respected or feared her. He just lacked a sense of humor and was too full of himself to engage in any sort of banter or mischief.

Phinas didn't fear her either, but he didn't take himself too seriously, and he had a sense of humor.

Jade glanced down at her blood-encrusted leathers. "Since I'm always vicious, my level of hotness doesn't change."

His grin widened. "I agree. It's a solid ten."

Stifling the urge to roll her eyes, she crouched next to Kagra. "How are you feeling?"

"Mad as hell. As soon as I can stand, I want us to resume training. This would never have happened to you."

"Everyone makes mistakes." Jade put her hand on Kagra's shoulder. "Get well first, and then we will resume training." She turned her head to look at the clan's doctor. "When can she leave?"

He walked over and spoke in a hushed voice. "I stitched her up, but I don't know how fast her inner wounds are healing. Your infirmary doesn't have the equipment to take a look inside of her. You probably have more experience in that than me."

Except for her and Kagra, no one else knew that their liberators were the descendants of gods, so Merlin couldn't talk about it within earshot of the other injured Kra-ell, and she couldn't ask him about it either. It made sense though, that immortals healed faster than them.

Thanks to their enhanced genetics, gods healed so fast that it almost seemed like magic. Their immortal descendants had probably inherited that trait, at least to some degree.

Jade nodded to communicate her understanding. "Kagra should be okay to walk to the bathroom and back, but she needs to rest for another day or two. It doesn't have to be in the infirmary, though. She can convalesce in her room."

"I'd rather keep an eye on her." Merlin looked at Phinas. "But she doesn't need a personal nurse. I'm sure you have better things to do than hang around here."

"I do." Phinas cast Kagra a brief smile before returning his gaze to Jade. "I just wanted to make sure that she was okay."

"I owe you a life—" Kagra started.

Jade snapped her hand faster than she did when she grabbed Phinas's throat and silenced Kagra with a hand on her mouth. "I've already pledged a life-debt to Phinas." She removed her hand. "You don't have to pledge yours as well."

Kagra frowned. "Why did you do that? It's my debt to pay."

"Your life is precious to me, and I'm grateful to Phinas for saving you. Enough said."

Given Kagra's sour expression, there was much more she wanted to say on the subject, but she obeyed Jade's command. "Thank you, Prime." She didn't even try to hide the note of sarcasm in her tone.

"Get some rest." Jade turned to glare at Phinas. "You should have woken me up a long time ago."

"I should have, but I didn't want to. You needed the rest."

She got in his face. "Next time, if there is a next time, I will not trust your promises."

"Ouch."

6

PHINAS

*P*hinas couldn't wipe the stupid grin off his face as he left the infirmary, and it stayed there while he searched for a secluded spot to call Kalugal.

It had been almost comical the way Jade had slapped her hand over Kagra's mouth to stop her from pledging a life-debt to him, and if that wasn't enough, she'd commanded her second to say nothing more on the subject.

Was he kidding himself by thinking that Jade wanted to owe him so he could collect on the debt?

And why the hell did he want her even more after her vicious show of fangs and red eyes?

She'd looked like a sexy demon. Dangerous, deadly, exciting.

Perhaps he had a subconscious death wish? Was that the source of his insane attraction to the Kra-ell leader?

Her commanding personality and palpable aggression weren't the only things that drew him to her, though.

Despite her hard-as-nails attitude, he'd sensed the vulnerability ever-present right under the tough façade. Jade was broken on the inside, and the glue holding the pieces together was her formidable will and her devotion to her people.

He respected that.

He understood that.

He could empathize with that.

Phinas had lost people he'd cared for, and he'd killed people on orders that he should have disobeyed, but his broken pieces were held together by a different bond.

While Jade carried the burden of her losses and her obligations on her shoulders and tried to keep herself from falling apart on her own, Phinas had Kalugal and the promise of better tomorrows helping him hold together the jagged shards of his soul.

When he found a quiet spot between two buildings, he leaned against a wall and pulled out his phone.

"Hello, Phinas," Kalugal answered. "Any news on Igor?"

"As you expected, he didn't show up."

Kalugal chuckled. "When you told me that there were no missed calls from him, I knew that he found out somehow. What are they planning to do next?"

"I don't know. There was a meeting in the human quarters, but I wasn't invited."

Kalugal huffed out a breath. "Kian can be insufferable. He accepted my help with open arms, but he still keeps things close to his chest and doesn't share. Did you manage to befriend the female you saved?"

Phinas grinned. "I did better than that. I befriended the notorious Jade. In her gratitude for saving her second-in-command, she swore a life-debt to me, which means that I can ask anything I want of her, and she's obligated to provide it."

His boss uttered a whistle. "I'm impressed. That's better than anything I was hoping to achieve. You know what I want."

Kalugal wanted information about the Kra-ell, and, if possible, cooperation, but Phinas wanted more than that.

"I do, but I need to wait for an opportune time. As you can imagine, she has her hands full, so it's not like I can sit her down for a chat."

"Naturally. I'll talk with Kian and volunteer your services for the foreseeable future. Once the Guardians leave, you will have her all to yourself."

"They are not going to leave so soon. Not with Igor still at large. Toven has to stay to ensure their safety."

"Right. But they can't stay forever, and they need someone to keep an eye on Jade to ensure that she's not mistreating the humans. You know how important that is to Kian and Annani. Since they can't spare more than one or two Guardians, who will be very unhappy to be stuck in freezing Karelia, Kian will be very happy when I offer for you to stay for a bit longer. I hope you don't mind."

"I can't say that I'm enjoying the weather out here, but it is beautiful and very serene." He chuckled. "That is when the clan is not blowing things up. But I wouldn't stay just to enjoy the forest and the numerous rivers and lakes. My only motivation is getting close to Jade, and not just because you asked me to do that."

"Other than the life-debt, how friendly did you get with her?"

"Very friendly, and I plan on getting much friendlier still."

Kalugal cleared his throat. "I appreciate your loyalty and your willingness to do anything I ask of you, but you have to know that I would never expect you to get that friendly with a female who repulses you."

A laugh bubbled up Phinas's throat. "Jade is the hottest female I've ever laid eyes on, and I can't wait to lay more than just my gaze on her. She's gorgeous, has a body to kill for, and she's powerful, honorable, and vicious like a viper."

He stopped himself before adding that he'd been hard from the moment she'd walked into the infirmary and sat down next to him. Rufsur had no problem talking like that with Kalugal, but Phinas had always opted to keep a professional distance out of respect for the male who had saved his life in more ways than one.

For a long moment, Kalugal didn't say anything, and then he cleared his throat again. "If you were repulsed by Aliya's occasional need for blood, how are you going to tolerate a female who can't subsist on anything else?"

"I've never said that Aliya's need for blood repulsed me. What made you think that?"

"You stopped seeing her after you took her hunting, so the rumor was that you were disgusted by her being a bloodsucker."

Phinas snorted. "Don't believe all the rumors you hear. That wasn't the reason I disengaged."

"Was it because of Vrog? Since when did you concede a competition to allow a rival to win?"

"Never. I just realized that Aliya wasn't for me. I was attracted to her for many reasons. She's a beautiful girl who is also extremely strong, physically and mentally. But during our hunt together, I got to know her better, and I discovered that emotionally, she's just a girl, young and inexperienced. Vrog loves being a teacher. I don't. I prefer older women who know what they want and how they want it."

7

JADE

*J*ade needed a shower and a change of clothes, not just because hers were filthy but also because they were unsuitable for winter in Karelia and uncomfortable. Except, the worry churning in her gut propelled her toward the human quarters where she'd been told she could find Tom.

She found him walking toward her, looking rested and wearing clean clothes.

Where had he gotten them?

They must have left clothing along with the provisions outside the compound and had gotten them after the dust had settled and everything had been taken care of. She'd seen the Guardians eating field rations, and they couldn't have carried them inside the exoskeletons.

"Good morning." He stopped in front of her. "Did you have a nice nap?"

Was he insinuating that she was a weakling who had taken time to rest while the rest of them had kept working to trap Igor?

"Did you? When I left you earlier, you and your mate were asleep on the couch."

He leaned closer and whispered in her ear. "I only need two to three hours of sleep a night, but my mate needs a little more. What are your sleep requirements?"

Show-off.

The gods prided themselves on how little sleep their bodies needed to keep operating at an optimal level, and she had no doubt that it was one of the first things they had genetically modified. That allowed them to do more each day, either learning or continuing to create miraculous enhancements for themselves.

"I need a little more. What are you going to do about Igor? By now, it's obvious that he knows."

Tom's expression was severe, but he didn't look too worried. "He might still come. The only indication we have to the contrary is that he hasn't called, which seems out of character for him."

"It is. He would have checked with Valstar first thing in the morning. Is it possible that he noticed something was off about the camera feeds?"

"If he watched carefully over an extended period of time, he might have noticed the loop, but even a paranoid guy like him is not likely to do that. He's too busy for that."

"He could have assigned one of the hybrids to do that. What about Veskar? Did Igor try to call him?"

Tom shook his head. "Even if he did, he wouldn't have been able to get any information out of Emmett. All of Safe Haven's communications are routed through a voice translator. It works similarly to the earpieces I showed you."

In all the commotion, she'd forgotten about the devices, but she would need them when the time arrived to end Igor.

"Can I have a pair?"

"With Igor gone, you don't need them, and I don't want you to block my compulsion."

Jade bristled. "You have nothing to fear from me. I owe you, and I will never turn against you unless you go back on your word to me. But what if Igor comes back and manages to overtake the Guardians waiting for him in the tunnel? Are you sure he can't compel you? And even if he can't, you might not be able to compel him either, and he can wrestle control from you over everyone here, including your Guardians. With their unwilling help, he can end even you."

"We all have earpieces." He pulled a pair from his pocket and showed them to her. "But your point is valid. I'll ask William to provide you and Kagra with a pair each."

"Thank you."

"How is Kagra doing?" he asked.

"She's better. She woke up before I left."

"Good." Tom put the earpieces back in his pocket. "I'm on my way to see Valstar. I might not have asked all the right questions when I interrogated him earlier. Maybe he'll have some valuable insight as to what Igor's next move will be, and he also might know how Igor found out about what happened to his compound."

Her fangs itched as they elongated into her mouth.

"I'll come with you."

"That's not a good idea. I need him calm, which he won't be if you show up with murder in your eyes." He gave her a crooked smile.

"Does it matter if he's calm or not?"

"Compulsion works better if the compelled is not agitated or terrified."

It was one of those 'aha' moments Jade occasionally experienced. "That explains so much. I always wondered why Igor appeared so calm and collected and why he never raised his voice or showed anger. I thought that he just had no feelings whatsoever, but he did it for his compulsion to work better."

Tom shrugged. "Maybe it's the other way around, and his compulsion worked better because he didn't show emotion. Were you terrified of him?"

She nodded. "Compulsion is a terrible weapon in the wrong hands. I would never freeze opponents so I could kill them with ease. It's not only incredibly cruel but also dishonorable."

Tom's eyes softened. "Is that what he did to your people?"

"Yes. And he will pay for it." She took a deep breath. "You might need my input when you question Valstar. I can control myself when I must, and I'm a very good actress. I have a lot of practice."

"I believe you. But I'd rather not have you there."

"Can you at least get me a phone so you can call me?"

"We don't have any spares with us, but we might have spare earpieces, and they are also good for communicating with my people and me." He pulled out his phone and typed on the screen.

Obviously, he didn't trust her with a phone that she could use to communicate with the outside world, but who would she call?

"William says that he can get them ready for you in fifteen minutes. He'll meet you in the common room of the human quarters."

"Thank you." She looked down at her bloodied leathers. "I planned on going to see my people, but fifteen minutes is not long enough for that. Tell William that I'll be there."

She would use the time to shower and change.

Tom typed on his phone some more. "If I have any questions for you while I'm questioning Valstar, I'll contact you via the earpieces."

8

TOVEN

*T*oven entered Valstar's suite of rooms expecting the prisoner to be chained to a chair. Instead, he found him chained to the bed and looking like a corpse.

He wasn't faking it, either. His skin was gray, and there were dark hollows under his eyes and cheekbones. Paired with the bug-like eyes, Valstar wasn't a pretty sight.

"He looks bad," Toven told the Guardian watching Igor's second-in-command. "What's wrong with him?"

"I need to feed," Valstar said, sounding feeble. "Jade drained me multiple times."

"Yeah," the Guardian confirmed. "He's been saying it over and over again, but where am I going to get him blood?"

Good question. The purebloods held in the basement were probably hungry as well.

Toven turned to the prisoner. "How can we feed you? Do you have blood stored in a freezer somewhere?"

Valstar shook his head. "I know that you will not let me hunt, so the only other option is a farm animal. Take me to them."

"I'm not letting you out of this room." He glanced at the Guardian. "Ask for an animal to be brought here."

The Guardian shook his head but tapped his earpiece anyway and communicated the request.

"They are going to ask the humans tending to the animals," he said.

Several long minutes passed until he got a response. "They can bring up a goat."

Valstar licked his lips. "That would do. Have them bring two. I'm starving, and I don't want to drain the animal."

It was strange that a male who had no qualms about slaughtering the males of his kind had compassion for animals, but perhaps it wasn't about that. The Kra-ell didn't kill the animals that provided them with nourishment. It was considered a waste, and in light of what Jade had told him, it made sense. After the gods had infected the animals on their planet with a virus, the Kra-ell had experienced centuries of lack and near starvation. Waste of food would be abhorrent to them, but the culling of excessive mouths who needed to be fed would not.

"Do as he asks." Toven pulled a chair next to the bed.

"Did you catch him?" Valstar asked.

There was no need to elaborate as to who he meant.

"No."

Valstar's big eyes widened even more. "He knows. You need to get everyone out of here."

"We disabled the explosives. He can't detonate them."

"He will come with an army, or he will send a fighter jet to bomb the compound. If he can't take his people back, he would rather destroy them than let them fall into enemy hands."

"Even his own daughter?"

Valstar snorted. "Igor cares only about power. He doesn't care about anyone, including his daughter."

"How about you? Do you care?"

Perhaps it wasn't the most important question to ask the male right now, but Toven was curious. The compulsion he imbued his tone with guaranteed an honest answer.

Valstar closed his eyes and let out a breath. "For too many years, I was only allowed to feel what Igor wanted me to feel, which was nothing. I was to serve him loyally and follow his orders. I don't know who I am anymore, let alone who I care for. But I know that I don't want my daughter and my sons to die today. Nor do I want any of the others to die just because Igor considers them his personal property."

Toven made a mental note to tell Jade what Valstar had said, but he doubted it would change her mind about killing the guy.

"I don't think he would destroy everyone in the compound before exhausting every other alternative first. He is nothing without his people. Besides, there is no reason to panic. Perhaps he's just delayed."

Valstar closed his eyes. "He knows."

"How? There were no missed calls from him, so he didn't even know that the communications were down for half the night, and he didn't try to call you or anyone else."

"That's how I know that he knows." Valstar opened his eyes and turned his head toward Toven. "He didn't have to call to know that the communications were down. He would have discovered that when he tried to access the feed from the surveillance cameras and couldn't get in. I hoped that he would assume a malfunction and try again after they were restored, but the fact that he hasn't called me yet indicates that he knows."

"He can suspect. But he has no way of knowing. He wouldn't attack before finding out what happened."

Valstar shook his head as much as the chains allowed him. "Igor knows several powerful oligarchs, and at least one that

I know of has access to the Russian satellite network. As soon as Igor suspected something was wrong, he would have compelled the oligarch to give him access to the network. Last night's explosions would have been clearly visible. His first assumption would have been an attack by the Russian military, but it would have taken him only a few minutes to find out that they were not involved. His next assumption would have been that we had been attacked by other Kra-ell who had somehow found out about us." Valstar's pale grayish skin turned even grayer. "To Igor, the compound falling into the hands of another group of Kra-ell is even worse than it falling to the gods."

Toven should have known that Valstar had guessed who he was.

Jade had taken one look at him and had known right away, but he had still hoped that the story they had spread about being human with enhanced abilities and superior weaponry would hold.

Still, he didn't confirm or deny it. Instead, he asked, "Why is that?"

Valstar closed his eyes. "That would take a long time to explain, and we don't have time. Not if you want to keep everyone alive."

Toven still didn't think that Valstar's panic was justified.

After spending many decades with a powerful compeller, the guy must have figured out every possible trick and loophole to manipulate around the compulsion. He might have convinced himself that the danger was imminent just so he could communicate it to Toven and make him do something hasty.

Except, why would he want them to evacuate the compound? Did he fear for himself and his children, or did he fear for Igor?

9

JADE

"So I just tap here?" Jade asked.

William leaned closer to look at her ear. "You need to push them further in. If the seal is not tight, the compulsion still might reach you."

"Got it."

It was an uncomfortable sensation, but it was well worth it if it protected her from compulsion, whether Igor's or Tom's.

Not that she would wear both of the devices at once in the god's presence. It wasn't what they had agreed on.

She tapped on the earpiece. "Did you manage to isolate the sound waves responsible for compulsion?"

"Not yet. Our doctors are busy with other things, but perhaps my mate will be able to dedicate some time to research this after she's done with the project she's working on now."

"What does she do?"

William opened his mouth, closed it, and opened it again. "I'd better not say. The project she's working on is top secret, and it's very important. That's why she couldn't come with me, and I miss her very much." He pulled out his phone and showed Jade the screen saver. "That's the love of my life. Kaia."

William's mate was a pretty blond girl with big red glasses and smart blue eyes who looked very young, but then it was hard to tell the age of those immortals. In that regard, they were like the gods whose genes they'd inherited.

Even an ancient god could look like a twenty-year-old.

"Your mate is beautiful, and she looks smart."

"She is." William put the phone in his pocket. "The Fates found the perfect mate for me, and I thank them every day for the incredible boon they've bestowed on me." He rubbed the bridge of his nose. "I was a lonely man before Kaia came into my life, and my existence was gray. Now I live in full color."

Something about that statement tugged at her heart.

Jade was lonely, and her world was gray, and not just because there was little sunlight in Karelia in the winter.

Even when she'd had a whole tribe surrounding her, she'd been lonely. Leadership came with a steep cost, and the rewards were probably not worth it, but to refuse the call and not accept the mantle when one was uniquely suited to carry it was dishonorable.

Leadership was the duty of those who were capable and strong enough to provide it.

She tapped again to disconnect. "Should I have Tom try to compel me to make sure that they work?"

"They work." William squared his shoulders. "I had them all tested before loading them on the plane."

She was tempted to ask him where he'd boarded that plane, and she knew he would probably tell her because he wasn't a Guardian, but it was none of her business. If Tom didn't want her to know, she didn't need to.

"Thank you."

"No problem." William handed her another pair. "Let me know if Kagra needs me to show her how to use them."

"I can show her. She doesn't need to bother you."

He nodded. "Very well. I'll see you later."

Jade left one device in her ear, put the other in one of the many pockets of her fatigues, and Kagra's pair in another, and headed to the basement of the office building where her people were held.

The Guardian on duty gave her a nod as he opened the door for her. "Good luck."

She arched a brow. "Did they give you trouble?"

"Not really, but that's only because they couldn't. There's a lot of grumbling going on."

"That's understandable." Jade took a deep breath before walking in.

She surveyed the cots lined up in neat rows and the pure-bloods sprawled on top of them.

Many of the females that had been captured by Igor years ago were either curled up or staring blankly at the ceiling, no doubt immersed in the grief that they had been compelled to suppress for so long.

Sometimes she'd envied those with weaker minds who had been relieved of their burdens by Igor's compulsion. But the truth was that she didn't want the grief taken away from her, no matter how much it hurt. It was the only way left for her to honor the memory of her sons and the other males.

Those who had been born in the compound, males and females alike, looked either anxious or angry, no doubt wondering what the future held for them.

As no one got up to greet her, Jade realized they must have assumed that she was a prisoner just like them.

"Jade." Borga waved her over. "I'm glad to see that you are alive."

Pavel raised his head and glared at her. "Can you explain

why I am here? I cooperated. I did everything that was asked of me."

Borga cast her a quizzical look. "What is he talking about?"

"I'll explain in a moment." Jade scanned the cots for her daughter.

She found Drova lying on a cot near the wall with her knees up, and her head resting on her folded arms. She was staring at the ceiling and ignoring her mother's arrival.

"I need everyone's attention," Jade said.

As more people sat up, Jade assumed a military stance, her legs about two feet apart and her sword hand resting on the hilt.

"I know you are all wondering about the reason for your confinement. Tom released you from Igor's compulsion, and he compelled you all to cooperate, but until Igor is caught, we can't risk someone making contact with him and warning him. Some of you might still be loyal to Igor or hope to gain favor with him by betraying the others."

"Are you close to catching him?" Drova asked.

"Regrettably, no. I don't know how he learned about the compound's liberation, but it would seem that he's aware of what's going on, and he's not coming back."

Drova snorted. "Liberation, my ass. Who are these people, and how did you get them to come here?"

Jade decided to ignore her daughter's impudent attitude and questions for now, and addressed the liberation part first. "For many of you, this is the first time in your lives that you have been free from Igor's compulsion. Tom had to assert his will over you for the time being, but he will remove it once Igor's threat is no longer an issue." She scanned the room searching for the females. "Many of you had their tribes slaughtered by Igor and his henchmen, and to add insult to injury, you were compelled to suppress the memo-

41

ries of loss and grief and forced to breed. Now you are free to think for yourselves, to remember and to mourn."

"Awesome." Drova clapped her hands. "Thank you for that."

Patience. Jade took a deep breath.

"I came here to reassure you that this situation is temporary. As soon as Igor is captured, life in the compound will return to normal, but we will no longer be under Igor's thumb, our traditions will no longer be ignored, and females will no longer be subjugated. The Mother's daughters will once again rise to lead the community."

This time it was Pavel who snorted. "Am I supposed to be happy about that?"

"Females are the natural leaders of our society. What Igor did was an abomination."

Pavel glared at her. "And what you propose is not? Why can't we all be free? Why can't all of us be equal?"

"Someone has to lead," Jade said. "And the Mother of All Life chose her daughters to lead the Kra-ell."

"Says who?" Pavel didn't back down. "I didn't hear the goddess speak to me. Did you?"

Patience.

"Those traditions were passed down from generation to generation, and back on the home planet, the priestesses gave voice to the Mother's wishes. We have none among us, but every Kra-ell female is the Mother's worldly embodiment."

Thankfully, the two priestesses who had accompanied the ship had not been among those Igor had found. To subjugate them would have been a terrible crime and a great offense to the Mother of All Life.

The royal twins had only been acolytes, but since they were royal, they would have carried the same authority.

Regrettably, they were gone. If anyone could have overpowered Igor, it would have been them, and the history of the settlers would have been very different.

Drova chuckled. "I'm a pureblooded Kra-ell female, and according to you I'm a prime, and yet the Mother has never said anything to me. Pavel is right. Our leader should be chosen based on merit, not gender, and not the amount of Kra-ell blood in their veins either. The hybrids have been mistreated for far too long."

There were no hybrids in the basement, but if there were, they would have applauded Drova.

Jade had given the hybrid situation a lot of thought during her years in captivity, and she'd vowed to the Mother that if she ever got free and led her own tribe again, she would treat them better than she had done before.

A good leader learned from her mistakes. She didn't try to excuse them away.

Pavel started clapping, and not surprisingly, most of the males joined him. But when all the young pureblooded females started clapping as well, and even some of the older ones, Jade was taken aback.

Perhaps Pavel and Drova were right, and it was time to toss out gender roles?

They had lived mostly in isolation, apart from the humans, but they watched movies, read books, and were influenced by democratic human societies. Would it be so bad to remove gender from the equation?

It didn't work all that well for humans. Males still dominated most of their societies, and females still had to fight for equal respect.

If the Kra-ell females didn't assert their will, the males would. Igor and his deviants were the perfect examples of that. Jade would never allow herself or the other females to be subjugated again.

When Kra-ell females were in charge, the males were not

subjugated. They served because that was their natural inclination. It wasn't a hardship. It was a choice. But Drova and Pavel had never lived in a proper Kra-ell community, so to them, female leadership seemed the same as Igor's, just gender-flipped.

Until they experienced it, no amount of explanation would convince them that it wasn't so.

"This is a new beginning for us, and I can promise you that nothing will be forced upon you, and no member will be subjugated, whether male or female, pureblood or hybrid, Kra-ell or human. We will figure out a system that will be acceptable to all of us as a community."

Jade hadn't expected to add the humans, but once the words had left her mouth, she'd felt the rightness of them. She could practically feel the Mother of All Life nodding her approval.

After all, humans were her children as well, and so were the gods.

Except, the gods had perverted the Mother's gifts with their genetic manipulations and made themselves into something that nature hadn't intended.

10

TOVEN

*W*hen the goats were brought in, Toven considered leaving the bedroom but then decided to stay and watch. He'd seen many things throughout his long life, but he'd never seen a vampiric creature drinking blood from a living animal, and he was curious.

"They don't seem nervous," he commented as the Guardian lifted Valstar so he could reach the goat. "Are you thralling them?"

Valstar nodded. "Something like that. If my hands were free, I would have petted the goat while I drank, and it would have calmed them further. It's different when I hunt, but domesticated animals can't be treated the same as wild ones."

"You will have to do without the use of your hands," Toven said.

"You compelled me to refrain from using my physical or mental power on any people in the compound, human, Kra-ell, hybrid, and other, which I took to mean your people. What could I possibly do?"

Toven shrugged. "There are ways to work around compulsion, and I'm sure you know every trick there is."

"You are a wise male." Valstar pulled up until his fangs were within reach of the animal's neck and struck.

The goat didn't even flinch, and the only indication of what was going on was the sucking sound that Valstar made.

It was disturbing but not as bad as Toven had expected. After witnessing the strange feeding a few times, it would probably bother him no more.

A few minutes later, Valstar retracted his fangs and licked the wounds closed.

"Bring the other one," he told the Guardian.

The entire feeding took less time than it would have taken Toven to eat a sandwich, and given that Valstar had been starved, it indicated that the purebloods didn't need a lot of blood to sustain them.

"Thank you," he said after he was done with the second goat. "I hope that wasn't my last meal."

Already he looked better, and the color returned to his face.

"That depends on Jade. I have no vendetta against you."

As the Guardian led the goats out, Valstar leveled his gaze at Toven. "If you let her kill me, you'll regret it. I can tell you things about Igor that she doesn't know." He chuckled. "There is a lot she doesn't know."

The guy was smart, saying the one thing that could convince Toven to keep him alive.

"What do you know that she doesn't?"

"A lot, but now is not the time for questions and answers. Please don't take my warning lightly. If you want to keep your people and mine alive, you need to evacuate the compound. I didn't exaggerate when I told you that Igor could bring an army here. He's probably working on it as we speak, and we are wasting precious time."

"If you want me to believe you, tell me one thing that Jade doesn't know about Igor and that you haven't told me already."

"The account numbers you got from me represent less than half of what he has. The rest is in bitcoin, and only he has access to it. He has several cold wallets in safe storage at different locations, and before you ask, none here that I know of. Even the best hackers in the world can't steal that from him until and unless he is caught and compelled to provide his seed phrases."

Toven didn't know much about cryptocurrency. With all the actual gold he controlled, he found little to be of interest in the so-called digital gold. Valstar's talk about cold wallets and seed phrases was meaningless to him. But now wasn't the time to ask about the particulars. Roni would know much more about it, and the kid could probably get to that money as well.

In any case, it was time to let Kian know that the ruse was up and that they needed to get the money out of the accounts before Igor transferred it somewhere else or even bought more bitcoin with it.

"Thank you for the information." Toven left the bedroom and walked out of Valstar's suite just as the Guardian returned.

Out in the corridor, Toven dialed Kian's number.

"Toven," Kian answered right away. "Any news?"

"I talked with Valstar. He says we need to evacuate as soon as possible. I also suggest we grab the funds before it's too late. Relocating the Kra-ell will not be cheap."

"Hold on a second. I'm calling Roni right now."

A moment later, Roni joined the conversation. "The money is still there, which is surprising. I'm moving it out right now."

"Will Igor be able to trace it?" Kian asked.

"Not once I'm done with it. I'm creating a maze."

"What about the bitcoin?" Toven asked. "Can you hack into that?"

"I can't," Roni said. "But there is enough money in the accounts to provide for the Kra-ell for the next fifty years, and that's after we cover our expenses. If they manage it wisely, it could last them forever. I need to get off the line now. I'll call you once it's done."

"Thank you, Roni," Kian said.

"So what do we do now?" Toven asked. "Do we heed Valstar's warning and get everyone out, or do we keep waiting for Igor to show up? We have earpieces, so I'm not worried about him compelling everyone to obey him, but I am worried about a Russian bomber shelling the compound."

There was a long moment of silence, with neither Kian nor Turner saying anything.

"Did you get Valstar to tell you if he knows or suspects how Igor found out?" Turner asked.

"He said that Igor didn't need to call to find out about the communications going down. He would have known that when he tried to access the surveillance footage, and according to Valstar, he does so often. When he suspected that something was off, he could have used one of his oligarch contacts to check the Russian military's satellite feed, and he would have seen the explosions. Valstar says that he would first assume that the Russian military is behind the attack, but that would be easy to confirm, and his next suspicion would be other Kra-ell, which might prompt him to destroy the compound along with everyone in it to prevent his people from falling into enemy hands."

"Interesting," Turner said. "Then he must assume that there are more powerful compellers among the missing Kra-ell. Did Valstar say anything about it?"

"He said that he knows a lot, so we should keep him alive

and since he was under my compulsion when he said that, I assume he didn't lie, but I can't be certain of that. He could have convinced himself that was the truth. We all know that there are ways around compulsion. In any case, though, we've already decided that we can't let Jade kill him for now."

"Didn't you promise her that you would let her do it?" Kian asked.

"I promised to let her kill Valstar after we catch Igor, but we don't have Igor, do we?"

Kian let out a breath. "Regrettably, we don't."

11

JADE

"We should hold elections," Pavel said. "First to choose candidates. Everyone will suggest three names, and the three who get the most votes get to compete. They will need to prepare a platform explaining their ideas for the future, and present them to an assembly, then they will have a debate, and after that, we will vote to choose the winner."

"We need more than just one elected official," Drova said. "We need representatives from each group, and we need a council."

"Why do we need all that?" Morgada asked. "There aren't that many of us, and we can all vote on proposals that each of us will be allowed to bring up for a vote."

Pavel chuckled. "Then nothing will ever get done, and we will spend all of our time arguing and trying to convince each other of this and that. One leader and a small council is the way to go."

Jade listened patiently while her people threw ideas around. It wasn't the time to decide on how their future would look, but her goal had been to calm frayed nerves, and discussing a better future gave the people hope.

The mood in the basement had improved dramatically.

Sitting on her cot, Drova had taken part in the discussion for a few more moments, but then she turned her attention back to Jade. "What are they going to do to Igor once they catch him?"

Jade was grateful for her not referring to Igor as her father.

"They are not going to do anything to him. He's my kill. Tom promised to leave him to me."

She'd expected Drova to protest, but her daughter nodded. "Morgada told me what he did to the males of your tribe." She looked at the female on the cot to her right and then back at Jade. "He killed your sons. My brothers."

It wasn't often that Jade felt tears well in her eyes, and it took a lot to fight them from spilling.

The Kra-ell did not cry. They got revenge.

"He did that to the families of all the females who weren't born in the compound. He froze us with the power of his compulsion, not giving our males a fighting chance. They didn't get to die honorably in battle and enter the fields of the brave. They were slaughtered like cattle while the females watched, frozen in place and unable to help."

Drova swallowed. "I don't believe in all that nonsense about the fields of the brave and the valley of the shamed, but what he did was vile."

"He also put a collar around your neck that was filled with explosives so you couldn't run, and as if that wasn't enough, he rigged this entire compound with explosives as well. The people who came to help us made sure he couldn't detonate them remotely."

Drova nodded. "Yeah, Pavel told us about that too. But you still didn't tell us who are these so-called liberators."

There were no tears in her daughter's eyes, not even a sheen, and Jade couldn't be prouder of her at that moment. Even though Igor was a shitty father, his blood still coursed through Drova's veins, and it must be difficult for her to deal with what Jade intended to do, but she understood, and she accepted.

Drova was a true Kra-ell warrior, even if she didn't know that yet.

"Our liberators are people with special paranormal abilities and advanced technology."

"How did they know about us? Where and how did you find them?"

"It was by sheer luck that I found a former member of my tribe, who had left decades before Igor slaughtered all of my males and enslaved the females. I contacted him in a clever way so Igor wouldn't suspect anything, and I gave him the coordinates of the compound. I hoped he had found other Kra-ell that would be able to help us, but instead, he brought the new friends he'd found among humans."

Jade didn't like lying, but she'd promised not to reveal the immortals' identity. Well, she'd been compelled, but she would have promised if Tom had asked her. Still, those who came from the home planet like she had would have recognized Tom's otherworldly beauty for what it was. No human or Kra-ell was that perfect.

"Maybe they are the descendants of the gods who colonized this planet first," Morgada said. "They had many thousands of years of a head start on us, and they probably enhanced some of the humans like they did us."

Drova gaped at the female. "What are you talking about? What gods?"

Jade lifted her hand to stop Morgada. "There is a lot you don't know about the Kra-ell past, but now is not the time for a history lesson."

"Come on, Jade," Pavel said. "Give us something. You and the other original settlers have kept secrets from us for long enough. Aren't we purebloods like you? What are you hiding and why?"

Perhaps Pavel was right, and it was time to tell the young generation about their history, the good and the bad, but perhaps not as much of the bad. She wanted them to feel pride in their heritage, to follow the Mother of All Life's traditions without sneering at their religion like it was something only primitives believed in.

They didn't understand that the belief in the Mother was part of their identity as Kra-ell, and without it, they were just a bunch of aliens squatting on a planet that wasn't theirs. They would have no reason to preserve the purity of their blood so their kind wouldn't disappear, and in time, all that would be left of them would be traces of their genes in their human descendants.

Jade let out a breath. "You already know that we came from another place in the universe. There are many species of humanoids, and no one knows who the progenitor was, but those who call themselves gods claim that title. They were our neighbors back home. They claimed to have made us in their image, and they did the same thing on Earth with humans. That's why humans are compatible with us, and we can produce offspring together."

"I wondered about that," Drova said. "Are the gods still around?"

"I've searched for them, but all I found was mythology. I assumed that they had either left or had been killed by their creations—the humans."

When a barrage of questions was hurled her way, Jade lifted her hand. "That's all for today."

Morgada nodded her approval. "I'm glad that you finally told them something. I never agreed with your edict of secrecy. The young ones need to know, or the knowledge will be lost."

KIAN

"There are three hundred and twenty-seven people living in the compound," Turner said after Toven had joined them via a video call. "And that's not counting our Guardians, Kalugal's men, William, Marcel, Sylvia, and Mia. Getting everyone out and pulling a disappearing act is going to be difficult. Yamanu can shroud them, but not indefinitely. He needs to sleep and replenish his reserves."

"Especially given that at least half of them look alien." Kian swiveled his chair around and picked up his tablet. "One or two can blend in using sunglasses to hide their eyes, but a bunch of tall, willowy people all wearing sunglasses would be noticed."

Onegus chuckled. "We could use the movie set cover. They could look like ogres, and people would still buy it."

"Igor won't," Turner said. "We have four trucks that can carry between thirty to forty people each. It should be enough for the humans, the children of the purebloods and hybrids, and the injured. The rest can head out on foot. I can arrange for more trucks to intercept them on the way and collect the rest."

"Where will we take them?" Toven asked.

"Finland. Igor seems to have connections in Russia, but he probably doesn't have them in Finland. The question is where to take them from there and how." He looked at Kian. "Any ideas?"

Kian shook his head. "I haven't given it much thought because the plan was to leave them where they are and let Jade lead them. The only involvement I had in mind was some loose supervision to make sure that the humans were not mistreated."

"You'll need more trucks for the animals," Toven interjected. "If the Kra-ell can hunt where we end up taking them, we can let the animals go free. But until we find a place for them to roam and hunt, we need to take the livestock with us so the purebloods, and probably some of the hybrids, have a fresh supply of blood. I don't think we could raid blood banks on the way to feed so many. Igor will have no problem finding us just by following the news about blood supply shortages."

It was a mess Kian didn't want to deal with, but at this point, there was no turning back. He couldn't abandon those people, and he had to finish what he had started. "We need to find them a farm or take them somewhere wild where they can hunt."

"I can find them a place in Finland," Turner said. "But it's not going to be a permanent solution. Igor will find them, and then all we did would be for nothing. He would just take over again. We need to get them as far away from their original location as possible, and we need to do so in a way that won't leave traceable tracks. They will need to be scanned for trackers, and that includes all their clothing and belongings."

When he was a kid, the best way to avoid trackers was to use a waterway, but that wasn't going to solve their problem in today's interconnected, satellite-monitored world. Igor wouldn't follow them by the footprints left in the mud.

However, thinking of water gave Kian an idea.

"We can use the cruise ship. It's still at the shipyard in Stockholm, but it is basically ready to sail. I can tell them to skip the final clean-up and cabin inspections and get it out of there. It will still need time to refuel and resupply, and that will take some time, but the biggest question is whether the captain is done prepping the new crew for the voyage to Long Beach. If all the stars align and the *Aurora* can leave within a day, I can direct it to Helsinki to pick them up."

"I wasn't aware that you found a crew," Turner said.

"It wasn't easy to find what I was looking for. I wanted people with impeccable military and civilian experience who could function well under stress. The core crew we ended up hiring is fully vetted and top-notch. For now, we only have a great captain and a skeleton crew, and that was enough to sail an empty ship to Long Beach, but it's not a fully operable cruise ship yet. That being said, we can have it loaded with food and other supplies for our guests, but the Kra-ell and the others will have to serve themselves."

"Let me remind you again," Toven said. "The Kra-ell can't eat regular food. We will have to bring the animals onboard. The question is whether we take the livestock from here or procure it in Helsinki."

Kian groaned. "I can't believe that I'm allowing our newly remodeled luxury cruise ship to be turned into Noah's ark. But it's going to happen either way and if we get the live-stock in Helsinki, it will leave unnecessary breadcrumbs for Igor to follow. We need to take the animals from the compound, but we don't have time to arrange for their trans-portation. What are we going to do? Run them through the woods?"

"That's an option," Toven said. "At least at the beginning of the exodus before we can get more trucks to pick up the rest of the people and the herd. The problem will be hiding them while they are passing through Karelia. A convoy that size would get noticed."

"We have Yamanu to shroud the convoy while it's passing through," Turner said. "But its passage will leave tracks. That being said, I don't think that a bunch of trucks hauling produce is such a rare occurrence in Karelia. There are many farms in the area, and they must ship produce on a regular basis. However, it might not be the right season. They were probably done harvesting several months ago."

"Animals get shipped all year round." Onegus pulled out his phone. "Let's see what they produce in Karelia." His eyes darted over the screen. "Forestry, iron ore mining, wood processing, paper mills, and trout. Fish seems to be their biggest export industry." He lifted his eyes. "Except for the fish, all those things are not seasonal. There is plenty of reason for trucks to pass through the area year-round."

"I heard that ice fishing was a thing, and that's going on in the winter." Turner cast Kian a sidelong glance. "How soon can your ship get to Helsinki?"

"The voyage will probably take between twelve to sixteen hours, but the *Aurora* still needs to be fueled and loaded with supplies. Those things are solvable but may take some additional time. I just hope that the captain has the crew ready."

"Let's assume thirty-six hours," Turner said. "It will take them four to six hours to get organized, leave the compound, get to the farm where the Guardians stayed overnight, and collect their things. By then, the trucks should arrive. From the farm, it's about a fourteen-hour drive to Helsinki. That's a total of eighteen to twenty hours, which leaves another sixteen to eighteen hours during which they will have to hide until the ship is ready to receive them. I need to find them a place to lay low for half the night and most of the next day."

He started typing on his laptop. "It needs to be outside the city, secluded, and big enough to accommodate four hundred guests and the animals, so it needs to be a hotel or a lodge with a large grassy area that is fenced in."

Everything was moving too fast for Kian's liking, and for a moment, he was tempted to halt the action. The Guardians could handle the Russian military provided that the force wasn't overwhelming and provided that they didn't attack from the sky. But even then, it would only be a temporary solution. The attacks would just keep coming.

There was no other way but to evacuate the compound.

He looked at Onegus. "We don't have to bring them all the way to Long Beach. In fact, I'd rather we didn't. We can drop them off somewhere on the way."

The chief lifted a brow. "Where?"

"In Colombia. The *Aurora* needs to make a stop there anyway to get equipped with the armaments I ordered, and the Kra-ell should do just fine in the jungle. It would be the perfect solution for them. They will have plenty of game to hunt, and they might even take care of the drug cartel problem over there." He chuckled. "Talk about killing two birds with one stone."

"Don't you want to keep an eye on them?" Onegus asked. "And what about the humans? Some of them would want to be set free."

Another groan left Kian's throat. "You are right. We can't erase a lifetime of memories, and compulsion needs to be periodically reinforced. They will need to be accessible to Toven."

Onegus nodded. "The good thing about a sea voyage is that it takes a long time. We don't have to decide anything right now. We can consider our options at leisure while they are en route."

13

JADE

*W*hen Jade's earpiece vibrated, and a moment later Tom's voice sounded in her ear, she was glad for the distraction.

Her explanation about what she assumed had happened to the gods had been followed by a barrage of questions that she didn't want to answer and dig herself deeper into a pit of lies.

She remembered to tap the device before answering. "Yes, I'm still in the basement."

"We need to evacuate. Get everyone out, have them collect only their most precious and necessary belongings, and assemble in the courtyard in half an hour."

She tensed. "What's going on?"

"Valstar thinks that Igor will get the Russian Army or Air Force involved and bomb the compound."

"I don't think he would do that before he exhausts all other means of retaking it."

The fact that Igor hadn't attempted to activate the explosives the compound was rigged with or the collars proved that he wasn't gung-ho about killing his people. But if he couldn't get them by any other means, she believed he would destroy them rather than let them get taken by humans or other Kra-ell.

"I agree," Tom said. "But he still might show up with a platoon of soldiers equipped with rocket launchers and such, and the casualties will be staggering. We prefer to leave."

"Where will you take us?"

"Let's discuss it on the way. Time is of the essence."

"Got it." She tapped the earpiece closed and addressed her people. "We are moving out. You are to collect only your most necessary belongings and assemble in the front courtyard in half an hour."

It was good that none of them owned much. All of her things would fit in a backpack or in a pillowcase since she didn't own one.

"What happened?" Pavel asked.

"Nothing yet, but Valstar thinks that Igor will show up with the Russian Army. They have weapons we can't defend against or survive."

"Is he still alive?"

"Regrettably, he is."

The door behind her opened, and the Guardian stepped in holding a machine gun. "Let's go, people."

If not for Tom's compulsion, any of the Kra-ell could have wrestled the weapon out of his hands, but even though there was no reason to do that, Jade had to fight the impulse to disarm him.

Showing up with a machine gun wasn't conducive to the spirit of cooperation, but she could understand why the immortals were wary of her people. They weren't used to interacting with beings who were physically much stronger than them.

As everyone filed out, Jade stood by the door, smiling at the children and murmuring reassuring words.

The little ones didn't understand what was going on, and they were scared. They were about to leave the only home they had known, hopefully for a better one.

When her earpiece vibrated again, she tapped on it. "The purebloods are all out. What about the hybrids and the humans?"

Igor's remaining cronies were held under guard in one of the offices, but she couldn't care less about what happened to them. As far as she was concerned, they could stay chained to the wall and die when the Russians bombarded the place.

"Sofia and Marcel are in charge of assembling the humans," Tom said. "The Guardians are escorting the hybrids. We have only four trucks, so it was decided that the humans, the injured, and the children would ride in them while the rest would follow on foot. We will be intercepted by more trucks on the way."

"Can you tell me where we are going?"

"Helsinki, but don't tell anyone."

"Of course."

"By the way, you'll be glad to know that we have all the money Igor had in his bank and brokerage accounts. Your people will be able to live very comfortably on that."

That was a surprise. Not that the immortals had been able to seize the money, but that they were going to give it to her.

"That's good news. How much was in there?" As the last of her people left the basement, she started up the stairs.

"I don't know, but it's plenty. Regrettably, it's not all of it. Igor kept about half of the money in bitcoin, and we couldn't access that."

Jade's fangs twitched as they elongated. "It's all stolen blood money, and I'm sure that most of it came from my tribe. We had several exceptional enterprises going, and we had big profits."

"I hope to hear all about it on the way."

She might have said too much, but it was ancient history now, so it didn't matter.

"The male who made all that possible was murdered. If Igor wasn't so simpleminded and greedy and exclusively focused on the females, the idiot could have made much more money by leaving that male alive."

14

SOFIA

"Where are we going?" Helmi clutched her childhood teddy bear to her chest.

That thing had slept in her bed since she was three years old, and it hadn't left even to make room for Tomos. It was mended in so many places that there was barely any fake fur left, but Sofia knew better than to make fun of the one-eyed, patched-up wonder.

Instead, she shifted her gaze to Marcel, who shook his head.

She knew where they were heading, but it was supposed to be a secret. They needed to evade Igor, and whatever force he might summon to attack the compound, and given that he could compel anyone in the Russian military to do whatever he would instruct them to do, she wasn't sure how they were going to pull it off.

"Somewhere safe." She wrapped her arm around her cousin's waist. "Did you pack everything?"

Helmi pointed to the pillowcase she'd stuffed with her clothes. "I left my books, and my CDs behind like you told me to. That's all the clothes I had and a few toiletries."

Her father and her aunts had packed their things and handed them over to the Guardians, who had loaded them on the trucks already. They and several others were herding the animals out of the opening that used to be the front gate. The purebloods were going to run until they could rendezvous with more trucks and use their mental powers to get the animals to follow.

"Come on." Sofia led her cousin out of the common room. "We are riding together."

"What about Marcel?"

"He's running with the rest of them."

Helmi frowned. "How is he going to keep up with the Kra-ell? They are so much faster."

As what Helmi had said sank in, Marcel's eyes widened. "I need to call Yamanu." He rushed out the door.

"The liberators will follow behind. They are trained soldiers, so I'm sure they can keep up." It was the best explanation Sofia could come up with.

"I wish I could see Tomos before we leave." Helmi's eyes darted around, looking for her boyfriend.

"You will see him once the other trucks intercept us. Marcel can probably get you permission to ride with Tomos."

When they got to the courtyard, and Helmi saw her boyfriend standing with the other hybrids, she tore out of Sofia's grip and rushed to him.

He opened his arms and caught her as she flung herself at him. Seemingly unperturbed by the other hybrids and purebloods watching the display of affection, he swung her around before crushing her to his chest and kissing her like there was no tomorrow.

Heck, maybe there wasn't, but Sofia smiled nonetheless. The two were so obviously in love, and if the Kra-ell weren't so blinded by their stupid beliefs, they would have realized that as well.

Scanning the gathered crowd, Sofia saw her mother talking to another hybrid female.

Should she approach her?

What was she going to say to her? Should she introduce her to Marcel?

Her musings were interrupted when Valstar entered the courtyard between two Guardians. He was in handcuffs, and his legs were chained as well, so all he could do was shuffle.

Her mother looked at him with a horrified expression on her face, but when she made a move to go to him, the other female put a hand on her shoulder and shook her head.

Did her mother care about her father?

Who knew? She'd never interacted with her only daughter to share her feelings with her.

Joanna was more of a stranger to Sofia than Jade or Kagra, and she barely knew the pureblooded females.

The bleating of sheep and goats interrupted that line of thought. Her father and several of the others herded the animals through the courtyard and out the front, where the humans were boarding the trucks.

Sofia was startled when Marcel suddenly appeared next to her. "You scared me."

"I'm sorry." He leaned to whisper in her ear. "I can't believe no one thought about the Guardians having to keep up appearances and walk at a human speed. Your cousin saved the day."

"What are they going to do?"

"Everyone will have to walk at a rate reasonable for well-trained humans. We can't risk letting the Kra-ell run ahead. If the Russian military shows up, though, we will have no choice but to show our hand. Eventually, we will have to reveal who we are anyway."

"Yeah, I guess it depends on how long your people have to

spend with the Kra-ell. The longer it is, the harder it's going to be to keep up appearances."

"It's going to be long." He smiled. "We are about to go on a cruise."

Sofia leaned back and frowned. "We are?"

He nodded and wrapped his arm around her shoulders so he could continue whispering in her ear. "The clan recently acquired a cruise ship and had it renovated at a shipyard in Stockholm. It was supposed to leave for Long Beach in a few days. Kian is dispatching it to the port of Helsinki to pick us up."

She pretended to kiss his cheek to whisper back. "Is he planning on bringing all the Kra-ell to your secret village?"

"I don't think so. He doesn't know what to do with them yet, but thankfully, our hacker was able to grab the money that Igor stole from all the tribes, so they will have enough to settle somewhere else. I heard South America mentioned, but don't say anything to anyone just yet. If there are spies among us, we don't want them to know where we are going."

She nodded. "Maybe we should start spreading rumors about different locations to confuse Igor?"

"That's not a bad idea. So where are we going?"

"Australia. They say it's a wild place. That's perfect for the Kra-ell."

"Or we can say that Jade wants to go back to China," Marcel suggested.

"That's a good one. China is so big."

"Right. One rumor can say Beijing and another Shanghai or some other place." His eyes brightened. "Or Lugu Lake. We have reason to believe that ancient Kra-ell resided there and influenced the local culture. I'll tell you all about it on the way."

15

PHINAS

*W*ith the compound in organized chaos, and people milling all around, it was difficult to find a secluded spot to call Kalugal, and the only place Phinas had found was a bathroom stall in the office building.

It was the middle of the night in California, but the boss wanted updates, and he was probably awake and waiting.

"I don't have much time," he said as soon as Kalugal answered. "Kian is taking the Kra-ell with the humans and the livestock to Helsinki, and from there, they are sailing on the cruise ship he got for the clan. What do you want me to do?"

"What is he doing with the Guardians?"

"Some of them are going back with Bhathian on the amphibian. They are taking the exoskeletons with them and boarding a chartered plane in St. Petersburg to take them home. The rest will be led by Yamanu, who will be instrumental in shrouding the convoy. They will take the light weaponry and accompany the Kra-ell. We are leaving the compound in a few minutes and heading to the farm where we left our camping equipment. We don't have enough trucks for everyone, so most of us are walking. Turner is sending more trucks to collect us on the way, and once we break camp, we will head to Helsinki, where we will spend the night until the ship gets there and is ready to cast off."

"How many Guardians are going with Bhathian, and how many are boarding the ship, and where is the ship heading?"

"Originally, it was supposed to sail to Long Beach, but Kian wants to drop the Kra-ell somewhere on the way, and I wasn't told what the options were. Yamanu asked how many of our men would accompany the ship. He needs to know how many Guardians he will need to take with him. I told him that I would have to ask you."

"Unless some of the men need to go home, take everyone to the ship. The cruise idea plays beautifully into my agenda of befriending the Kra-ell. It will take almost a month for the ship to reach Long Beach, and since there will be more of us than the Guardians, we will form a stronger connection with the Kra-ell. But if the Kra-ell are dropped off on the way, you will continue with the ship back home. I hope the men will have no problem with such a long voyage."

"I don't think they will. I was told that the ship is luxurious."

"Of course, it is, but don't forget that it has no service staff. Everyone will have to pitch in, you and the men included. Make a good impression on our new friends."

It shouldn't have surprised Phinas that Kalugal knew more than even Bhathian and Yamanu about the clan's ship.

"I didn't know that there was no serving staff. Are you sure? Neither Yamanu nor Bhathian mentioned that."

"I'm sure. The ship was supposed to be delivered to the Long Beach port, and Kian hired only a skeleton crew to do that. Nevertheless, I'm sure it will be an enjoyable experience." He chuckled. "Especially for you. Did you have a chance to get even friendlier with the infamous Jade?"

"When? It's a madhouse out here. Everyone is scrambling to evacuate the compound as soon as possible, and that includes the livestock because the Kra-ell need a fresh supply of blood on hand, and they can't get it at sea. Can you imagine a luxury cruise ship with goats and sheep running around?"

Kalugal barked out a laugh. "I can't. Are they bringing the chickens along too?"

Phinas frowned. "How did you know about the chickens? I didn't tell you that."

"Yamanu told Kian about eating the best chicken he ever had. Organic and pasture-raised."

Phinas didn't ask how Kalugal had heard a conversation between Yamanu and Kian. His boss had his mysterious ways of finding out things he shouldn't have been able to.

"I don't think the chickens are coming. They feed the humans, not the Kra-ell, and the humans can get food at any port."

"I'm glad that they are taking the livestock. Otherwise, the Kra-ell would have to snack on the humans and the immortals, and I wouldn't have been happy about them using my men like blood bags."

Thinking about Jade snacking on him got Phinas hard in an instant, and as he adjusted himself, he realized why Kalugal had said that.

"You did that on purpose," he accused.

"Obviously. I'm curious about your reaction. Was it a turn-on or a turn-off?"

"Definitely a turn-on. Jade can snack on me anytime she wants. I wonder if what I eat makes a difference in how I taste."

Would his blood taste sweet if he ate a lot of sugar? Or tart if he ate berries?

Kalugal groaned. "That was a bit too much information."

Phinas chuckled. "You asked, and I answered. If I have anything more to report, I'll call you again."

"Please do."

16

KIAN

*O*negus put the phone down and turned to face Kian and Turner. "They are out of the compound. What's the status with the trucks?"

"ETA about two hours," Turner said. "If the immortals didn't need to moderate their speed, they could have reached the farm on foot and started breaking camp before the trucks arrived."

Kian looked up from his computer screen. "We have no choice. I don't want the Kra-ell or the humans to know who their liberators are. If we offload them somewhere in South America, it would be better if they don't know that immortals exist. If we bring them here on the other hand, which I'm not at all inclined to do, we will obviously have to tell them."

Turner leveled his penetrating stare at Kian and leaned back in his chair. "What are your objections to bringing them to the village?"

"Isn't that obvious?"

"Not at all. You've already allowed three former members of Jade's tribe to join the clan, and the experience was positive. Having this group as allies will shore up our defenses against Navuh's warriors and against other Kra-ell."

Kian returned Turner's stare. The guy was usually the more cautious among them, and his stance on the Kra-ell was out of character. "We have no reason to trust them not to turn on us or betray us when it will serve them to do so. That's one. In addition, Igor will be searching for them, and bringing them here might lead him to us. There must be at least a dozen more reasons that I can't think of right now, but I'm sure they will come to me later. I'm surprised that you are advocating for them."

"I'm not." Turner leaned forward. "I'm just starting a discussion. Do you know the saying about keeping your friends close and your enemies closer? That's why Kalugal volunteered his men not only to join the mission but also to escort the Kra-ell on the cruise."

"It has occurred to me." Kian let out a breath. "Nevertheless, I'm glad he did that because I can't leave all of the Guardians we sent for this mission to babysit this group. I don't like leaving the village without an adequate force to defend it."

"Speaking of Guardians." Onegus swiveled his chair to face Kian. "Yamanu wants Mey to join him on the cruise, and I just got a text from Arwel asking if he and Jin could go as well. Yamanu doesn't want to spend a month without his mate, and the ladies are curious about their relatives."

Kian felt a muscle tic in his jaw. "I don't want to endanger any more females. It's bad enough that Mia and Sofia are going with the ship, and I'm very glad that Sylvia is flying home from Helsinki. I wanted her to go back with the Guardians on the amphibian, but William asked her to stay with him in case he needs her to disable surveillance cameras when the convoy passes through the city and the port."

Turner glanced at him over the screen of his laptop. "Two

more females won't really make a difference." He kept on typing. "It would be interesting to get Arwel's opinion on the Kra-ell's feelings. From what I have observed about the three hybrids we know, they are not much different from us. The purebloods front a tough façade, but I wouldn't be surprised if on the inside they are just as vulnerable as the gods, the immortals, and even the humans."

Onegus chuckled. "Except for you, Turner. You are like our Spock. Always the voice of logic."

Turner smirked. "I take that as a compliment."

"It was meant as such. Anyway, I have no problem admitting my feelings, and I can tell you both that I will be very happy to see Toven back in the village. When he's here, I have an added peace of mind knowing that we have such a powerful compeller on our side. If we are ever attacked, I'm sure he would be a great help, freezing our enemies with a verbal command."

"I would like to see him back as well," Turner said. "But we need him and Mia to go with the Kra-ell to keep them in check and to defend them in case Igor shows up with a pirate armada."

"Are pirates still a thing?" Onegus asked.

"Surprisingly, they are." Kian swiveled his laptop around for Onegus to see the article he'd been reading. "*Best Management Practices to Deter Piracy*. They encourage vessels to register their voyages, so the navy knows to protect them. There is also a list of self-protective measures a vessel can take to make itself less of a target for pirates, but they are BS, like rigging the deck with razor wire, rigging firehoses to spray seawater over the side of the ship, and having a pirate alarm. They have other ridiculous suggestions like setting up mannequins posing as armed guards or firing flares at the pirates. Any merchant ship with a valuable cargo that has to sail through pirate-infested waters needs to hire an armed escort, which is what I want to do, but for different reasons." He looked at Turner. "I planned on retrofitting the ship in Colombia with some advanced defensive and offensive weapon systems, but for now the *Aurora* is defenseless. Do you know anyone who provides security to ships crossing the Atlantic?"

Hopefully, the guy knew someone with a navy submarine that could stealthily escort the cruise ship, not only during the Kra-ell voyage, but also during the wedding celebrations that were planned for next month but would probably have to be postponed.

Alena wouldn't be happy, or rather Orion wouldn't be. He was more anxious for them to get married than she was.

"I can make a few inquiries and find us an escort," Turner said. "I'm not sure that Igor would be able to do the same. He doesn't have the contacts I do."

"Don't be so sure," Onegus said. "He can come onboard any Russian naval ship and compel the captain to act as his pirate."

"True." Kian glanced at Turner. "It's not easy to hijack a navy ship, though. Even if the captain severs communications with command, he can't disappear with the ship. Not in the age of satellites. And a rogue ship would be hunted down."

"It can be done," Turner said. "The sea is vast, and vessels disappear all the time. A satellite capable of detecting a small to medium-sized vessel will usually only be able to scan a limited area based on its overhead pass, making it unlikely that the ship it's looking for passes through that exact area at the time it's scanning for it. But regardless, ships communicate with both ground stations and satellites via a dedicated system that tracks their position, heading, course, and more. But for the most part, these trackers can be disabled locally on the ship. It might be more complicated than that to achieve on a Russian navy vessel though. "

This was actually great news. "That means that our cruise ship can disappear, and Igor won't be able to find it."

"He can find out its final destination," Turner asserted. "There is no way to hide the ship from him when it passes through the Panama Canal."

"I'd rather chance it, offload the cargo in Colombia, and bring the ship to its original destination as planned."

Turner shrugged. "Ultimately, it's your decision. I'm just the advisor."

Kian glanced at the timer on his laptop. "We need to tell Leon that they have to evacuate Safe Haven, but I hate dropping the news on him at four in the morning. Igor will probably be busy trying to chase his people, but if he can't find them, he might turn his sights to the only other lead he has. We also need to collect the two hybrids stranded in the area."

"What do you want to do with them?" Onegus asked.

"Lock them in the keep until we figure out what to do with the rest of them. I don't want Igor getting them back."

Onegus smiled. "It's good that we had the foresight to attach a tracker to their car. We know where to find them."

Kian nodded. "Call Leon. We shouldn't waste any time."

"What about the paranormals?" Onegus asked. "What do we do with them?"

"Good question. How many are left in the program?"

"Let me check." Onegus pulled up a file on his laptop. "Nine."

"Tell Eleanor to send them on a vacation. She can claim a family emergency, and with her gone, there will be no one to run the program. We might still catch Igor, so there is no point in making permanent arrangements. I would rather not lose Safe Haven after all we have invested in the place."

Turner chuckled. "If we catch Igor, we can return the

Kra-ell to their compound and be done with them, but personally, I prefer them where I can keep an eye on them."

Onegus nodded in agreement. "Speaking of trackers, we have to assume that many of the compound's occupants are implanted with them. They might not all have sophisticated devices like the one we removed from Sofia, but even a simpler version will be just as effective. The only difference is that it will be easier to find."

KIAN

*K*ian pulled out his phone. "I hope that William's communication disrupter can help with that. We don't have time to run all three hundred and twenty-seven people and their belongings through an MRI machine and take the trackers out before we let them board the ship."

"Hello, boss." William sounded out of breath. "What can I do for you?"

"Are you walking?"

William chuckled. "Fates forbid. I'm in the van, but there were a lot of things to take care of before leaving. I helped Charlie and Morris move the drone piloting equipment and controls from the van to the amphibian and set them up. We need the drones to provide us with aerial cover on the way to Helsinki, so I left my mods intact. I will trigger the self-destruct circuitry as soon as the drones touch down for the last time. The modifications I installed will be fried, and no one will be able to reverse engineer or realize what exactly was added to the drones. We don't want that technology falling into Igor's or Russian's hands, or for that matter, into the hands of Turner's hired crew."

Regrettably, the military drones were far too large to transport and required a stretch of runway to take off that the cruise ship didn't have, otherwise Kian would have loved to have them on board and use them to defend it.

"Of course. I have a question for you. We have to assume that many of the compound's people have trackers in them. Can your disrupter scramble the signals so they can't be followed?"

"It can, and I activated it before we left the compound, but I will have to turn it off once we reach Helsinki. If suddenly scores of people lose their phone signal across such a major metropolis, too much attention will be drawn, and Igor might be able to figure out where we are heading even without having access to the trackers."

"That's not good." Kian raked his fingers through his hair. "Any suggestions about what can be done in that regard?"

"Not readily. If the location Turner finds for us to spend the night is remote, I can keep the scrambler on until we enter the city the next day."

"Can't you make it so it only affects a small area?"

"We have people in fifteen trucks, and we don't know who has trackers in them. Five more trucks carry livestock. To cover the entire convoy, I'll have to scramble a large area. I can turn it on again once everyone is on board the ship, but I will have to turn it off once the ship casts off. Communication between the ship and port authorities is required, and we want to avoid being blocked or chased because the authorities could not communicate with us. Likewise, a port-assigned pilot will come on board to navigate the ship until it fully clears the port zone, so communication will need to remain available for that duration. But now that I think on it, the Baltic Sea is narrow, and its shipping lanes are concentrated. It makes little sense to scramble signals while we sail through it because the ship will be tracked by many ground stations and passing vessels. Igor will have no problem finding us while we are in the Baltic. Certainly not if he gains access to a Russian, Finnish, or NATO military tracking system. Once we leave the Baltic Sea and enter the North Sea, though, and certainly in the North Atlantic, I can turn the scrambler back on and we can basically disappear."

Kian didn't want William on that ship. Marcel could take over for him, and they needed William back in the village, but that was a discussion for later. "Maybe we should remove the trackers before they board the ship."

Turner held Kian's gaze for a moment. "Even if Merlin works around the clock, it will take several days to do, not to mention the difficulty of getting our hands on an MRI machine first. We can't wait that long. We have to get an MRI on the ship before it leaves the port and do the scanning and removal en route. They can dump the trackers in the water before reaching the North Sea and disappear."

"But Igor will know that his people boarded a ship, and as William just noted, he will have no problem following, either with a Russian naval vessel, a submarine, or virtually. He wants them back and he is not going to give up on them."

"I don't see a way around it unless you want them to hole up in some remote location in Finland and hope that it will take him a while to track the convoy without the help of the trackers, but I don't think it would. He doesn't need to rely solely on the trackers to follow and locate the convoy. There aren't that many roads going through Karelia, and even with Yamanu's shrouding, Igor can find breadcrumbs that will lead him to his people."

"Yeah, in the shape of sheep and goat droppings." William

chuckled. "Thankfully, they didn't raise cows in the compound, or those clues would have been bigger and stinkier."

PHINAS

*P*hinas scanned the field, searching for Jade among the Guardians that were taking down the tents and packing up the rest of their stuff.

As the only female out there, she was hard to miss, but with her height and striking looks, she would have stood out even in a crowd of women.

Jade was beautiful despite putting zero effort into it. Her long black hair was gathered in a high ponytail, and she was wearing nothing special.

The black tactical pants were loose, providing plenty of pockets to store things. She was probably wearing a thermal layer underneath that was similar to the Henley shirt peeking out from the open collar of her tactical jacket. Absent were the sword and the scabbard, but he was sure she had a full arsenal of daggers and throwing knives hidden in her pants and boots.

One thing was for sure. He would never again startle her by approaching her from behind, and risk a dagger into his gut or a hand crushing his windpipe.

That shouldn't make him want her even more, but Phinas

had already established that Jade affected him in strange ways.

It wasn't only the sexual attraction, though. He respected and admired her.

She didn't have to be out there with the men, helping take down the tents. She could've waited in the van where the heater was working, and Toven and Mia were chatting with William and Yamanu.

But maybe that was precisely why she was out there with the Guardians, taking down tents.

Spending more time with Toven meant answering more questions. Regrettably, Phinas hadn't been invited to take part in the history lesson she'd promised Toven, and he'd only heard about it later from Yamanu, who hadn't volunteered to share any details.

Eventually, the information would find its way to Kalugal, as it always did, and his boss would most likely share it with him and Rufsur, but Phinas didn't want to wait.

As soon as he managed to pierce through Jade's formidable protective shields, he would learn as much as he could get her to reveal.

"Hello, beautiful," he said from a few feet away. "You cleaned up nicely, although I have to admit that the other outfit was the stuff of wet dreams."

The see-through mesh shirt and tight leather pants hadn't been practical in the nearly freezing temperature, but it was a hot look.

She looked every inch like the badass she was.

Jade cast him a glance over her shoulder. "When did you have time to dream about me?"

"I've been daydreaming about you since the first moment I laid eyes on you." He helped her fold the tent she'd taken down. "Did you dream about me?"

She looked at him with those huge eyes of hers. "You

entered my thoughts once or twice, but I don't daydream about males unless I'm plotting to kill them."

Chuckling, Phinas lifted his hands in the air. "Then I'm very glad that you only thought about me. I don't want to be on your kill list."

Jade put a hand over her chest. "Never. I owe you a life-debt. I'll die to protect you."

She'd said it with such conviction that Phinas had no doubt that she would do just that. His band of adopted brothers would die for him, too, as he would for them, but they had never pledged such a vow to each other.

He dipped his head. "Thank you. I hope you will never have to defend me."

Tilting her head, she regarded him with a frown. "Tell me something, Phinas. Why weren't you put in charge of any of the Kra-ell? Are you second class to the Guardians?"

The female didn't beat around the bush, and she had the tact of a bull in a china shop.

"The Guardians are on active duty, while my men and I had retired a long time ago. We didn't keep up our training as vigilantly as we should have, and that's why we are just assisting and not assuming leadership positions."

She gave him a once-over. "You look in excellent shape to me."

"Thank you. So do you."

"I train daily." She handed him the bag containing the tent.

When he pretended to sag under the weight, a smile tugged at her lips, which had been his intention. The act of pretending to be human had been unnecessary.

The humans and Jade's people were waiting for them in the trucks, and the only ones on the field were the Guardians, Kalugal's men, and Jade.

Immortals were not nearly as strong as the Kra-ell, but

they weren't as weak as humans. It was an advantage for the Kra-ell, and supposedly, their females got turned on by fighting their males for dominance.

Jade could overpower him with ease, which was probably a turn-off for her, but she was responding to his flirting, so maybe she was curious about having sex with an immortal.

He would be more than happy to satisfy her curiosity and show her what an immortal male with vast experience and endless stamina could do for her.

She would be glorious. He had no doubt of that.

"I would love to train with you one day." He cast her a suggestive look. "Perhaps later, we could wrestle between the sheets."

He had a feeling that Jade would appreciate his directness, but if he was wrong, his boldness could backfire.

19

JADE

The immortal was so refreshingly bold.

Human females might have considered his approach presumptuous or even rude, but Jade appreciated the directness. Still, she was Kra-ell, and now that she didn't need to obey Igor's rules, she would never again have sex that she didn't initiate. Phinas didn't know the Kra-ell ways, but he would have to learn to regard her with more respect and wait to be invited instead of issuing the invitation first.

The one exception to that was a life-debt.

He could ask anything he wanted, and she would have to deliver. If he asked for sex, though, it would be on her terms.

"Does that line work for you? Or do you just thrall women to wrestle you in bed?" She didn't wait for him to answer as she moved to the next tent.

"Do I look like the kind of guy who has to thrall a woman to get her naked?"

He didn't. He was a fine male specimen, but he was no match for her physically, and that was regrettable.

Jade had never taken a human to her bed or even a

hybrid, and the idea of sex with a male she could overpower effortlessly didn't appeal to her. Then again, as a Kra-ell female her duty was to choose the best male to breed with, and immortals had significant advantages over the Kra-ell. If a child resulted from the union, it would be better protected against injury, heal faster, and perhaps possess other abilities that the gods gave to their hybrid descendants with humans but not to the Kra-ell.

She cast him a quick glance. "For a human, you're good-looking, but you need to work on your game. Especially around me."

He cracked a grin. "I don't play games, and neither do you. You're not human, and neither am I. Therefore, human rules of conduct don't apply to us." He took the folded tent from her and stuffed it in its bag.

Jade looked around the campground to see if there was anything left to do, but all the tents were down, and nearly all of the equipment had been taken to the trucks already. "In principle, you are right, but there are nuances you need to learn, and I don't have time to explain them. We need to move out."

Undeterred, Phinas cast her a grin that revealed his slightly elongated fangs. Jade had no doubt that he had done it on purpose to show her that he was attracted to her. "I can't wait to hear all about those nuances. We should resume this conversation as soon as we can." He leaned and pecked her on the cheek. "Until we meet again, beautiful."

Dumbfounded, she watched him collect the two tents, four sleeping bags, and other miscellaneous equipment and carry everything to the truck.

No one had ever taken such familiar liberties with her. Not even her own sons or daughter.

"Jade!" Tom called her over. "You are riding with us."

"Not if I can help it," she muttered under her breath.

She'd managed to avoid walking next to Tom until they were intercepted by the additional trucks, and she'd hopped on one to avoid riding with him on the way to the farm.

Jade hoped her luck would hold and she wouldn't have to ride with him all the way to Helsinki. Being stuck in the command van for so many hours with the compeller, she might be forced to reveal too much.

He would ask a lot of questions, which she would have no choice but to answer, and keeping the few secrets she didn't want him to get out of her would be that much harder.

Casting a quick look at Phinas's back, she considered using him as an excuse.

She could tell Tom that she was interested in the male and that she wanted to ride in the truck with him. It wouldn't even be a lie.

She wanted to continue the silly human-style banter they'd been enjoying.

Phinas amused her, and the smiles she'd given him had been real for a change, not the kind that were meant to intimidate or manipulate.

Heck, she didn't even remember what he'd said that had amused her, and given that Igor and Valstar were still alive, it was a miracle she'd found anything funny or that it could take her mind off revenge for even a few moments.

It had been so long since anything or anyone had managed to distract her from the bottomless pit of grief and rage that had taken permanent residence in her chest.

There had been brief moments of peace when Drova had been born. On occasion, the baby's sweet smiles had managed to loosen the tight vise gripping Jade's dark heart, but it was difficult to enjoy the child when her older brothers hadn't gotten a chance to live and father children of their own. They didn't even get to die an honorable death in battle.

Walking over to the van, Jade peered inside through the open side door. "It looks cramped in here. I'd better ride in one of the trucks." She started to pivot on her heel.

"Stop," Tom commanded. "You're coming with us."

Jade arched a brow. "Why? Are you afraid I'm going to run?"

He'd compelled the other Kra-ell to obey the Guardians who were in charge of them and commanded them not to get farther than fifty feet away from the Guardian they were assigned to.

He hadn't compelled her.

Tom let out a long-suffering sigh. "Do you always assume the worst about people?"

She lifted her other brow. "Shouldn't I?"

"No, you shouldn't. I understand why you do, though." He shook his head. "You are part of this command, so you ride in the command van."

"Yamanu is not in the van, and he's in charge of all the Guardians."

"He is in the lead truck for a good reason." Tom leaned closer. "He can do things that even I can't. He can hide the entire convoy from human eyes, but if there are other vehicles on the road, he has to let them see ours to avoid them crashing into us."

She narrowed her eyes at him. "There is no way Yamanu can do more than you. It doesn't work like that."

"He has more practice. I haven't used such massive shrouding in eons."

"How old are you?"

"Old." He motioned for her to get in.

He was probably younger than she was, but since she hadn't actually lived all those years she'd spent in stasis, perhaps it didn't count. Then again, she'd been through enough torment and anguish to last anyone several lifetimes, and that was what mattered.

"What position will the van have in the convoy?" she asked as she put her foot on the step.

"One before last."

"Makes sense." She climbed into the cramped interior.

Tom's mate was strapped into a seat with a security belt, and another female who Jade hadn't met yet sat next to her.

William was in the back, immersed in whatever was on the screen of his computer, and a Guardian sat behind the wheel.

"Hi. I'm Sylvia." The woman offered Jade her hand.

She was pretty, but not perfectly beautiful like a goddess, which meant that she was an immortal.

"Hi." Jade shook it. "Handshaking is a human custom."

"Does it bother you?" Sylvia asked.

Jade sat across from her on the bench. "It has been a very long time since I pretended to be human. At first, I found it strange, but I got used to it."

"What do the Kra-ell do for greetings?"

"We nod to acknowledge our superiors. Otherwise, we ignore each other unless we have something to say."

Sylvia stifled a grimace. "That's efficient, just not very friendly."

"We are not friendly people." Jade thought about what she'd said for a moment. "I take that back. We don't express friendliness in the way humans do, but we are tribal people, so bonds of friendship are important to us. In fact, they are crucial for our survival."

Sylvia's expression softened. "That makes much more sense to me."

Jade wasn't friendly, but Kagra definitely was. Did that make Kagra a better leader? Or could Kagra allow herself to be friendly because she wasn't the leader?

Now that they were free, Kagra might want to split and get a tribe of her own, but that was as ill-advised now as it had been all the other times when she'd brought it up before they had been captured. There was strength in numbers, and they needed it now even more than they needed it then.

20

TOVEN

*A*s the van pulled out, Jade leaned back. "What doesn't make sense to me is that Igor didn't show up and didn't arrive with Russian troops in tow, either. There aren't that many paved roads in Karelia, so if any force was coming, we should have crossed paths with it, and if he sent the Russian Air Force to bomb the compound, we would have heard the explosions."

Toven nodded. "I had the same thoughts. William launched one of the small surveillance drones to be our eyes from above, and so far, he has seen no activity. We also have the large military drones we used during the attack circling the entire area at a low altitude overhead, and so far, there has been no troop movement or other military aircraft that we could detect in the area. Perhaps Igor hasn't been able to get organized yet."

"He had plenty of time," Jade said. "He wouldn't want to lose our trail." She looked at William. "Are you running that disrupter of yours?"

He nodded. "Igor can't trace the trackers if that's what you mean, and if he sends humans to track us, they won't see past

Yamanu's shrouding. If he comes in person, though, he will have no problem finding a convoy of twenty trucks and a van."

Jade appeared to be focused inwardly for a spell before she raised her eyes to him again. "If Igor doesn't attack us on our way, he must have figured out another way to get what he wants. What worries me is that we are clueless as to what that might be. Underestimating Igor is a mistake typically done only once, if you catch my drift."

"Loud and clear," Toven said. "But you are not telling me anything I don't know. I'm a strong compeller as well, and I have an army of trained immortal warriors with me. Still, I'm moving your people out, and I wouldn't do that if I underestimated Igor."

His answer seemed to satisfy Jade, but only partially. "Perhaps Valstar knows what Igor would do in a situation like this. He should be here in the van with you."

Toven chuckled. "I didn't want to put the two of you in the same vehicle, and I prefer your company to his."

He had many more questions for Jade, and when they arrived at the place that Turner had found for them outside of Helsinki, he would pose the same questions to Valstar.

Toven didn't expect either of them to flat-out lie, but both were strong, and both had lived under Igor's thumb for a long time, so they had plenty of experience withholding information from a compeller.

Given Jade's hard stare, she knew why he wanted her in the van for the next twelve hours. "As much as I detest Valstar, I wouldn't end his miserable life before we've wrung all the information out of him that might help us catch Igor. But after we catch his boss, they are both mine."

Toven dipped his head. "I will keep my promise. Their lives are yours to do with as you please."

"I'm counting on it." She briefly flicked her gaze to Mia

before leveling her unnerving eyes on him. "I also might be more pleasing to the eye than Valstar, but I'm sure that's not why you wanted me here."

He smiled. "You whetted my appetite with your brief history account, and I'm curious to learn more. You said that the Kra-ell were not technologically advanced, and yet you embarked on an interstellar voyage across the universe. Were you sent by the gods?"

Jade nodded. "When the gods' king demanded that we start settling on other planets, he also offered to get us there. The ship we arrived in belonged to the gods, but it was a piece of crap vessel that should have been decommissioned ages prior. Instead of the voyage taking two hundred and twenty-three years, it took over seven thousand. I'm surprised any of us survived in the stasis pods and even more surprised that we survived the explosion. I don't know if it was a malfunction, which is possible given how old the ship was when it started the voyage, not to mention how old it was when it arrived at its destination. But I suspect that it was sabotage. I just don't know why or by whose hands."

Toven was still reeling from the seven-thousand-years figure.

The Kra-ell must have left shortly after his parents had been exiled. At the time of Toven's birth, his parents had only been on Earth for a few centuries, but it hadn't been his father's first visit, nor was it Ahn's or Athor's. They had taken part in much earlier expeditions. The difference was that this time, they had been left behind for good.

They had been exiled and banished for their part in the rebellion.

Not that they had told him any of that.

His father hadn't talked about a rebellion or an exile. Most of the other gods who had been born on Earth hadn't even been told that their kind had arrived from somewhere else. Ekin was a little less tight-lipped than Ahn, so he'd let a few things slip, giving Toven the impression that the gods had arrived voluntarily and that, at some point, communications with home had been severed, probably because something terrible had happened back there.

Mortdh, who had been one of the exiles, had thrown hints around for centuries, but he was unhinged, and Toven had dismissed his half-brother's remarks as the rantings of a lunatic.

"How many settlers were on the ship?" Sylvia asked.

When Jade seemed reluctant to answer, Toven added with a touch of compulsion, "I would like to know that as well."

"Twelve hundred, but most didn't make it, and we can safely assume that Igor collected all the survivors and killed off most of the males to even the ratio between males and females."

That was a lot of people.

"How many original purebloods were in the compound?" Toven asked.

"Igor's pod had twenty members, sixteen males, and four females. Of the six pureblooded females he took from my tribe, only three were from the original group, including myself, and the other three were born on Earth. From other tribes, he took fifteen more original pureblooded females."

Toven wrapped his arm around Mia's shoulders. "I assume that you are talking about escape pods?"

Jade nodded. "The stasis pods were ejected from the mother ship before it was destroyed. They had some propulsion capability, and they got dispersed over a very wide area. Most probably ended up in the Arctic Ocean."

That made them extremely difficult to retrieve, if not impossible.

"How did Igor know where to find you and the others?"

She chuckled. "I tried to get him to tell me that for years. I don't know."

William lifted his head. "We found a tracker in Sofia. It's a very sophisticated piece of equipment, but since she's a young human, he must have gotten her implanted with it. Perhaps all of the original settlers had implants in them, and Igor either had a stash of them or removed them from himself and his inner-circle buddies."

"I'm not aware of having a tracker in me." Jade grimaced. "Although I wouldn't put it past the gods to trick us and put it in us after we went into stasis."

"How was that done?" Toven asked. "We can only put someone in stasis using our venom."

21

JADE

"It wasn't done with venom, that's for sure." Jade pursed her lips. "We each had an individual pod within the larger escape pod, and the gods hooked us up to all kinds of tubes that were supposed to put us into stasis and keep us healthy during the voyage. I counted to five, and it was lights out for me, as the humans say." She huffed out a breath. "The next time I opened my eyes, seven thousand years had passed. Obviously, I didn't know that right away. I knew that much more time had elapsed than it should have because we were all in pretty bad shape, and we crash-landed with our escape pod creating a crater the size of a stadium. One of our males was able to resurrect the equipment, but we thought that it was still malfunctioning and that the number it displayed was incorrect. When we got out, made it to civilization, and oriented ourselves, it was a shock to discover how advanced humans were, and it confirmed that number. It took us seven thousand years to reach our destination."

Sylvia tilted her head. "Seven thousand exactly?"

"A little longer than that. Why?"

"If it were exactly seven thousand, then it would have been sabotage for sure."

"Well, it was more than that, but I still think that it was done on purpose."

"Do you think it was done by the gods?" Mia asked.

Jade shrugged. "Why send us across the universe? They could have programmed the ship to self-destruct closer to home."

"Because your queen would have known that," Toven said. "By the time your ship arrived at its destination, the queen was long gone, and all your relatives were gone as well, and there was no one to investigate what happened."

"We were supposed to settle in and prepare things for more Kra-ell to arrive, and we were also supposed to provide the exiled gods with labor in payment for the voyage. If the king didn't want the exiled gods to get workers, he could have sent us somewhere else."

Tom lifted a pair of sad eyes at her. "What if your ship wasn't the only one that exploded? What if the king was sending all the Kra-ell on old ships to get rid of them?"

"That wouldn't have been a practical way to get rid of us. Even though the ship was old and it wasn't a great loss, there were only twelve hundred Kra-ell on board. That wasn't enough to tip the head-count scale in the gods' favor."

She'd speculated on that endlessly for years, and one scenario was that someone had found out that the royal twins were on board, and the sabotage had been an assassination. Her guess as to the identity of the assassin was Igor, of course.

But why send an assassin?

Not everyone approved of the queen or of the peace treaty she'd brokered, so it could have been a retaliation. But since the twins had been consecrated to the priesthood, they hadn't been meant to be the next rulers. Besides, they had left, so what was the point of killing them seven thousand years later?

The gods had even less of a motive to assassinate the queen's children, especially since the peace treaty was so tenuous.

Why had they been smuggled on the ship in the first place, though?

Had the queen feared for their lives? Maybe she'd received threats?

If she had, Jade hadn't heard about it.

Throughout their lives, the twins had been kept in seclusion in the Mother's main temple, dedicated from birth to serve the goddess, and no one had known what they looked like.

It was unusual for a male to be dedicated to the priesthood, but the head priestess had made an exception for the prince because twins were extremely rare for the Kra-ell, almost unheard of, and the belief was that they were born sharing a single soul.

There had been rumors about their incredible compulsion powers, but that wasn't surprising. The queen was the most powerful Kra-ell compeller, so it made sense that her children were powerful as well.

Jade had been a junior commander in the Queen's Guard for only five years before drawing the lottery number that had put her on the settlers' ship, but during that time, she'd seen the twins walking the palace garden on several occasions. They'd both been veiled and covered in loose clothing from head to toe, but she'd memorized their bearing and their gait, which she had recognized when they had been escorted to the pod right next to hers.

That had been just one clue, though.

The second clue that those were no ordinary Kra-ell was that their pod had an equal number of males and females, which Jade was sure wasn't the case for any of the other pods. And the last clue was the god technician who had tended to them. The guy was anxious and jumpy, and he couldn't wait to get them and their other pod members hooked up, so he could seal them in.

Jade had only ever shared her suspicions with Kagra, and since Jade didn't have proof that the twins had been aboard the ship, keeping it away from Tom hadn't been difficult. He'd demanded true facts from her, not speculations.

However, she was convinced that Igor knew that the royal twins were onboard, despite never mentioning it. And if the ship had indeed been sabotaged, he was just ruthless enough to have done it.

It was all speculation, though, and no matter how many times Jade turned it over in her head, things just didn't add up. She was either missing pieces of the puzzle or had created a conspiracy theory where there had been none.

Still, if the queen had felt the need to hide her children on the other side of the galaxy, there must have been a reason for that, and Igor might have been sent to end them. He might have caused the explosion to cover his tracks, but he couldn't have been the one who'd made the voyage take so much longer than it had been supposed to.

However much thought Jade had dedicated to the subject, she couldn't find a reason for Igor to delay the ship's arrival for so long.

Someone else must have done that.

"I'm about seven thousand years old," Tom said. "I was born about the time that you embarked on your journey. My parents arrived only a couple of centuries earlier, which from a gods' time perspective is not long, and yet no one ever mentioned a shipment of workers or the Kra-ell. I don't think they knew you were coming."

Jade tilted her head. "Did they say what their mission here was?"

"My parents didn't, but my brother threw hints around." Tom snorted. "He was a nonconformist. I guess you could call him a rebel. The older gods didn't talk about their past or why they left their home."

"It's so weird," Mia said. "Why were they so secretive? And why were the Kra-ell sent here to supposedly help the gods, but no one told the gods that they were coming?"

"I smell a rat." Sylvia leaned her elbow on her knee and her chin on her fist. "A conspiracy. I can understand the gods hiding the fact that they had been exiled for committing treason from their children. It would have cast them in a bad light and could have given their kids rebellious ideas. But if they were expecting the arrival of a ship full of Kra-ell, they would have prepared the younger generation for the guests. If they wanted to keep their past a secret, they might have wanted to prevent the ship from getting to its destination, but I can't see how they could have caused the malfunction that delayed its arrival by thousands of years. They couldn't do that from Earth, and since they had no contact with their home planet, they couldn't have asked their former rebel friends to sabotage it for them either."

Tom cleared his throat. "I'm not sure exactly when all communications were severed." He sighed. "I was one of the first gods born on Earth, and my father wasn't as secretive with me. The other young gods weren't even told that we were extraterrestrials."

His mate lifted her eyes to him. "But if you knew, why didn't you tell the others?"

"Ahn forbade it, and his word was law. No one dared to disobey." He smiled. "Except for my father, that is. Ekin found clever ways of working around Ahn's commands."

"I don't get it," Sylvia said. "Ahn answered to the council, and the council included all the gods of voting age. How could he have forbidden something without securing the council's approval?"

Tom smiled. "The same way Kian sometimes does things without consulting the council. In matters involving the security of the clan, he can make executive decisions without asking for anyone's approval."

Interesting. It seemed that Kian was the one in charge, not Tom.

"Is Kian one of the surviving gods?" Jade asked.

Tom hesitated for a moment before answering. "He's not. He's an immortal."

"So, how come he's in charge?"

Mia avoided her eyes, and Sylvia got busy examining her fingernails.

Tom closed his eyes. "I guess you deserve some information as well, but I need to compel you to keep it to yourself."

Jade widened her eyes, which she knew made her look even more alien than normal. "Who am I going to tell? You've already compelled me to keep your identity and that of your people a secret, and aside from me, only Kagra knows who you are. Do you want me to keep it from Kagra as well?"

"Yes. For now. We still don't know what we are going to do with you and your people, and the less they know about us, the better."

"I disagree. I don't know how many of you there are, but it can't be too many, and there are only a couple of hundred of us, including the hybrids. We should stick together."

The truth was that she hadn't thought along those lines until that moment. When Tom had first approached her, her objective had been to eliminate Igor and his close circle of murderers. Once that was achieved, she'd expected them to leave her at the compound to lead it, and to keep a loose eye on her. Maybe even appoint a liaison. But now that her people were being forced to resettle, joining Tom's clan seemed like the best option.

Even though their hacker had managed to secure the money, it wouldn't be easy to resettle a large group of people who looked different enough to stand out and who were traveling with children and livestock.

22

TOVEN

*J*ade's suggestion had surprised Toven on two accounts.

First, how had she guessed that there were only a few hundred of them?

Secondly, he would have never expected her to relinquish sole authority over the Kra-ell in exchange for security, but perhaps he'd been wrong about her.

Not that what she'd suggested was in the cards. Kian would never agree to invite the Kra-ell to join the clan.

"It's not up to me. As you've observed, I'm not the leader of this community. In fact, I'm a recent addition, and although I've been accepted and welcomed, I'm not even on the council, nor do I hold any official position. I volunteered to help because I'm the strongest compeller the clan has." He tightened his arm around Mia's shoulders. "I was also blessed with a mate who enhances my powers."

Jade gave Mia an appreciative once-over. "That's why you dragged your crippled mate into enemy territory. The gods are not high on my list of good people, but the one quality

I've always appreciated about them was their devotion to their mates."

Mia groaned. "I know that I shouldn't expect you to know anything about political correctness, but just for future reference, it's rude to call someone a cripple."

Jade dipped her head. "I meant no offense, but the fact is that you don't have legs. Is there a better way to refer to your condition?"

"Definitely. Disabled or challenged are acceptable terms, but I like it best when people just ignore my legs. Before I started regrowing them, I used prostheses very effectively, and my mobility wasn't restricted. Most people didn't even notice that I had difficulty walking or that my gait was a little stiff. But when I turned immortal and started regrowing my legs, I could no longer wear them because it put pressure on the stumps. It would have impacted the growth."

As Mia had blurted out about turning immortal, Toven tensed, expecting Jade's next question.

She frowned. "What do you mean you turned immortal? You are either born immortal or human. No one can turn immortal." When Mia looked to Toven for help, Jade leveled her eyes at him. "I should have known that the gods would bring their genetic knowhow to Earth. Can you turn anyone immortal?"

It was an odd statement. The gods created humans, so they had to bring their genetic knowhow with them, but Toven had never heard of the gods turning humans into immortals or changing them in any way. They might have done that at some point, hundreds of thousands of years ago, jumpstarting the leap from ape-like creatures to homo sapiens by using their own DNA, but from then on, it was just evolution.

"Perhaps the first gods who came to Earth manipulated the genetics of the proto-humans and helped them leap ahead of natural evolution, but the group of gods I was part of did not have advanced genetic abilities. We discovered how to activate Dormants by chance."

Jade looked skeptical. "What's a Dormant?"

"A Dormant is a child of an immortal female with a human male. They are born human but carry the immortal genes, which can be activated with venom."

Jade tilted her head. "What about a child born to an immortal male and a human mother?"

"They don't carry the genes. They are only inherited through the mothers. Even a Dormant mother who hasn't been activated gives her children the genes of immortality."

He could practically see the proverbial wheels spinning in Jade's brain as she processed what he'd just told her.

"So if a child is born to a hybrid female and a human male, she is a carrier of long-lived genes?"

"We don't know whether it works the same for the Kra-ell. Obviously, Marcel hopes that it does."

Jade's eyes widened. "Sofia's mother is a hybrid. Can she turn Kra-ell?"

"A hybrid Kra-ell. But as I said, we don't know if it works. What we do know is that a hybrid Kra-ell's venom can't activate one of our Dormants. Emmett was intimate with one for a long time, but she didn't transition until she took an immortal mate."

In the back of the van, William groaned. "You shouldn't have told her that."

Toven had a feeling that William was right. Looking into Jade's dark eyes, he said, "You can't ever tell anyone about that. Not even Kagra."

She nodded. "If it worked for the children of the males, it would have been huge. It could have given us a new lease on life. But our females don't breed with humans. There is no need and, frankly, no inclination either. We are programmed to seek the best breeders for our offspring, and the natural choice is pureblooded males. As it is, there are not enough of us even for them, and that's after Igor's selective slaughter. I wish there was a way to change our genetics, so we had an equal number of female and male births. That would have solved a lot of problems."

"Perhaps the solution was always in front of you," Sylvia said. "If the Kra-ell females chose human males to father their children, they would have produced hybrids who were capable of transmitting the Kra-ell genes to the next generation, and since those hybrids had half of their DNA from their human fathers, their children could have a more evenly distributed gender birth ratio."

That was an interesting hypothesis.

Vlad, Mey, and Jin were good examples of the kind of offspring a union between an immortal Dormant and a hybrid Kra-ell could produce. It would be interesting to see whether their children would be predominantly male or more evenly gender-distributed.

Jade shook her head. "We can't experiment like that. There are too few pureblooded and hybrid females, and we are having as many children as we can. Our fertility is much better than the gods', but it's a fraction of that of the humans."

23

PHINAS

*K*arelia's roads were full of potholes and every time the truck hit one, which seemed to happen every couple of minutes, Kagra winced and some of the other injured Kra-ell stifled groans.

By now they were all well enough to sit, with the exception of Kagra, who should have been lying down but had refused to and was paying the price for it.

Phinas got up and walked over to Merlin. "Can't you give Kagra and some of the others more painkillers?"

"I offered." The doctor's lips twisted in a grimace. "They refused. These people are stubborn as oxen. Hell, let me rephrase. I'm sure that they could outdo any ox." Merlin leaned closer to whisper in Phinas's ear. "They consider getting injured a failure, and I think that they are punishing themselves by refusing to take painkillers."

"I suspect that you are right." Phinas glanced around to see if anyone was listening in before leaning closer to Merlin. "Did you bring your sleeping potion? We can knock them out with that."

Merlin shook his head. "I have it, but I'm saving it for an emergency."

"What kind of an emergency are you expecting?"

"It doesn't only work on them. If Igor shows up with an army, the potion might be useful."

"It's not going to do any good against machine guns or rockets."

Merlin pursed his lips. "He's not going to open fire on his people. He wants them back."

"The Kra-ell are resilient, and they heal fast. Igor will assume that most of them will recover, and since he doesn't give a shit about the humans, which includes us because that's what he thinks, it makes perfect sense for him to open fire on the convoy."

Merlin smoothed a hand over his nearly white beard. "You might be right. How come you are not concerned?"

Phinas patted the machine gun slung over his chest. "I'll meet fire with fire."

He and the others had donated their Kevlar vests and hats to protect the children and the humans, and as the exoskeletons had to go back with the amphibian to make room in the trucks, he had no protective gear. But Phinas wasn't worried. It wouldn't be the first time he'd been riddled with bullets. Unless he was hit with a rocket to the head or the heart, he would survive most other injuries.

"Give me the pills and a bottle of water, and I'll convince Kagra to take them."

Merlin pulled a pill bottle out of his pocket, a water canteen from his crate, and handed them to Phinas. "Good luck with that."

"I don't need luck." He tapped his temple. "I'll use cunning and my knowledge of female psychology."

Merlin snorted. "This, I would like to see."

"Watch and learn, my friend." He gave the doctor one last smile before returning to his seat next to Kagra.

Leaning her head against the side of the truck, she had her eyes closed, and her lips pressed together.

"Are you okay?" he asked.

"I'll live," she murmured.

"Yes, you will. And you will fight again."

"You'd better believe it." She didn't even open her eyes.

"It might be sooner than you think. Igor might attack us en route. We expect him to show up with the Russian military and open fire."

She cracked her eyes open. "I don't even have a weapon to fight with."

"You have your fangs and your nails." He took her hand and lifted it to examine her nails. "How hard are they?"

"Hard." She pulled her hand out of his grip. "Are you flirting with me, Phinas?"

"What gave you that impression?"

"That's the second time you've held my hand."

"No offense, but I have my sights set on your boss. Especially since she owes me a life-debt. She said I can ask for anything, and she'll deliver."

Kagra's lips twitched with a smile. "She likes you, so I'm glad you weren't flirting with me. Jade and I decided a long time ago that we would not share males. We are too close to each other for that to work. Usually, females of the same tribe share all the males, but Jade and I divided ours between us. The others could have anyone they wanted, though, and they did."

Phinas lifted his hands. "Do you know the human phrase 'too much information?'"

She smiled again. "I watch a lot of American movies. I know what it means. You don't want to hear about Jade's past sexual exploits."

"Precisely. Let's talk about Igor's imminent attack instead. You are in no shape to fight because you are in too much pain. Your internal organs are most likely healed enough not to tear if you fight, but the pain will make you fear that they will and it will slow you down." He pulled out the container Merlin had given him. "If you can't swallow pills, I can ask the doctor to give you a shot."

"I can swallow." She eyed the container suspiciously. "How big are they, and how many do I need to take?"

"Merlin said that you need six." Phinas opened the container and shook out six small tablets into the palm of his hand. "They are small."

He had a feeling Kagra had very little experience with pills or swallowing any solids, for that matter. She lived on a liquid diet.

She looked at his hand and grimaced. "One isn't big, but six are. Maybe I should take them one at a time?"

"Whatever works for you." He twisted the cap off the water container and handed it to her.

She gagged on each pill, but she didn't give up and took them all.

"Good job." He patted her knee. "You'll start feeling better soon."

A few minutes later, her features smoothed out, and she let out a sigh. "I feel like I do when I drink too much vodka."

Interesting.

"Did you have that reaction before?"

She shook her head. "When Merlin gave me shots for the pain before, I passed out. This just feels like a pleasant buzz." She rubbed a hand over the flat expanse of her stomach. "I'm all warm inside, and I'm a little floaty."

Perhaps it was underhanded of him, but Phinas wasn't going to waste the opportunity to ask Kagra about her boss.

"Did Jade have a favorite?"

Kagra cast him an amused sidelong glance. "Me. I was her favorite."

"I meant from among the males."

"She liked each of them for different reasons, but she didn't favor any one of them over the others."

KIAN

"Thank you." Kian took the paper cup from Aliya. "It was very thoughtful of you to bring us breakfast."

She smiled shyly. "I wish I could take credit for the idea, but Syssi texted me and asked if I could do that. Naturally, I was more than happy to help in any way I could." She looked at him expectantly.

"Jade and the others are free, but their captor is at large, so we had to evacuate them from their compound. We are working on a plan to bring them somewhere safe."

She held his gaze, expecting him to elaborate, but he didn't have time to indulge her.

Smart girl that she was, Aliya dipped her head. "Thank you. You have mine and Vrog's eternal gratitude."

"You're welcome, but I'm doing it as part of the clan's humanitarian effort and for security reasons."

"Nevertheless. We are grateful." She turned on her heel and left the room.

Removing the lid, Kian took a sip of coffee and leaned back. The war room didn't have windows, and he missed the view of the village from his office. He loved watching the sunrise and the café filling up with the morning crowd, but it didn't seem like he was going to get a break today.

There was still so much to be done, so much to decide on, and even Turner wasn't as confident as he usually was about the overall plan. They had bits and pieces, things that had to be done, like securing an MRI device in Helsinki and loading it on the *Aurora* and finding a naval security detail for this voyage and the next. After that, he planned to charter the ship for private executive cruises and make back what he'd spent on her.

The original itinerary of the ship was to sail through the Panama Canal and head to a secluded dock in Colombia, where it would be retrofitted with advanced weapon systems that he couldn't get on board in Europe.

Kian had promised Alena a wedding cruise, but there were so many risks involved in having the entire clan, including Annani, on a floating target. The Guardians' combined might and the technological superiority of the clan would be useless against a torpedo, a missile or a bomb.

Any adversary with access to such weapons could fatally injure the ship. The immortals weren't easy to kill, and most would probably survive the initial attack, but their enemies could finish the job by picking off the swimming survivors one at a time at their leisure.

It wasn't very likely that Navuh would find out about the cruise and attack, but Kian couldn't count on that, and he needed to be ready for even the most remote possibility of an ambush at sea. Given that Alena was pregnant and growing larger by the day, he couldn't delay the wedding by much. The ship had to get to Colombia, get fitted with armaments, and arrive at Long Beach more or less on schedule.

The plan was far from perfect, and Turner wanted to bring the Kra-ell to Long Beach, but perhaps they could combine their cerebral prowess and come up with a solution that would satisfy them both.

Putting his cup on the conference table, Kian covered it with the lid to preserve the coffee's temperature. "I have to keep the ship's original itinerary. Since we are heading to Colombia anyway to arm the vessel, we can unload our cargo first, either there or at one of the neighboring countries, and then have it rigged with the weapons we ordered. That would introduce a delay, and the contractor we hired to do the fitting of the weapons systems on board might get antsy, but I'm paying him enough to work around my schedule." He looked at Turner. "What was the name of your friend over there? Stefano? Maybe he can help us settle the Kra-ell somewhere near his place. Do they have jungles nearby?"

"His name is Arturo Sandoval, and I'm sure he'll be more than happy to help settle the Kra-ell and keep an eye on them for you as well. But do you want him to?"

Kian winced. "Good point."

"I see a few problems with that. Until the cruise ship reaches Colombia, it is defenseless and easily found. The longer it is at sea, and the clearer its course, the easier it will be for Igor to come up with a plan of attack. I'm securing an escort, but the submarine I have in mind has a limited range, and it won't be able to follow the ship across the ocean to the Panama Canal without at least two fueling stops, and it most certainly won't be able to follow it through the canal, and we'll need to find a different escort for the Pacific, which will further complicate things. This will present additional challenges, risks, and delays. Also, in case we are proven correct, and Igor sends a military vessel to hunt our ship, I want to control where the battle will take place. If the *Aurora* sustains catastrophic damage, I don't want it to be in the middle of the Pacific where we can't send rescue vessels to retrieve the people in short order."

As usual, Turner's assessment was spot on. "What do you suggest?"

"Let's see." Turner leaned back, braced his elbow on his fist, and stroked his jaw with two fingers. "Even after we get rid of the trackers and dump them in the sea, Igor will know which ship his people are on. If the *Aurora* manages to outrun whoever he sends to follow it and reach the Atlantic, it has a good chance of evading detection. But once in the Panama Canal, it's once again very easy to find. For obvious reasons, the passage cannot be shrouded or thralled, or compelled away. There are just too many people and resources along the way. In addition, there are many operators in that part of the world whom Igor can reach out to and compel to give chase and do damage. All it would take to sink the cruise ship is ramming another big vessel into it."

Kian lifted his hands. "Okay, you win. We have to offload the Kra-ell before the ship reaches the Panama Canal and make it very clear that we don't have any passengers on board. I would much rather avoid getting our newly-remodeled luxury cruise ship that my sister is supposed to get married on damaged or destroyed."

"Right," Onegus said. "We need to bring the Kra-ell to a location that can accommodate a cruise ship, but that's not densely populated or heavily guarded, and it needs to be closer to Helsinki to minimize their time at sea." He turned to his laptop and brought up the world map. "Where can we take close to four hundred people and a large cargo of livestock?"

KIAN

*T*urner kept rubbing his chin for a long moment, the faraway look in his eyes one that Kian had seen many times before, while the guy's brain worked out a solution to a difficult problem.

"Our best bet is the southwest coast of Greenland. It meets all three criteria."

Kian brought up a map of Greenland. "Why the southwest coast? The eastern coast of Greenland is closer to Helsinki."

"The eastern seaboard of Greenland doesn't have a dock large enough for a ship that size, and there is no airfield nearby with a runway long enough for the size of the plane that will be required to airlift our passengers out of there. Even the one on the south coast that I'm considering can only accommodate small and midsize aircraft. We will need to charter two narrow-body passenger jets."

"What about the livestock?" Onegus asked. "Can we leave it there?"

"Of course." Turner reached for his coffee cup. "Local farmers would be more than happy to collect however many heads of livestock we leave for them."

"How come you are so familiar with Greenland?" Kian asked.

"It's a long story." Turner took a sip from his coffee cup. "The port I'm thinking of is adjacent to an airfield that was built by the US Air Force." Turner paused to take another sip from his coffee. "The seaport and airport are both tiny, and so is the community that supports both. That will make shrouding and thralling everyone in the vicinity easy, which is crucial for transporting four hundred undocumented travelers and overcoming the typical port-of-entry documentation. It will also make it much easier to circumvent any surveillance."

Kian leaned forward. "The type of aircraft you are talking about can't cross the Atlantic and fly all the way to the western coast of South America. Where do you propose we take the Kra-ell?"

Turner shrugged. "The airliners can layover in some remote airport in Canada to refuel and continue to our airstrip. I don't think they are too big to land there."

"They might not be, but I'd rather not paint a large arrow pointing to our runway. Two approaching jetliners landing in a tower-less airfield will draw a lot of unwanted attention in the crowded Southern California airspace. They should be directed to an active but semi-private airfield that, from time to time, receives jetliner traffic from private parties somewhere out in the boonies. We can bus them from there. But that is beside the point. I am not comfortable with so many Kra-ell in the village. Even with Toven controlling them and ensuring their compliance with our instructions and demands, there are too many of them, and they will change the way we live. In addition, they have their particular nutritional needs, and I'm not ready to have sheep and goats grazing in the village. Then there is the issue of the humans and what to do with them."

"You need to bring the subject to the council and let them decide," Turner said. "You know my opinion."

"This is a security issue, so I don't have to get the council's approval for not accepting the Kra-ell, but I will need it if we decide that it is best to bring them here." Kian flicked his gaze to Onegus. "What do you think?"

"The issues you raised are all valid, and we need to work them out, but think of the alternative. Are we comfortable with such a large group of Kra-ell somewhere where we cannot monitor them? If Jade immediately guessed who Toven was, the other purebloods from the original pods might have guessed it as well, and we can't thrall them to forget what they know. If we don't catch Igor and eliminate him, we can't dismiss the possibility of him tracking them down and taking over again. Only this time, he could get out of Jade everything she already knows about us. In my opinion, those risks far outweigh the difficulties and risks of keeping the Kra-ell right where we can keep an eye on them."

Kian hated to admit it, but Onegus wasn't wrong.

Was he right, though?

The truth was somewhere in the middle, but no matter what was decided, it would require some sort of compromise.

Security was the only thing he wasn't willing to compromise on.

Turner cleared his throat. "Both options are problematic and will require a shift in how we run our security, and they will most likely impact our way of life as well. But of the two, I'd much rather have the Kra-ell closely monitored, routinely compelled to neutralize any threat they might pose, and heavily guarded. These objectives can only be achieved by bringing them to the village."

Kian knew he was in the minority, but he wasn't ready to concede yet. "We can't spare the Guardian manpower to effectively guard them. I could slap security cuffs on the adults, but then I won't be any better than Igor. We are supposed to be their liberators, not their new masters. On the other hand, I don't know these people, I can't anticipate their behavior, and I can't allow them to roam free in our midst. They are simply too powerful."

Turner's lips lifted in a conspiratorial smile. "As we've discussed before, Kalugal is taking great interest in the Kra-ell, and from what we've heard from Toven, his lieutenant fancies Jade. Surprisingly, she hasn't taken his head off yet, so she's not averse to his flirting, either. Maybe there is a match there, and if there is, Kalugal might allow the Kra-ell in his section. Since so many Guardians have moved to the third phase, there are plenty of vacancies in the original part of the village to relocate everyone residing in the second phase, and it can be easily annexed to Kalugal's. All you'll have to do is reinforce the fence surrounding it and open it on Kalugal's side. Once Toven is done with their initial compulsion, Kalugal can keep it up on an ongoing basis, with Toven and Mia providing an occasional deep boost. We even have the adjacent canyon area to provide pasture for the animals. That will save you the need to clear it of weeds every year ahead of the fire season."

Kian grimaced. "I still remember the smell of farm animals, and I don't want it anywhere near my house. But that's a minor consideration that we will find a solution for."

Looking at both Onegus and Turner, Kian addressed the last remaining obstacle, signaling his acceptance of the proposed solution. "What would you suggest we do with the humans? They have decades of memories that can't be erased, and even if that wasn't a problem or could be mitigated with compulsion, many of them are so habituated to serving the Kra-ell that they will be afraid to live on their own."

"Let's cross that bridge when we get to it," Turner said. "We have logistics to figure out."

"True." Kian closed his eyes for a brief moment. "I will need to run this by the council and by my mother."

"Naturally." Turner went back to typing on his laptop. "I'll inform the captain of the course we need him to plot."

Onegus nodded. "I'll notify Yamanu and Toven of the change of plans."

26

ELEANOR

"We need to evacuate Safe Haven," Leon dropped the bomb Eleanor had been dreading. "It's only temporary until we catch Igor."

When he'd called at five in the morning and asked her and Emmett to come to his office, she'd guessed that was the reason, but she'd hoped it wasn't.

Her gut tied up in knots, she flicked her gaze to Emmett, who looked as if all the blood had left his face.

"How are they going to catch him?" Emmett asked.

"The assumption is that he will want his people back and will follow the trackers implanted in at least some of them. All Toven and the Guardians need is for him to show up. With their earpieces blocking his compulsion and Toven at the ready, they will apprehend him easily."

"I don't understand." Eleanor frowned. "Kian is doing everything he can to get the Kra-ell safely to the ship and evade Igor. How does that mesh with catching him?"

Leon shrugged. "If they make it easy for Igor, he will know that they are setting a trap for him. Besides, Kian is not as worried about him as much as he is about the human forces Igor might compel to help him. We don't want to be forced to fight them, and we don't want to cause an international incident while transporting aliens."

"That's a sticky situation," Emmett said.

"In your opinion, what's more important?" Eleanor asked. "Getting the Kra-ell away from Igor or catching him?"

Leon pursed his lips. "The most important thing is to prevent Igor from getting them back. He can do a lot of damage without them, but he's much less of a threat on his own. If we are lucky, we will lure him out to sea and catch him there."

"I hope the plan works," Emmett murmured. "I really don't want to abandon Safe Haven. It's my baby, my life's achievement, and I love it here."

"I don't want to leave either," Leon said. "We invested a lot of money in the facility, and Ana and I love it here. But it is what it is."

"What do I do with the paranormals?" Eleanor asked.

"They are not immortal, and they don't know anything, so they can stay if they want. But the holidays are coming up, so I'm sure that they would appreciate a vacation back home."

"That will solve the problem for a couple of weeks." Eleanor got up and lifted Cecilia off the windowsill. "What if we can't catch Igor?"

She sat back down and stroked the cat's soft fur. The warmth and the contented purring eased the anxious knot in her gut.

"Then we will come up with a different solution," Leon said. "You will have to resign from the program, and Emmett will have to deliver televised sermons." He shifted his eyes to Emmett. "You can claim some rare autoimmune syndrome that prevents you from interacting with people."

Emmett groaned. "I need to be with the people, to soak up their energy and their adoration. I live for those moments." He let his head drop back and uttered a mournful groan.

Eleanor rolled her eyes. "I think that Leon's idea has merit, and it's certainly better than nothing." She turned to the Guardian. "Can we move the paranormal program somewhere else? We still didn't test whether any of them are Dormants. The ladies are more difficult to test, and regrettably, the Guardians didn't feel any special affinity toward them or toward the men. But since the males are easy to test, we should give them a chance."

"You are right. After they come back from their vacation and this latest crisis is over, I'll ask Kian's permission to start testing the men. But that's a worry for another time. Right now, you need to talk to the paranormals, tell them that you had some sort of a family emergency, and send them on vacation. We need to get out of here."

"What about the two hybrids assigned to Sofia?"

"I have it covered. I sent two Guardians to retrieve them. Kian doesn't want them to join Igor. The fewer people he has around him, the better."

"Where are we taking them?"

"After we remove their trackers, we will take them to the dungeon in the keep."

Emmett let out a dramatic sigh. "I hated being locked up down there. The Kra-ell need sunlight and air."

"It's only temporary," Leon said. "When Kian decides what he wants to do with the Kra-ell, those two will join the rest."

"I have a better idea." Eleanor kept petting the cat. "If Igor wants the two hybrids and calls them to him, we can follow them. Instead of collecting them and taking them to the keep, it's better to leave them where they are and put a couple of Guardians to tail them."

Leon winced. "We are a little short on Guardians at the moment, which is another reason Kian wants us back in the village. Igor might call those two or not. I'll give Onegus a call and tell him what you suggested."

"Are you taking Cecilia with you?"

Leon shifted his gaze to the cat and smiled. "That's another question for Onegus. We will need to take the tracker out of her, and I don't know if he's ready to do that yet."

"There is no more reason to pretend that Sofia is here," Emmett said. "If we take the tracker out, William can take it apart to see where it was made."

27

KIAN

*O*negus put his phone down, lifted the cup of coffee that was probably cold by now, and finished the last of what was in it. "Yamanu wasn't happy about the change of plan. He had his heart set on a month-long vacation with his mate, and now it's shortened to eight days."

"They can still cancel their plans," Kian said. "They didn't leave yet, did they?"

The three were taking a commercial flight to Helsinki, and since no one in their right mind flew to Finland in the winter, getting last-minute tickets hadn't been a problem.

"No, not yet, but Yamanu still wants Mey to come, and Jin and Arwel are going as well. We will soon have twenty-five of the Guardians back, so I don't mind that Arwel is leaving."

"I don't mind that either," Kian muttered under his breath. "What I mind is Mey and Jin on the ship and Mia and Sofia, not to mention Toven. What if Sofia starts transitioning? They have Merlin, and the ship has a clinic, but I planned on outfitting it in Long Beach, so it has no medical equipment in the clinic yet."

"We are getting an MRI," Turner said. "We might as well get the rest of the equipment delivered as well."

Kian arched a brow. "Did you find one for sale in Helsinki?"

"Bridget found a compact MRI in Turku of all places, and it's already making its way to Helsinki. It will get there before the ship docks. I'm sure Bridget can find everything else that's needed for the clinic locally. I'll let her know to get on it."

Kian hadn't even known that Bridget was assisting Turner, but he should have guessed. The two were a dynamic duo.

"Thanks. And thank Bridget for me as well."

"Sure thing," Turner murmured from behind the screen of his laptop.

"Did you talk with your submariner friend?" Kian asked.

"Not yet." Turner lifted his head. "I'm going to call him once I'm done preparing instructions for him."

"Are you sure he's still in business? You said he retired from the navy over twenty years ago."

Turner smiled. "I know for a fact that he's still taking jobs. I've recommended him to an associate of mine, who used him not too long ago and was very happy with his service. Besides, Nils is never going to quit. He's threatened to do it many times over the years, but he loves what he does too much to let go."

"In case he says no, do you have an alternative?"

"I always do, but it won't be necessary. Nils will come through."

When Kian heard Onegus's phone ping, he turned to the chief with a questioning look.

"It's from Leon. He wants to discuss another option regarding the hybrids. Do you want to call him, or do you want me to do it?"

"I'll call him. I hope we are not too late and the two haven't already disappeared. They could've returned the rental car with the tracker in it and given us the slip."

Onegus shook his head. "That's not likely unless they also found the trackers we put in their backpacks."

"Let's find out." Kian dialed the Guardian's number.

"Hello, boss," Leon answered. "I'll keep it short. Eleanor says that we shouldn't pick up the hybrids. We should follow them instead. If Igor tries to retrieve them, they can lead us to him."

"Good point." Kian rapped his fingers on the tabletop. "Make it so. Put two Guardians on them. They need to have earpieces, tranquilizer darts, and regular guns on them."

Turner lifted his head. "That might not be a good idea. We already know that Igor is super careful and suspicious. If he tells them to come to him, he will do so in a way that will allow him to watch whether they have a tail. If he catches our Guardians, he can compel them to reveal everything they know. It's not worth the risk."

Kian considered it for a moment. "The chances of us catching Igor while he chases his people are slim. We are doing everything we can to keep him from getting to them. Once the dust settles and the Kra-ell are safe, those hybrids might be the only lead we have left."

"We can use Tim," Onegus said. "Jade can describe Igor to him even over the phone, and he can send her pictures of his work in progress. Once he's done, we can use face recognition to find him when he passes through an airport."

"He's too careful to get caught like that." Turner rubbed a spot between his brows as if he was fighting a headache. "He will wear a disguise and the special glasses that elude facial recognition."

"So what do you suggest we do?" Onegus asked.

"I can send a human team to follow the hybrids. If they get caught, they can't tell Igor anything. If we get a good description of him, they can eliminate him for us. As much as I would love to interrogate Igor and learn what he knows, he's too dangerous to capture. The instructions should be kill on sight."

Kian nodded. "I agree, but how do you explain to your human assassins what it takes to kill a Kra-ell?"

"I'll tell them that he's jacked on drugs, super paranoid, and super strong. The only way to take him out is from afar with a small rocket aimed at his head."

Onegus grimaced. "Gruesome, but effective. Just make sure that you instruct them to avoid any collateral damage."

"That might be unavoidable. He will keep the Kra-ell he has close to him."

"I meant innocent bystanders."

"I'll tell them to do their best."

"So, what's the plan?" Leon asked. "Do I send Guardians to watch the hybrids until a human team takes over?"

"Yes. But if they head to the airport before my team arrives, tell the Guardians to follow and verify the flight they are on, but no more. I will have another human team pick up the tail at the destination."

"Got it," Leon said.

"Anything else?" Kian asked.

"The cat. There is no reason to leave the tracker inside of it. Gertrude said that she could take it out, so we are bringing the cat with us, but the question is how to transport the device so William can tinker with it. Supposedly, it doesn't transmit when it's not in a living body, but I don't want to risk it. I can put it inside a thick lead box, but maybe I should ask William what he recommends."

"Do you have a scrambler?" Kian asked.

"I have a small one, but we can't use it on a plane. If you

want me to use it, I will have to send it with the Guardians driving the moving van with the equipment from the lab."

Kian lifted his gaze to Turner. "What do you think?"

"Use a scrambler, and don't bring the tracker to the village. If it came from the gods' planet, it could contain technology we are not familiar with that can transmit through lead and could be impervious to the scrambler."

"If so, William's scrambler would have been ineffective, and Igor would have caught up to them by now."

Turner nodded. "You have a point. But since we can't be sure, I suggest caution. Igor discovering the location of the village is much worse than him discovering where his people are."

"You heard the man," Kian told Leon.

"I did. I'll give instructions to the Guardians driving the moving truck to take it with them and leave it at our downtown warehouse."

Kian looked at Turner. "Good enough? Or do you want us to put it in a safe deposit box in a bank?"

"The warehouse is good. William equipped it with so many security features that it's safer than a bank vault."

Kian returned his attention to Leon. "Anything else you need from me?"

"No, that's it. Eleanor is sending the paranormals, the doctor assigned to them, and the kitchen staff on vacation. Emmett is seriously depressed, and the Guardians are packing up all the sensitive equipment from the lab and our offices. I'm waiting for the moving van to get here. I'll send two guys to follow the hybrids, and when they are in position, I'll tell Gertrude to remove the tracker from the cat. It will be interesting to see what they do once it's out."

"Very well. Let me know if there is a problem."

"Will do."

28

CAPTAIN NILS PETERSON

*N*ils poured himself an afternoon tea and headed out to the porch for a smoke.

This time of year the air was brisk and the wind biting, but his wife did not permit smoking inside, so he'd put on a thick sweater, wrapped a scarf around his neck, and pulled on the cap she'd knitted for him last Christmas.

The smoking den he'd set up for himself on the porch overlooked the harbor, and his open man-cave included a comfortable armchair, a side table with a good reading lamp, and most importantly, a high-BTU gas heater to keep him warm and toasty.

When his phone rang, he didn't recognize the number and let the call go to voicemail. In his line of business, getting calls from unknown numbers was the norm rather than the exception, but he never answered before hearing the message first.

A moment later, he checked the mail and heard a voice he hadn't heard in a while.

"It's Turner. I'll call again in five. Pick up the phone."

Over the years, Turner had sent several referrals his way, but they hadn't worked together in at least a decade.

When the phone rang precisely five minutes later, Nils answered with a smile. "Hello, old friend. What a pleasant surprise. How have you been?"

"Very well. I retired a few years ago and now run a private operation. I specialize in hostage retrieval."

"Sounds exciting. How is business?"

"Booming. How is yours?"

"More or less the same. I'm thinking about retiring." Nils took a drag from his cigar. "I'm getting too old for all this crap."

Turner chuckled. "Guys like us don't retire. We get retired."

"That's what I'm afraid of. Against all odds, I managed to stay alive into my sixties and have enough to live on comfortably for what's left of my life. I can do without all the excitement."

"I doubt you can stay away from the sea for more than a week, but you do what's good for you. Before you give retirement a try, though, you need to take the job I'm offering. It might give you the extra cushion to retire comfortably."

His enigmatic friend never bothered with much preamble.

"What's the job?"

"A good friend of mine has a cruise ship that he suspects might get attacked at sea. It will depart Helsinki in about thirty hours and head toward Greenland. I need a heavily armed submarine escort to the Port of Narsaq on its southern coast."

After the long years Nils had known Turner and run clandestine operations for him, he'd thought that he would never be surprised by any request Turner might make, but he should have known better.

A cruise ship? That was new.

"What exactly are you expecting to encounter?"

"Frankly, we are not certain. We believe the aggressor will try to disable and possibly sink the ship to force the passengers off it. While that could be done by attaching detonation devices to the hull, the more likely scenario is an attack with a missile or a torpedo. And because he will need to collect the two hundred or so individuals he is after, I believe we will be dealing with an attacking ship rather than a sub. Therefore, he'll probably get a cruiser-size vessel."

Nils had great respect for the man's mind, but he needed to know what Turner was basing his assumptions on.

"How did you arrive at that conclusion?"

"The aggressor is interested in the passengers and wants them alive. So he will not bomb the ship out of the water and kill all onboard. Taking over by scaling and rappelling would require far more planning and equipment than he has the time or the ability to put together, so that is not an option either. Stealth sabotage would require trained commandos to which he isn't likely to have access. Once he gets the passengers, he also needs to transport them, so we can rule out a sub or a small gunship. It has to be a cruiser."

Tensing, Nils sat up straight. "I am unaware of any such vessel in our neck of the woods that is not flying the Russian flag. Are you proposing that we sink a Russian cruiser? And why would the Russian navy want to attack a civilian cruise ship? What are you not telling me?"

That last one was a question he did not expect an answer for. It was always only the 'need to know,' and even that was kept to a bare minimum. Turner shared only what was absolutely necessary.

"We believe that the aggressor has the means to do just that by way of funds or coercion or both. This will not be a

Russian navy sanctioned operation, even if one of its ships is involved."

Well, that changed the picture. If Nils disabled a rogue ship that might have caused an unsanctioned international incident, the Russians wouldn't be too upset. They might even be thankful, as long as no one found out that it had been done by a private operator. They would want to take credit for it.

Stubbing out his cigar, he asked, "When did you say the cruise ship is leaving Helsinki?"

"In about thirty hours."

"There is no way I can get the crew and sub ready for this mission so fast. I need at least forty-eight hours. We are moored in an island far to the west, so we can meet up with the cruise ship when it passes by, but that will leave her exposed for most of the way through the Baltic Sea."

Nils imagined he could hear the well-oiled wheels turning in Turner's head as he considered his input.

"It isn't likely that the ship will be attacked in the Baltic. It's too close to the territorial waters of the surrounding countries, where other navy vessels, not to mention military aircraft of all kinds, are a short hop away. The aggressor will opt to attack as far away from land as possible so that calls for help from the ship will take many hours to be responded to by ships or aircraft arriving at the scene. He will need time to sink the ship, collect those he is interested in from the water, and put a safe distance between himself and any incoming rescue vessels. None of these objectives could be met while in the Baltic."

"I see that you have it all figured out."

"I do, but I needed to know that I can count on your help before making the final arrangements. I will instruct the cruise ship captain to hug the coast all the way to Bergen and make the crossing of the North Sea toward the Shetland

Islands there. The proximity to land will provide the cruise ship with some measure of security, but once it leaves the Shetlands behind, we should expect to have at most twenty-four to thirty-six hours before the attack will take place. By that point, anyone responding to a distress call would be many hours away."

Nils considered his options.

A mission so fraught with risks should be planned and thought through with care, not rushed into head-on. An armed altercation with a navy vessel was not the same as stealthily transporting goods and personnel, which was most of what he had been doing for the past decade and a half. He hadn't seen action in so long that he had almost forgotten the rush it used to give him.

He could decline.

Correction, he should decline, but he knew that he wouldn't.

All his talk about retirement and getting tired of the excitement was a lot of bull. The truth was that he was bored with the small-fish operations that kept the lights on. The risks were minimal, but so were the rewards, and the excitement was nil.

Just thinking about a mission of this caliber made his muscles twitch in anticipation. Frankly, he had known that he would say yes to Turner within the first ten seconds of the call.

"Give me a couple of hours to make some calls to make sure I can pull it off for you in time."

"I can't wait that long. If you can't do that, I need to get someone else."

Now Nils tensed for a different reason.

He didn't want Turner to find someone else for this mission. He could already taste it.

"Don't worry. I'll make it happen. Consider it done."

"Excellent. That's what I wanted to hear. What's your price?"

Nils smiled. "I will let you know in a couple of hours, but don't worry. Given our long and successful history of cooperation, I will not take advantage of the tight spot you are in. I'll give you a fair price."

"I'm counting on that. Thank you, Nils."

As soon as Turner ended the call, Nils called Rob Farland, his indispensable second-in-command, and left a message on his secure voicemail. "We are hunting for a big fish, and we need to get on it ASAP. Assemble the crew and have everyone ready in twenty-four hours. I'm taking care of the necessary supplies. "

Supplies were code for munitions.

The line was supposedly secure, but one could never be too careful, and nothing he left in a recorded message could be used to incriminate him.

A couple of moments later, he got a reply. "Aye, aye, captain."

29

JADE

"*This* is so fancy." Kagra walked over to the bed and sat down.

The wedding venue Tom's people had secured for the night was much nicer than anything Jade had expected, but she'd stayed in some luxury hotels during her travels, and she knew what fancy looked like.

This wasn't it, but it was perfect for their needs.

It was outside of town and had over a hundred guest rooms, rolling hills on one side and the Baltic Sea on the other. Including the Guardians and Phinas's men, nearly four hundred people needed a bed and shower. The staff had been told to vacate the premises so there were no strangers they needed to hide from, and they could use the staff quarters to house more people.

Her and Kagra's room faced the sea, and she loved watching the vast expanse of water and the ice floating in the bay. So far this year, the winter had been mild, so the ice floaters didn't form a solid mass yet. In harsher winters, ice breakers were used to carve out a corridor for ships to sail between the major ports.

Had that been the case, it might have deterred Igor from securing a Russian ship to follow them, but that also could have meant the clan's cruise ship couldn't have gotten from the shipyard in Stockholm to the port of Helsinki.

"Come. Check it out." Kagra patted the mattress. "It's so comfy. I've never stayed in a room this nice. Have you?"

"During my travels, I stayed in nice hotels." She sat next to Kagra. "And I slept on comfortable mattresses."

Their accommodations back in China hadn't been nearly as lavish, and her room in Igor's compound was spartan, but it was sufficient.

Jade wasn't picky. The fact that she had served the queen back in the day and lived on the palace grounds didn't mean that she'd lived like royalty. She'd slept in the barracks with the rest of the guards.

When she'd stayed in fancy hotels, it had been for business, and she'd needed to appear wealthy. Otherwise, she would have opted for more modest accommodations.

Kagra leaned back on her forearms. "Tom's clan must have incredible connections in addition to deep pockets. I don't know how they got us this place on such short notice."

"I told Tom they could use the funds they had taken from Igor to finance our rescue. I owe them enough as it is. I don't want to owe them even more."

"Are you sure they are going to give us what's left after they pay themselves for our liberation?"

Jade shrugged. "Tom has given me his word, but you know how much I trust the promises of a god. To be fair, though, so far he has delivered on every promise, so I'm inclined to believe him."

Kagra toed her boots off. "I'm bone tired and want to go to sleep, but I'm filthy and need to shower. Do you mind if I go first?"

"Go ahead. I managed to shower before we left."

"Thanks." Kagra pushed to her socked feet and lifted her boots off the floor. "Do you want to go to the sauna after we shower? Phinas told me that it's a Finnish tradition to have a bridal sauna. The bride and her girlfriends have a party in the sauna before the wedding."

It shouldn't have bothered her that Kagra had spent twelve hours with Phinas, talking and getting to know him, while Jade had been stuck in the command van and had pretended to sleep for most of it to avoid Tom's never-ending string of questions.

But it did bother her, and that wasn't good.

Jealousy and possessiveness were not only character flaws, but they were also considered a sin in the eyes of the Mother of All Life.

"Did you pump him for information?"

The guilty look on Kagra's face indicated the opposite. "Their doctor gave me pain medication. I didn't want to take it, but Phinas convinced me that I would be better prepared to fight when I wasn't in pain, so I took them, and they made me overly talkative."

Jade glared at her. "There is a reason we avoid them as much as possible. They act like alcohol or *tpaba* on us. What did you tell him?"

"Nothing important. He asked a lot of questions about you."

That shouldn't have pleased Jade as much as it did. "And what did you tell him about me?"

Kagra grinned. "I made you sound like a goddess and the best leader possible for our people. I told him about your selflessness and the risks you took to teach our young the ways of the Mother under Igor's nose. I also told him that you are an incredible fighter and won against all the males of our former tribe."

As Jade winced, Kagra's smile wilted. "It felt good to talk

about the old days with someone. But I might have said too much about how we ran our old compound."

"Like what?"

"Like compelling the humans to serve us. Back then, it wasn't a big deal because the Chinese government treated them much worse than we did, but nowadays, it sounds like we were slave owners."

Jade nodded. "I thought about that often during our years of captivity. These people must have felt the same about us as we did about our captors. The only differences between Igor and us were that we didn't slaughter their families, and most of them came to work for us voluntarily. They just didn't know what they were signing up for and that employment was for life."

"Would you have done things differently if given a chance?"

Jade nodded. "I would have been upfront about what was involved in working for us, and I would have compelled those who didn't want to forfeit their freedom to forget what I told them and let them go. I would have probably paid those who chose the security we offered better as well."

"Would you have set free those who wanted to leave?"

Jade shook her head. "The security of my people superseded all other considerations. I couldn't release those who worked for us and bred with our males to tell the world about us."

"Igor released them, and the world is still as ignorant about our existence as it was two decades ago."

"Igor is a much more powerful compeller than I am. Besides, we were no longer there, so there was no risk involved in releasing them. The humans could have told tall stories about us until they were blue in the face, but no one would have believed them without proof."

30

PHINAS

"I'm going to the sauna." Phinas slung a towel over his shoulder. "Either of you want to join me?"

Dandor cast him an incredulous look. "In your underwear, a T-shirt, and barefoot? It's freezing out there."

"It's not like we packed for a vacation. Besides, we are immortals." Phinas thumped his chest. "I bet the Kra-ell don't have a problem with the cold."

Boleck pulled the blanket under his chin. "I heard that the Finns enjoy saunas in the nude. Do they have separate rooms for males and females?"

"I don't know."

Boleck turned on his side. "I'm going to sleep. If there are naked ladies in the sauna, come get me."

"I'm going to sleep as well," Dandor said. "It's four o'clock in the morning, and I want to get some shut-eye before we start hustling again. When are we boarding the ship?"

"When it's ready, which should be this afternoon or evening." Phinas opened the door. "If either of you change your mind, you know where to find me."

As he trudged through the snow to the building where

the saunas were located, Phinas hoped that he would find Jade enjoying one of the rooms. According to the brochure, the venue offered different types of saunas, wet, dry, and smoked.

Finnish saunas were the dry heat kind, not steam, and given where Phinas had grown up, he'd experienced enough dry heat to last him his entire immortal lifetime. Then Navuh had moved the brotherhood to a tropical island, and the humid heat wasn't an improvement, but at least the island was pretty.

Then again, it was freezing cold as Dandor had said, and Phinas's feet were getting numb, so some heat, even the dry kind, would be welcome. But he wasn't going to the sauna to enjoy it. He hoped to meet Jade, but given what he'd learned from Kagra, there was little chance of that.

According to her second, Jade was all work and no play. During the long years of her captivity, the Kra-ell leader had denied herself pleasure as penance for failing to protect her people. Kagra claimed that Jade hadn't been forced to become Igor's prime, and that she'd chosen to do it as additional atonement.

That type of person wouldn't enjoy a sauna in the middle of the night, but hope was a powerful thing, and perhaps fate would smile on him.

As Phinas entered the building, he was immediately enveloped in heat, which was a tremendous relief. The sauna rooms were lined up on both sides of the wide corridor; some of them were small, only big enough for two or three people, while others were large enough to accommodate a small party, and thankfully they all had small windows he could peek through to see whether there was anyone inside.

Most were empty, which wasn't surprising given the hour of the night, but some were occupied, which explained the heat permeating the building. Several Guardians were in one

of the larger rooms, enjoying beers in the nude. Their bois-
terous laughter made him smile, and if he didn't find Jade, he
was going to join them and share a couple of beers with
them, provided that they had any to spare.

The next several rooms were empty, one had a couple of
human females who were wrapped in towels, and the one
next to it was where he found Jade and Kagra, both glori-
ously naked.

They had no breasts to speak of, but their bodies were
slender, graceful, and feminine. Their long limbs didn't look
overly muscled, but their appearance was deceptive. Phinas
had experienced firsthand how powerful Kra-ell females
were, and he had only tumbled with an untrained hybrid.
Those two were probably twice as strong as Aliya and ten
times as lethal.

Should he knock and go in?

Could they sense him standing outside the door and
ogling them?

Well, not them. He had eyes only for Jade. Not that Kagra
wasn't pleasing to look at, but he wasn't attracted to her.

Jade's inner strength was what drew him to her. Even as
relaxed as she appeared now, there was a hard line to her
expression, a determination to fight to the very end, to do
everything in her power to lead her people to freedom.

He found her formidable will sexy as hell.

Were the Kra-ell females as comfortable with their nudity
as their immortal cousins?

There was only one way to find out.

Draping a hand over his eyes, he opened the door. "May I
join you, ladies? Or am I not allowed to gaze upon your
beautiful naked bodies?"

Jade chuckled. "If you know that our bodies are beautiful,
you've already seen them, so you might as well come in."

Grinning, he dropped his hand. "Hallelujah, praise the

sweet Fates, and thank you." He went in, closed the door behind him, and sauntered to the bench opposite the two females.

Jade eyed him with an amused smirk lifting the corners of her lush lips. "Are you going to take your shirt and those swimming trunks off? If you're not comfortable getting naked with us, you'll have to leave."

He was glad she'd mistaken his dark gray undershorts for swimming trunks.

"I'm very comfortable with my body." He put the towel on the bench next to him, whipped his shirt over his head, and put it over the towel. Turning around, he gave Kagra and Jade his rearview as he took off the undershorts.

"Very nice," Jade said as he turned to face them with his shaft at half-mast.

It would have been at full mast if Kagra wasn't there. Phinas was proud of his body, but he didn't like to parade it like a show horse.

"Thank you." He gave them a bow before sitting down and crossing his legs to hide his package.

It wasn't that he was embarrassed. As humans and immortals went, he was well endowed, but for all he knew, the Kra-ell might be hung like horses.

Besides, both ladies were sitting with their legs crossed and hiding their feminine treasures, so he could at least try to be a gentleman and do the same instead of flaunting his assets.

31

JADE

"I'd better head to bed." Kagra pretended to rise with effort.

She'd been fine on the way to the sauna.

Jade cast her a glare. "You were the one who insisted on coming here, and now you're leaving?"

Kagra grabbed her underwear and shimmied into them. "I'm recovering from a nearly fatal injury." She took her long-sleeved thermal shirt and pulled it over her head. "Merlin said that I need to rest as much as possible." She turned her back to Phinas and winked at Jade.

"Traitor," Jade mouthed.

"You're welcome," Kagra mouthed back and then turned to Phinas. "See you later, as they say in the movies." She padded out of the room and closed the door behind her.

The female watched way too many American movies. That was not how the Kra-ell behaved when they were prowling for a bed partner. Jade didn't need to create special circumstances to be alone with Phinas, and she didn't need to flirt with him and drop hints like human females did. If she wanted him, all she had to do was issue an invitation, and he could either accept or decline.

Not that there was a chance he would say no to her. The immortal was attracted to her.

Still, sex wasn't the only thing she wanted from Phinas.

She wanted information about the political makeup of the clan and why his people cooperated with Tom's but didn't become one unit with them. She wanted to find out about his boss, the guy named Kalugal, and what role he played in the clan's leadership. Those things couldn't be achieved by a simple invitation to her bed. She needed to play the flirting game that humans engaged in and apparently immortals as well.

Jade needed Phinas to fall for her, and she had no clue how to do that.

Perhaps she should have watched more of those romantic movies Kagra favored, but the truth was that they nauseated her. The female leads in those silly movies were so weak, so pliable, and even the men were mostly spoiled and soft.

Shifting her gaze to Phinas, she saw him watching her intently, but to his credit, his gaze was focused on her face and not her breasts or lower.

Well, her breasts were nonexistent compared to those of human and immortal females. She'd only met two so far. Mia was tiny all over with small breasts to match, but Sylvia had an impressive cleavage.

"Why are you looking at me like that?" she asked.

"Like what?"

"Like you are trying to read my thoughts. I hope it's not one of your paranormal talents."

He smiled. "I have no special talents. I can thrall and shroud, but nothing compared to Yamanu's god-like ability."

"Tom says that even he can't do what Yamanu can. He says that he's out of practice."

Phinas shrugged. "If you're asking whether I can verify that statement, the answer is no. I don't know Tom well. He's a relative newcomer to the clan."

She tilted her head, her long black hair cascading down her front and covering her left breast. "Are you and your men newcomers as well?"

He nodded.

"Why are you collectively called Kalugal's men?"

"Because he's our boss, and we came with him."

Phinas wasn't lying, but he wasn't telling her everything either. He was holding back. Perhaps she needed to flirt with him first to soften him up.

What was she supposed to say? That she found him attractive? Would he consider it too forward? If the immortals were like human males, they didn't like aggressive females, but Jade didn't know what the rules of engagement were.

She really should have paid more attention to those awful movies.

"Your form is pleasing." She gave his body a once-over. "Do you train a lot?"

He was about her height but at least three times as broad and muscular. Not that it mattered. She could still overpower him effortlessly. It was a wonder the gods hadn't improved their descendants' physical strength over the millennia she'd been in stasis.

Given his satisfied grin, it had been the right thing to say.

"I train for about an hour every day. What about you?"

"At least three hours, sometimes more if I'm training someone else."

"Do you enjoy that?"

She tilted her head. "Which part? Training myself or others?"

"Both."

"I enjoy all aspects of training, but teaching the most. It gives me great satisfaction when someone I trained excels."

"What if they best you?"

She laughed. "It hasn't happened yet, but I will feel pride when it does." As a memory of Drova offering her a hand up surfaced, the smile slid off Jade's face. "There was one time when my daughter managed to best me, but that wasn't because of her skill. I was distracted. Still, she did well, and I was proud of her accomplishment."

"Where is she now?"

"In a room with three other pureblooded females and a Guardian posted outside."

"I'm sorry," Phinas said. "I hope she and the others will be allowed more freedom on the ship."

PHINAS

*I*t wasn't the strangest conversation Phinas had ever had with a female, but given that they were both naked, it was certainly novel. They were like a couple of buddies hanging out in the sauna and talking shop, with the minor distraction of a raging erection.

Not that there was anything minor about it.

Jade shrugged. "I don't know why they bother. If Drova wasn't compelled to cooperate, she could easily overpower the guard. I trained her well. It's unnecessary to keep her and the others locked up and guarded."

She sounded proud of her daughter, and given who the girl's father was, it wasn't obvious.

Phinas's heart ached for the female and what she'd been through.

He knew what it meant to be forced to breed with the enemy. His mother was a Dormant who'd given Navuh's army eight warriors and four Dormant breeders, each from a different father, and each against her will, and yet she'd loved her children and had done the best she could for them given her circumstances.

His sisters were long gone, and out of his seven brothers, six were still alive and served Navuh.

Phinas had been the odd man out, gifted or maybe cursed with intelligence and compassion the others didn't possess. Perhaps his father had been different.

"We are being vigilant," he said. "You don't want Igor to find you and take over again, do you?"

"Of course not. But if I was in charge of the operation, I would have just posted guards at key access points. Your William disabled all communications, so it's not like any of the Kra-ell or the humans can sneak into an office and call Igor even if they were inclined to." Her eyes widened. "I forgot all about the human descendants away at the university. We will need to collect them. They won't know what happened to their families."

Phinas was surprised that she cared. Kalugal had told him that everyone described Jade as a heartless bitch who didn't give a damn about the humans in her old compound or Igor's.

"I'm sure their families told Yamanu about them. In the meantime, it's unclear where we are taking you, so there is no point in collecting them. On second thought, perhaps we should get to them before Igor does it first. He might do that out of spite."

Jade shook her head. "Igor doesn't do anything out of spite because he's devoid of feelings. He's a calculating bastard who believes that the goal justifies the means."

"What's his goal?"

She shrugged. "In the short term, it was a Kra-ell society that was patriarchal and not matriarchal. In the long run, who knows? He's not the sharing type."

Phinas closed his eyes and leaned his head against the wood panel behind him. He was sitting in a sauna with a gorgeous naked female, both of them sweaty and glistening, and they were talking politics.

It didn't get much more pathetic than that.

How could he turn this tanker in the right direction?

"Did I say something to upset you?" Jade asked. "Or are you tired and want to call it a night?"

He opened his eyes and smiled. "I enjoy talking to you. Hell, I enjoy being with you, and I wouldn't mind calling it a night if we retired to the bedroom together, but I'm out of my element with you. You are unlike any female I've met before, and I don't know how to court you."

"You don't need to court me. I owe you a life-debt, and you can ask anything you want of me."

Phinas flinched. "Let's make one thing clear. I will never use that vow to get you to have sex with me. In fact, I don't plan on ever invoking your vow to demand anything of you. Not even a cup of coffee."

Jade frowned, looking offended. "Why not? Am I so vile that you can't fathom asking anything of me?"

He lifted his hands in the air. "What I said must have been lost in translation. I appreciate your gratitude and am willing to accept a thank you, but nothing more than that. I didn't save Kagra as a favor to you."

"You have to let me repay the debt. If you don't, it will shame me."

"That's nonsense."

Her eyes flickered red. "Don't belittle my beliefs. I owe you a life-debt, and if you don't collect, you will sentence me to forever walk in the valley of the shamed. I've worked very hard to earn my place in the fields of the brave."

Religion was irrational, but it was powerful, and he couldn't change her mind, but he could trick her.

"Does it matter what I ask for?"

She narrowed her huge eyes at him. "Don't make it something insignificant. That would shame me just as much as you not collecting on the debt at all."

Damn it. She wasn't easy to trick.

"Do you know what the Finns like to do after they get all hot and toasty in a sauna?"

She winced. "They like to dunk themselves in ice water."

"You are not a fan."

"I'm not."

"Can you swim?"

She shook her head. "I never tried."

"Then that's what I want as payment. I want you to come with me to the beach, and I'll teach you to swim."

Her huge eyes turned even bigger, and then she blinked. "The water is freezing. Can't you think of something else? I'd much rather escort you to your bedroom and show you how the Kra-ell have sex."

If he wasn't sitting with his legs crossed and cutting the blood supply to his shaft, it would have jumped to attention.

"I'm sharing a room with two other guys, I'm not an exhibitionist, and I'd much rather show you how the immortals make love than learn how the Kra-ell do it. I promise you that you will enjoy it much more than anything you experienced with your purebloods."

33

JADE

*P*hinas's words did something unexpected to Jade. They made her curious, and she'd never been curious about making gentle love.

Love.

It was such a human concept.

The Kra-ell didn't believe in love. There was affection and lust, loyalty and devotion, friendship and camaraderie, but not love. The word was vague and therefore meaningless.

It was also weak.

Love was supposed to be unconditional, and that was what made the concept absurd. Except for lust, which was instinctive because it was necessary for procreation, every emotion worth anything had to be earned. Affection and friendship weren't freely given to the undeserving, and that was even more true for loyalty and devotion, which occupied the top tier on the scale of emotions.

Motherhood was the closest Jade had experienced to feeling love, but that had been fueled by the instinct to nurture and protect the young, which nearly every animal had. It wasn't a choice, and it couldn't be applied to the males who were necessary to the creation of new life.

The only criterion applied should be the kind of offspring they could produce.

Jade had appreciated her sons' fathers, had even admired one of them for his sharp mind, and had enjoyed the rough coupling the males had provided. She mourned their deaths and missed them as much as she'd missed all the other lost members of her tribe, but that was the extent of her feelings for them.

Still, Kagra had enjoyed softer forms of intimacy, and she'd recommended that Jade try them.

Jade had been mildly intrigued, but it hadn't been in the cards until she'd met Phinas.

Kagra had experimented with hybrid males, but Jade had a reputation to uphold, and humans had never been an option.

An immortal male was a different story, though, and Phinas was a natural choice.

He was the commander of Kalugal's men, Tom and the Guardians seemed to respect him, he was intelligent, a good fighter, had a good sense of humor, was good-looking, and most importantly, he could give her immortal offspring. Tom had said that only the immortal mothers transferred their immortal genes to their children, but that was when immortals bred with humans. A union between an immortal male and a pureblooded Kra-ell female might produce different results.

She was long-lived, so perhaps her genes only needed reinforcement from his. After all, they were both related to the gods.

But then, so were humans.

There was the issue of the prohibition on coupling with gods, but Phinas wasn't a god, so technically she wouldn't be breaking any laws by being with him.

Besides, Jade was a long way from home, in distance as well as in time, and she could make her own rules as long as they didn't contradict the Mother's teachings.

Except, the gods back home hadn't allowed unions between gods and Kra-ell either, and a hybrid child was considered an abomination, so maybe Phinas was not allowed to breed with anyone other than immortal females.

Jade had never been clear on the reasons for the strong taboo. Was it just pride and the wish to preserve the purity of their races? Or was there a biological reason?

She believed that it was the former. If both gods and Kra-ell could breed with humans and produce healthy offspring, there was no reason to believe that a union between a god and a Kra-ell would produce an abomination.

Nevertheless, Phinas might believe that.

Thankfully she wasn't in her fertile cycle, so he had nothing to worry about, and by the time she was fertile again, she would find out his people's stance on the subject.

She would also have time to decide whether she wanted to be the first one to put the taboo to the test.

"Ready for your first lesson?" Phinas rose to his feet and offered her a hand up.

With his shaft right in front of her face, she had to pry her eyes from it to lift them to his luminous gaze. When she smiled, exposing her fangs, his shaft twitched and bobbed in excitement.

Was he turned on by her fangs?

Would he welcome her bite?

She hoped so. Drawing blood from a bed partner was a major part of a Kra-ell mating ritual for a reason. It was extremely pleasurable for the taker and the giver and resulted in a powerful climax for both.

"I hope you're not talking about swimming in the icy water," she purred.

Instead of answering her question, he lifted his hand and brushed his fingers over the curve of her cheek. "Your skin is so soft."

Without much thought, she shifted her face into the touch, leaning her cheek against the palm of his hand.

He sucked in a breath, and as she tugged on his hand and pulled him down to the bench, he didn't resist.

She pushed on his chest, guiding him to his back. "The wood must have all burned out. It's getting a little cooler in here." She leaned into him.

"I don't know about that. To me, it feels hotter." His hand closed over the nape of her neck.

Letting him pull her head down, she kissed him.

Phinas parted his lips for her, and as she pushed her tongue into his mouth and flicked it over his, he wrapped his arms around her back and pulled her flat on top of him.

He let her explore him for as long as she pleased, and even though his erection was hard like a steel rod against her belly, he didn't rush her. Caressing her back, he kissed her back softly, unhurriedly.

As he weaved his fingers through her long hair and cupped her bottom, the tenderness of his gentle touch was so different from anything she'd experienced before.

Jade let go of his mouth and trailed a line of kisses down his neck, nipping his salty skin with her sharp fangs but never drawing blood. She followed with her tongue, soothing and healing the small scrapes on contact.

Did Phinas find the implied threat of her fangs as thrilling as a pureblooded male would?

If the twitch of his shaft was any indication, he did.

Sliding lower down his sweat-slicked body, she licked the skin on his chest, and as she traced the defined lines of his pectorals and his abdominals, she marveled at the sculpted perfection of him.

Phinas was a beautiful specimen, a testament to the perfected genes he had inherited from the gods.

They were manipulative bastards who worshiped perfection, but they knew how to make everything beautiful, including themselves and their offspring.

As Phinas kept himself still, with only his hands moving over her back, Jade wondered whether he was afraid to move lest he spurred her aggression, or whether he was enjoying what she was doing so much that he didn't want her to stop.

His impressive restraint held until she slid further down, and her hardened nipples brushed over his erection. He jerked, and when she settled between his legs and kissed his shaft, he bucked up, nearly toppling them both to the floor.

"Careful." She smiled up at him. "This ledge is very narrow."

"I won't move." He belied his words by gripping her waist. "You're so slim that my fingers touch when my hands encircle your middle."

She stilled. "Does that turn you off?"

A laugh bubbled out of him as he lifted his hips. "Does that look like a turn-off to you?"

"Maybe you haven't been with a female for a while." She curled her hand around his length and moved it up and down. "Males are ruled by their baser needs. A touch in the right place is all that's needed to elicit a response. They are simple creatures."

"They are," he groaned. "But I'm not. You're the hottest female I've ever met. Never doubt that."

She gave him a smile. "I don't have confidence issues, and you don't need to smother me with flattery. I'm just curious about our differences. I've never been with a male who wasn't a pureblooded Kra-ell."

34

PHINAS

*P*hinas had guessed as much, but hearing Jade confirm it excited him. He liked being the first non-Kra-ell to show her a new way to make love.

No pressure.

If he disappointed her, not only would he bear the shame, but he would also shame all his immortal brethren.

But it was worth it. He was an old immortal, and novelty was his life's spice.

"I'm fascinated by you." He ran his fingers through her long hair, marveling at the silky texture.

"What exactly are you fascinated by?" She flicked her tongue over the tip of his shaft, licking off a drop of precum.

"Everything, but at this moment, I'm fascinated by your tongue. It's long, pointy, and it has a dark triangle at the tip."

Smiling, she stuck her tongue out and wiggled it like a snake. "The tongue is a highly erogenous zone for us, and it's also a status symbol. The darker the triangle, the more royal blood we have in us."

That was an interesting tidbit of information. He'd

noticed that the triangle on Kagra's tongue was much lighter. It was just a darker shade of pink.

No wonder Jade had been the leader of her tribe. She was related to the royals.

"How much royal blood do you have in you?"

"Very little. The royals have triangles that are all black. They are much more distinct. Mine is nothing special, but not many settlers had royal blood in them, so out here, it gets more respect than it had back home."

He wanted to know how close Jade had been to the Kraell queen, but now he had sex on his mind, and talking could wait for later.

"I find your tongue very sexy, especially when I imagine it around my shaft."

A mischievous grin lifted the corners of her lips. "Like this?" She flicked her tongue out, wrapped it around his shaft, and squeezed.

"Fates, Jade. I must have died and gone to heaven."

Talk about novelty. The things Jade could do with her tongue were the stuff of the most outlandish fantasies. Not that he'd ever fantasized about a tongue like that because he hadn't known that it existed.

Had Jade given this pleasure to the pureblooded males she'd been with?

She'd had no reason to go out of her way to provide pleasure to the males of her tribe who'd been her subordinates, but perhaps Igor had forced her to do that for him.

At the thought, a hiss left Phinas's lips, and his erection deflated.

Letting go of his shaft, Jade looked at him in alarm. "Did I hurt you?"

"No, beautiful, you didn't." He cupped her cheek. "I just let a random thought upset me."

"What was it?"

He wasn't going to mention her servitude to Igor while she was anywhere near his shaft, and perhaps he should never bring it up at all. If she wanted to talk about it, he would listen, but he wouldn't ask.

Jade was a proud female, and she might prefer to bury the past along with the male whose head she was about to chop off.

He forced a smile. "Nothing that should enter this space at this moment."

She nodded. "Shadows of the past have a way of intruding at the most inopportune moments."

Gripping him gently at the base, she flicked her incredible tongue around the top portion of his erection, and as she started moving it up and down, the pleasure was so intense that Phinas knew he had to stop her, or he would shoot his load in seconds.

He could be up and ready for the second round in moments, but this was his first time with Jade, and starting up by filling her mouth with his seed was not the way to go.

Stifling a groan, he cupped her cheek, letting her know he wanted her to stop. "My turn. I promised to show you how immortals make love."

When she unwrapped her tongue, leaving his shaft wet and bereft, he mourned the loss of the sensation.

"And how is that?" Jade asked.

As Phinas folded his arms around her and flipped her under him, he knew he could do that only because she allowed it.

The memory of trying to catch Aliya was still fresh in his mind. She'd handed him his ass and then some, and he'd been attracted to her strength as well, but he'd made the mistake of not seeing the fragile young soul inside the powerful body.

Jade was cut from a very different cloth than the former member of her tribe.

It was like comparing a kitten to a lioness.

Dipping his head, he took her mouth in a kiss that was just a shade on the dominant side to test the waters, and when she responded by wrapping her long arms around him and squeezing his buttocks, he had his answer and got even rougher.

As the flare in Jade's arousal sent a wave of her feminine scent to his nostrils, it was very similar to the scent of the immortal females he'd been with, only more potent.

Maybe the Kra-ell and the immortals weren't so different after all.

Snaking his hand between their bodies, he brushed his fingers over the moist petals guarding her sheath, and as he trailed them over the bundle of nerves at their top, he was happy to discover that Jade's anatomy wasn't different from that of other females he'd been with, human and immortal.

She moaned, her enormous eyes rolling back in her head, and then her hand was between their bodies, covering his and guiding his fingers inside of her.

As he pushed with two fingers and started pumping, she kept her hand over his, her knuckles rubbing against his erection and providing friction that in his heightened state of arousal would make him climax in no time.

He moved his fingers faster, harder, his hips churning and grinding his shaft over Jade's knuckles, and when he dipped his head and grazed his fangs over her nipple, she let out a sound he'd never heard before, and her body shuddered under him.

Her climax snapped Phinas's restraint, and as his seed erupted between their bodies, he sank his fangs into Jade's neck, only dimly aware that she was offering it to him without a fight.

35

JADE

*T*hroughout her adult life, Jade had gotten many bites, and she'd been ready for the venom's aphrodisiac effects and the euphoria that followed, but the Kra-ell had much less venom, only enough to make the bite pleasurable instead of painful.

What she'd experienced after getting bitten by pureblooded Kra-ell males couldn't compare to what she was experiencing now. The rush of pleasure washing over her pulled a string of climaxes from her, leaving her limp and pliant under the heavy weight of Phinas's muscled body.

Jade didn't mind the weight.

She didn't mind being under him instead of on top of him.

She didn't mind anything.

For the first time in longer than she could remember, Jade was at peace, floating on the clouds of euphoria but still tethered to the ground. If her body hadn't been so used to venom, she would have probably blacked out, and the tether would have snapped.

It could have been wonderful to leave her corporeal body

for a little while and float in a dream-like state, but it wasn't meant to be.

Not for her.

Her tether was made of duty and responsibility, and she could never let it snap.

Jade opened her eyes and looked into the warmth of Phinas's amber gaze. His eyes, which were normally brown, were illuminated from the inside, turning his irises into twin jewels. His fangs had retracted, though, which was a shame.

He looked feral with them fully elongated.

Sexy. Virile.

"You have beautiful eyes." She lifted her hand and cupped his cheek.

He chuckled. "Thank you. I'm sorry about the poor performance. I promise to do better next time."

"You did fine." She put her hands on his waist, lifted him off her, sat up, and sat him down beside her. "We should hit the showers before we head back to our rooms." She reached for the bucket of water, ladled some, and poured it over the sticky aftermath of their passion.

He took the bucket and the ladle as she passed them to him, but he didn't move to wash himself.

Holding the ladle, he gaped at her. "Fine? That's the worst performance evaluation I've ever gotten. I will forever walk in the valley of the shamed."

Rolling her eyes, she slapped his arm playfully. "Don't make fun of my beliefs."

"I'm not making fun of them. I feel ashamed. I have to make it up to you and turn fine into fabulous. I'm already primed for another round."

Jade glanced at his hardening erection. "That's impressive. It would have taken a Kra-ell pureblood a few moments longer." She shifted her gaze to his eyes. "I enjoyed our interlude very much even though it was different than what I'm used to, and your venom bite was exquisite."

It was odd that he needed reassurance from her.

Hell, it was weird that he was still there, and they were talking.

Kra-ell didn't converse after sex, and the male left as soon as it was over.

Sex the Kra-ell way was a simple affair. All her partners needed to do was overpower her, and nature did the rest. The fight was the foreplay, and being subdued was the primer for climaxing. Everything progressed fast from that moment on, and as soon as it was over, the male was supposed to leave.

Phinas let out a breath. "It's shameful for an immortal male to let the venom do his work for him. I'm glad that I managed to give you at least one orgasm before the bite."

It was so strange to spend time analyzing the sex, but it wasn't unpleasant, and surprisingly, Jade was not counting the moments until Phinas left. She enjoyed his closeness, and she was not in a rush to leave either.

"We are still learning each other in more ways than one, and first times are always awkward. I still remember mine. I was so scared."

He pursed his lips. "I don't believe you. You are not afraid of anything."

"I'm afraid of many things, I just don't let fear rule me. I was scared, the male I chose to invite was as inexperienced as I was, and he was terrified as well. Instead of fighting for dominance, we kind of danced around each other, not knowing what to do."

"How old were you?"

"Twenty. That's the age of consent for the Kra-ell." She smiled at him. "For the males. Females are free to invite males as soon as they believe they are ready, but we were not supposed to invite any male younger than twenty to our beds."

"Interesting. It's seventeen for us, and we live longer. It should have been the other way around."

"Perhaps." She leaned against the back panel and closed her eyes. "I feel languid, and I haven't felt that way for so long." She opened her eyes and slanted him a smile. "It's your doing. You deserve a visit to the fields of the brave just for that. It's one hell of an accomplishment."

Phinas laughed. "I thought it was blasphemy to invoke your religion in such an irreverent way."

"It is for you, not for me."

"Got it." He scooted closer so their thighs and arms were touching and took her hand. "If I am to do better next time, I need more feedback than the dreaded word fine. Obviously, I wasn't too rough, but was I rough enough?"

Jade released a long breath. "I'm not in the habit of analyzing the nuances of pleasure. We are both relaxed after climaxing, we are having a nice, civilized conversation afterward, and I still want to have sex with you again. That should be good enough."

When he smiled, his fangs seemed longer, and his eyes started glowing again. "Do you want to have sex with me now?"

Jade shook her head. "It's almost morning, and I need to catch a few hours of sleep. We will have plenty of opportunities to continue our sexual training on the ship." She let her head fall back against the wood-paneled wall and closed her eyes.

36

PHINAS

*S*exual training.

What a strange way to refer to lovemaking. It might have been a lost-in-translation thing, but when Jade used the term in that fashion, Phinas found it arousing.

Hell, everything she did was sexy to him, except when she used the word fine to describe his performance.

Strangely, though, he wasn't as embarrassed as he should be.

He was Jade's first immortal lover and, as such, a representative of all immortal males. He should have wowed her, left her breathless and panting for more.

He had failed miserably at that, but she'd said he'd satisfied her, and Jade wasn't the type who would say that to stroke a male's ego.

She'd meant it.

But then, she'd also said that she needed to catch up on sleep, but she hadn't shown any indication of wanting to leave, and neither did he.

It felt good being with her, just sitting next to her and talking, and he was too tired to analyze what it meant, only that it wasn't like him. He'd almost never spent the night with a hookup, and if he had, it was because he'd fallen asleep, or it hadn't been safe to leave the lady alone.

"You didn't tell me the rest of the story." He gave Jade's hand a gentle squeeze.

She smiled without opening her eyes. "About my first time?"

"It's the only story you told me, so yeah. The last thing you said was that you didn't fight for dominance and danced around each other instead."

"We circled each other for a few moments, and then he sighed and lowered his arms. He didn't want to fight me, but giving up would have shamed him, and he wouldn't have gotten any other invitations. I didn't want to be responsible for that. So I told him we would pretend to train, and I'd show him a few new moves I'd learned recently. I demonstrated the first move, we practiced it a few times, and when he got better at it, he took over." Jade opened her eyes. "It went smoothly from there. Regrettably, our union did not result in conception. I chose that male because he was smart, not because he was the strongest warrior I knew. I wanted a smart child."

Phinas frowned. "You wanted to get pregnant after your first time?"

"Of course." She looked at him as if his question was dumb. "Every adult Kra-ell female's duty is to produce as many offspring as possible. When we are in our fertile cycle, that's the only reason for breeding. We do it for pleasure only when we are not fertile."

"Are you fertile now?"

She shook her head. "I wouldn't be here if I was."

Her words were like a kick to the gut. "Am I not good enough for you to breed with? You only want pureblooded children?"

She cast him a sidelong glance. "Are you allowed to father a half-breed child?"

"I'm not asking anyone's permission."

"I might not have phrased it correctly." She tapped her long fingers on her bare knee. "Back home, gods and Kra-ell didn't breed, and a mixed offspring was considered an abomination. I don't know whether that's true or they just wanted to preserve the purity of the races, and I also don't know your people's stance on the subject."

"We didn't even know that Kra-ell existed, so we didn't have any rules against producing children with them, but fate put your Vrog in the path of one of the clan females, and they produced a child, who grew up to be a wonderful man. I don't know him personally, but I've heard only good things about him."

Jade's eyes briefly flashed turquoise. "I would like to meet him."

"I wish I could promise you that, but it's not up to me."

Jade sighed. "Your mighty Kian, right?"

"He's not mine, but yeah. He makes the rules."

"I thought he needed to listen to the council."

Phinas chuckled. "I'm not entirely clear on how the clan governs itself and what Kian needs the council's approval on. I think that whenever safety is the issue, he doesn't need to confer with them unless he wants to."

She nodded. "From what Tom told me, I know that Kian does not allow humans into the clan except for some special circumstances."

"That's true."

"So that means he doesn't allow the immortal males to produce children with human females either because their offspring will be human."

"I don't think there is a law about it. It's more of a recommendation. Fortunately, it's not much of a concern.

168

Immortal fertility is very low, and the chances of us getting a female pregnant are almost negligible." He turned to look into her eyes. "So you have nothing to worry about me getting you pregnant even when you are in your fertile cycle. Regardless, I don't like being considered as not good enough to father your child."

She nodded, not bothering to deny it. "It's not about being good enough or not. Before you told me about Vrog's son, I was wary of being the first to risk such an experiment. That's why I would like to meet him. I want to see what combination of Kra-ell and immortal attributes he has."

"As I said, I don't know him, so I can't tell you. I think he's a graphic artist."

She pursed her lips. "That must have come from his mother's side. The gods are into art. The Kra-ell, not as much."

Phinas came from a society that sneered at art, so he wasn't surprised that the Kra-ell didn't appreciate it either.

"I'm curious." He tilted his head. "Was the aversion to mixing gods and Kra-ell a cultural thing, or was it law?"

"The gods were forbidden to take Kra-ell into their beds, and the Kra-ell were forbidden to take gods. Both societies outlawed it."

"Why?"

Jade let out a sigh. "Why are members of one human caste forbidden to marry members of another? Why can't people from different religions get a religious wedding unless one of them converts to the other?"

"I don't know," Phinas said. "I don't understand that."

"The polite explanation is that every group wants to preserve its authentic essence, but the truth is that every group thinks that it's better than the other and doesn't want to dilute what it considers its superior blood."

37

DARLENE

"Welcome back." Darlene hugged Gilbert. "Are you done with everything you set out to do?"

"The house is ready to be rented out, and I have a realtor taking care of that. The building projects are going well, but sales are sluggish. With interest rates going crazy, people can't afford mortgages."

He looked worried, and there were dark circles under his eyes.

"How bad is it?" Eric asked his brother.

"Bad. I got the construction loan before the rate hikes, but the loan has an adjustable rate, so the monthly payments went up a lot, and I'm not selling enough houses to cover the loan payments. I met with the bank manager and the under-writer, and they are willing to extend the loan, but they can't budge on the rate. I will be lucky if I break even on both projects." He raked his fingers through his thinning hair. "It wasn't the best time to leave everything behind and manage things remotely, but it is what it is." He cast a loving glance at Karen. "It's just money, right?"

"Right." Karen nodded. "At least we don't need to worry

about going bankrupt. We have everything we need here in the village, and when we transition successfully, we won't need medical insurance either."

"You don't need it now," Eric said. "Bridget and Julian can take care of almost any medical problem."

Gilbert lifted his hands in the air. "We are not destitute yet, and I can still afford medical insurance for my family. However, that's not the case for many Americans. Who can afford premiums of over two grand a month and in addition pay hundreds and sometimes thousands in copays? If I knew I was about to turn immortal, I wouldn't have done the colonoscopy I was charged eighteen hundred dollars copay for."

Karen frowned. "You didn't tell me that you had a colonoscopy. When was that?"

Gilbert blanched. "Remember when I was feeling dizzy, and the doctor said I was anemic?"

"Yeah. She told you to take iron supplements, and you decided to eat more meat instead."

"She wanted me to have a colonoscopy to see if there was any internal bleeding. I didn't want to worry you, so I had it done, and everything was fine. My colon is beautifully clean."

Karen shook her head. "We might not be married on paper, but I'm your partner in sickness and in health. You should have told me."

As the two continued arguing, Darlene ducked into the kitchen, and Eric followed her.

"He should have told her," she said quietly. "I would have been so mad if you pulled something like that on me."

Eric wrapped his arms around her and kissed her forehead. "I promise to always tell you everything. Gilbert is just a stubborn ox, and he thinks men should deal with their problems on their own. Keeping everything inside is part of his oldest-son's syndrome. He always took care of me and our sister and he never complained about anything."

"Speaking of Gabi. When are you going to talk to her about all this? She's not getting any younger either."

"She's thirty-eight, so she has time. I can't deal with Gilbert and Karen's transition and with Gabi at the same time."

"Why? Is she a handful?"

He chuckled. "Gabriella Emerson is more than a handful. She's a whirlwind."

"She sounds exciting. Let's introduce her to Max."

Eric's smile vanished. "No way. Not after what he did with us. That's just gross."

Darlene huffed. "You keep saying that Max's part was marginal, and that he was just the venom donor. Then suddenly, it's a problem to introduce him to your sister?"

"Yeah, it is. I don't want him telling her the details of what the three of us did."

"He wouldn't do that."

Eric arched a brow. "You think? If he falls in love with her, he will tell her everything. Didn't we agree moments ago that there should be no secrets between mates?"

Darlene let out an exasperated breath. "I only suggested introducing them. They might not even like each other."

"They will. Max is a fun guy, and Gabi is a fun girl. Most men can't handle her, but Max will have no problem with her spunk or her big mouth."

Eric was wonderful, but he had a tendency to make contradicting statements. One moment he was against intro-ducing Max and Gabi, and the next, he was stating that they were perfect for each other.

Maybe he just needed to ponder this a little longer and organize his thoughts.

"Let's cut up the watermelon. I promised the boys a treat after dinner."

"Right." Eric opened the fridge and pulled out the twenty-pounder that they had gotten earlier that day. "Do you think it's big enough?" He hefted it in his arms.

She laughed. "I'm sure."

38

ERIC

*W*hen the doorbell rang, Darlene rushed out of the kitchen, but Cheryl beat her to the door.

"I'm sorry I'm late." Kaia hugged her sister. "William called, and we talked for over an hour. I miss him so badly." She smiled apologetically at Darlene as she took off her puffer coat and hung it on a peg next to the door.

"No worries. I saved you a plate."

"Thank you, but I'll just join you for dessert. I snacked while talking." She walked over to the twins and kissed each one on both cheeks.

"When is William coming back?" Darlene asked.

"Hopefully, tomorrow. He's going to escort the Kra-ell to the ship, and Marcel will take over from there. I'm so glad that he's not going with them." Kaia pulled out a chair next to Gilbert. "Welcome back. I missed you too." She leaned over to kiss him on both cheeks. "How are things at home?"

"This is home now." Eric put the bowl with watermelon chunks on the dining table. "The one up north is just a house."

"It's ready to be rented out." Gilbert shifted his gaze to

Eric. "You and I need to unload the moving truck. It has been sitting there for over a week."

The Guardians had returned with the truck on Monday and left it in the parking garage. They had shipped out the next day, and Eric was too busy with Darlene and her transition to help move things out.

"No problem. I'm sorry I didn't do it earlier." He looked at his mate. "While Darlene was transitioning, I couldn't think of anything else, and later, I forgot all about the truck." He glanced at Karen. "You should have reminded me."

She waved a dismissive hand. "The entire village was in turmoil about the Guardians and Kalugal's men leaving. Everything in the truck could wait."

As Darlene and Karen chatted about what was in the truck and where it was going, and Kaia and Cheryl fed the little ones watermelon, Eric turned his attention to his brother. "When are you going for it?"

Gilbert winced. "I don't know if I can do it now that the business is teetering. I heard that Kian, Onegus, and Turner have been stuck in the war room for two days, and they are probably going to stay very busy until the mission is over. I can't ask Kian for advice or help, so I can't check out. If I want to save what's left of my so-called fortune, I need to be aware of what's going on."

That was the problem with being a small, independent builder. There was potential for great profits but just as much for catastrophic losses.

"I can look after the business while you are transitioning. We did that before when you and Karen went on vacation."

"It's not the same." Gilbert took a sip of water. "I was always available on the phone and via email to anyone who needed to contact me, and when you didn't know what to do, you called me. Who are you going to call when I'm out?"

"Kian. If something comes up that I can't handle, I'm sure

he can spare a moment or two no matter what's going on. Besides, the crisis will be over in a few days. If William is coming back, it can't be too bad out there."

Gilbert stabbed a watermelon chunk with his fork. "Since I need to wait for Toven to return, this discussion is irrelevant." He put the chunk into his mouth.

Eric leaned his elbows on his knees. "You can ask someone else to induce you. Stop pussyfooting around and just go for it. Karen can transition right after you do with the help of a donor's venom. It wasn't that bad with Max. It would have gone even smoother if not for the damn immortal instincts."

The left corner of Gilbert's lips curled up. "Are you still feeling insanely possessive over Darlene? Or did the hormones calm down a little?"

From across the table, Darlene gave him a warning look.

"If anything, they got worse. I want to snarl at any male looking at her." He cast her an air kiss. "She was always beautiful, but now she's stunning."

She was still the same woman he'd fallen in love with, just younger looking, more vibrant, and with stamina to match his.

"Immortality rocks." He smiled at her before returning his gaze to Gilbert. "Darlene says that we shouldn't wait and tell Gabi, but I want you and Karen to transition before we tackle Gabriella. I don't want her to know that you are doing anything potentially dangerous. The freak-out will be epic."

Gilbert winced. "Yeah. Since Mom and Dad died, Gabi can't tolerate any upheaval. That's why I didn't tell Karen about the colonoscopy. I'm used to hiding from Gabi anything that's potentially worrisome or upsetting."

Eric nodded. "Poor Gabriela. Of the three of us, she took it the hardest."

"She was the youngest."

"Imagine how relieved she'll be when she learns that we are practically indestructible. That's the best gift you could ever give her."

Gilbert snorted. "You can stop campaigning. You've already sold me on the idea." He smoothed his fingers over his face as if checking for stubble. "Any suggestion as to who can fulfill Max's role for us?"

"As your inducer?"

"Not for that. I'm not taking any chances. I'm waiting for Toven to return. I meant for Karen."

"I have a couple of candidates, but we will focus on finding a venom donor for Karen after you are safely on the other side. You need to take care of your transition first. You should ask Orion to induce you. He's a demigod, so his venom should be almost as potent as his father's."

"I'll think about it." Gilbert stuffed another chunk of watermelon into his mouth.

39

PHINAS

"You look worried." Dandor fell in step with Phinas. "Is there trouble?"

Not the kind that Dandor imagined, but yeah. What had happened last night with Jade bothered Phinas more than it should, but he wasn't about to share it with the guy.

"That's what the meeting is about, and you'll get the update along with everyone else." He opened the door to the conference room where his men had assembled.

As it turned out, the venue wasn't just for weddings. It was also a corporate retreat with two large conference rooms. Right now, one was occupied by the Guardians and the other by Kalugal's men.

Phinas and Yamanu had decided to deliver the news to each group separately.

When Phinas stood in front of the men, they stopped their conversations and turned to face him.

"So here is the situation. As you know, we are boarding the ship in about an hour and a half, but we are not sailing back home as planned. Instead, we are going to Greenland, where we will be picked up by chartered planes and fly home."

He still didn't know where the Kra-ell were going, but he doubted it would be to the village. Kian would never allow them in. He'd asked Yamanu about that, but the head Guardian said it hadn't been decided yet.

"Why the change of plans?" Chad asked.

"The consensus is that Igor will try to get his people back, but he will not know where to find them until William turns off the communication disrupter, which he will have to do when the convoy enters the port. The assumption is that as soon as Igor learns that his people are on a ship, he will get his hands on another vessel and follow. He might compel a merchant ship captain to accidentally ram into ours, and when the ship starts taking in water and we have to abandon ship, he will take part in the rescue and collect his people. That could happen even when we are close to the port. The other possibility is that he will take over a Russian naval vessel, follow us out to sea, and launch a torpedo or missile to disable or sink our ship. The effect will be the same. We will have to abandon ship, and he will collect the survivors. He will assume that his people will survive in the frigid water, and he doesn't care what happens to the humans."

Chad raised his hand. "Who does he think took his people? He can't know that we are not human."

Phinas nodded. "I agree, but no one knows what Igor is thinking or what he will do next. It's all guesswork."

"I'm just thinking what I would do if I were Igor," Chad said. "If he thinks that humans took his people, which he has no reason to doubt because he doesn't know about us, he will for sure try to sink the ship and then take his sweet time to fish the survivors out of the water. That way, he will kill all the humans who will freeze to death and save only the Kra-ell and maybe the hybrids."

"They have kids with them," Dandor said. "The pure-blooded kids will probably be okay, but the hybrid kids don't start manifesting Kra-ell characteristics until puberty. They are probably not as resilient yet."

"Igor doesn't care." Phinas let out a breath. "Did Navuh ever care about collateral damage?"

Silence stretched over the room, and the men avoided each other's eyes.

They had all done things they wished they hadn't, following orders they shouldn't have followed. It didn't matter that refusing orders would have resulted in their execution.

Sometimes it was better to die with honor than live with shame.

One of the things he admired most about Jade was that, to her best ability, she lived her life honorably. Not that it had done her any good.

She didn't have peace of mind any more than he had.

Most people only saw the fierce leader, but he'd glimpsed the pain she was hiding, the guilt and the shame for the slaughter she couldn't have prevented.

But what if she could have?

Had Jade known Igor before boarding the mother ship? Had she suspected an attack on her tribe?

Aliya had told him that Jade had been very strict about security, so she must have suspected something, and he doubted that she'd been worried about humans.

With her compulsion ability, she could have handled humans with ease.

Perhaps she feared the gods?

Yamanu had given him a brief summary of what Jade had told Toven about the relationship between the Kra-ell and the gods, and that the original gods had been exiled to Earth as penance for their share in the Kra-ell uprising.

But if those gods had been Kra-ell sympathizers, why would Jade fear them?

She wouldn't.

She must have feared her own people, and since she was a strong compeller, she must have known about Igor and his incredible powers. She could have prepared her people better.

Not that Phinas knew how she could have done that. The clan had discovered only recently that compulsion was carried over sound waves and that it could be blocked with special earpieces.

Jade couldn't have known that twenty-some years ago.

"What are we supposed to do if and when the ship sinks?" Boleck asked.

It took Phinas a split second to return his mind to the present. "Survive, and help as many others as possible, particularly the children. They are the most vulnerable and will die the fastest in cold water. You will have mere moments to get to them and keep them warm. Hopefully, it won't come to that. Kian contracted an armed submarine to follow the ship and protect it. The most likely scenario is that we will enjoy a pleasant ten-day cruise with the Kra-ell, providing us with ample opportunities to befriend them and learn more about them. Kalugal wants us to become allies."

Phinas didn't understand why Kalugal wanted a leg up with the Kra-ell. It didn't matter if the Kra-ell were on friendlier terms with the clan or with Kalugal's faction. In everything security related, they were supposed to fully cooperate. Annani had cemented the accord with compulsion, but it hadn't been necessary. It was in both their peoples' best interest to join forces against Navuh and the Brotherhood.

Before Igor's attack, Jade's tribe had been involved in the communication business, and even though more than two decades had passed, she might still have some connections in China. Perhaps Kalugal had some joint business endeavor in mind? Maybe Kalugal wanted to help his brother with his fashion business there? Although, that didn't make sense either. Lokan was doing that on Navuh's dime, so it wasn't as if he would personally profit from the business's success, and no one wanted to make Navuh richer.

It was difficult to guess what was going on in Kalugal's mind. The guy was so smart that he was usually a hundred steps ahead of everyone around him. He must have a goal in mind that was years in the making for which he would need the Kra-ell.

Dandor snorted. "So that's why you were sweet-talking their leader. I wondered why you went after a female like her."

Phinas bristled at the implied insult, but he forced his fangs to stay dormant. "Jade is beautiful, courageous, and smart. She's most worthy of my attention, and I'm honored to have gained her friendship and trust."

Being a smart male, Dandor lifted his hands in the universal sign for peace. "To each his own. I just like my females a lot softer."

Chad snorted. "That's why you don't get booty calls from clan females. If you want soft, you need to limit yourself to human women."

Dandor looked at Chad with mirth dancing in his eyes. "I wouldn't call it limiting. I have millions of soft, sweet females to choose from. You can have all the immortal and Kra-ell ones. How many are there? Three hundred? Good luck finding the one perfect for you."

40

JADE

*J*ade collected her things and stuffed them in a pillowcase. Back in the day, before Igor had murdered her family and ruined everything she'd worked for, she used to travel with designer luggage filled with designer outfits.

It felt like another lifetime, and it was hard to believe that those things had ever mattered to her.

Nevertheless, she didn't want Phinas to see her carrying a pillowcase stuffed with her meager belongings. The only thing of value on her was the sword strapped to her hips, and even that wasn't anything special. It was a crappy sword that was too heavy for a human to carry, which probably meant that it had been inexpensive.

With the money Igor had stolen from her and the other tribes, he could have afforded the best, but then he most likely hadn't wanted them to have good weapons. It wasn't as if they would ever do battle against the humans using swords and javelins. Those weapons were good only for training, and Igor had wanted his people in good shape.

Kagra slung her own makeshift pack over her shoulder

and glared at her. "Are you going to tell me what you and Phinas did last night? Or are you going to keep me in suspense until we get to the ship?"

"First of all, it wasn't last night, it was this morning, and secondly, I don't have to tell you anything." Jade opened the door and took one last look at the room they had occupied for the last fifteen hours. "Come on. We need to help the humans load the animals on the trucks before it gets dark."

"It's not fair." Kagra pouted. "I tell you everything."

She told her too much.

Kagra was a capable and fearsome warrior, but sometimes she behaved like a young human and mistakenly thought of Jade as a mother figure, or worse, a best friend.

Jade was Kagra's commander first, her friend second, and never her mother. Thankfully, Kagra's mother was alive and well, or as well as any of them could be after what had happened to them.

"We talked." Jade continued down the corridor toward the exit.

Kagra snorted. "I bet you did more than talk. He was devouring you with his eyes, and you were not indifferent to him either. I'm dying to know if the immortals are good sex partners."

"Why?" Jade cast her an amused look. "Did any of them catch your eye?"

"Yamanu looks delicious. I love how tall and broad-shouldered he is, and he's always smiling. That's such a refreshing change from all the males in our compound. The purebloods are too full of themselves, the hybrids are too sour, and the humans are too timid."

"He's taken, and the immortals are exclusive with each other."

"How do you know he's taken?"

"Tom told me that Yamanu's mate is joining us on the

cruise." She slanted a glance at Kagra. "It seems that the immortals inherited the gods' unhealthy attachment to their mates. He can't be without her for even a few days. You'll have to choose someone else."

"All you told me about the gods was that they were not to be trusted and that they made themselves look too perfect. So how should I know?"

"Now you do." Jade opened the building's front door. "I need to check on Drova."

"I'll come with you." Kagra moved her pillowcase to her other shoulder. "Why do you refer to their devotion to their mates as unhealthy?"

"It's unnatural, and it makes them weak. A warrior like Yamanu shouldn't be crippled by his inability to stay away from his mate."

"Do you think they tinkered with their genes to create such a strong attachment between mates?"

Jade shrugged. "Who knows? But it fits the pattern. The gods wanted to perfect everything about themselves, so they might have incorporated loyalty and devotion into their genetic makeup instead of leaving it to free will. But the leadership of gods was famous for feeding their population with beautiful propaganda to get them to accept limitations their elite was exempt from. They might have convinced the people that getting their genes altered to ensure fidelity was the right thing to do and took their free will away from them. Unlike what the Eternal King preached to the populous, he had scores of concubines and his official wife and produced numerous offspring. Others in positions of power probably did the same."

"Do you know that for sure, or are you speculating?"

"It wasn't a secret that the Eternal King had many concubines and many children, so he obviously wasn't exclusive with his official wife. On the other hand, I also heard stories about gods who were so strongly bonded to each other that they couldn't stand to be apart. If the stories are true, different genetics is the only explanation."

"Not necessarily. Maybe those who married for love were loyal, and those who had arranged political matings were not."

"Perhaps. I know that the history we were taught was slanted against the gods and meant to make us look great, but I always thought that messing with nature and trying to make everything perfect was wrong. Who knows how many mistakes they've made along the way? They might have left scores of planets populated by monsters."

Kagra snorted. "We are monsters too, and so are the gods, and so are their other creations like the humans. Beauty and ugliness are in the eye of the beholder, and neither defines monsters. Actions do."

"Wise words." Jade clapped her second on her back.

41

MARCEL

"I'll take your things." Marcel took the two stuffed pillowcases from Sofia's father.

The air was cold, around thirty-seven degrees Fahrenheit, but neither Sofia, Helmi, nor Jarmo seemed bothered by the cold. The humans were wrapped in warm puffer jackets, scarves, hats, and gloves, and their cheeks were pinked from the cold, but no one even commented on the weather.

Perhaps because it wasn't raining or snowing, they considered it a nice evening. The sun was setting, though, and at night it got even colder.

Winter in the Scottish Highlands hadn't been any better, but Marcel had spent so many years in sunny Southern California that he'd forgotten what real cold was like. Nevertheless, he was immortal, and he was supposed to be less sensitive to temperature extremes.

Working in the lab had made him go soft.

"Thank you." Jarmo gave him a fond smile. "I'm thankful that the Kra-ell can control the herd. Otherwise, it would have been difficult to load them into the trucks. They didn't enjoy the long journey here."

As he walked away, Helmi scrunched her nose in disgust. "I didn't enjoy cleaning the trucks after them either." She shifted her gaze to Marcel. "Is there any chance that I can ride with Tomos this time?"

"The port is only a couple of hours away, and you have the entire cruise to spend as much time with Tomos as you want. As soon as we are out at sea, he will be free to roam the ship."

Her eyes brightened. "Can we get a cabin together?"

Marcel didn't know what kind of ship Kian had gotten, but if it had enough guest rooms for the entire clan, there was a good chance that Helmi could get her wish.

"I don't see why not." He looked back at the venue's front door. "Should we wait for Isla and Hannele?"

Helmi waved a dismissive hand. "They are not ready yet. We can go." She huffed out a breath. "I just wish I knew where we were going." She cast Marcel a sidelong glance. "Can't you give me a hint?"

"It hasn't been decided yet. The first priority is to get you away from Igor and put you somewhere he cannot find you. Given that he can get his hands on any information he needs, that's not an easy task. Fortunately, this is not our first rodeo, and I'm sure the brains in the war room are working on a solution."

"Rodeo?' Sofia asked. "Isn't that bullfighting?"

"No fighting is involved unless you count the struggle to stay on top of the bull or horse as he's trying to dislodge the rider. It's a skill competition."

"Oh, I get it." Sofia smiled. "So, saying that it's not your first rodeo means that you are skilled at what you do."

"Precisely."

"English." Helmi shook her head. "It has so many idioms. My mother bugged me about watching too many movies, saying that I was wasting my time on nonsense, but that's how I learned to speak it so well." She winked at Sofia. "With your help, of course."

Sofia's cheeks pinked as she smiled at Marcel. "I read a lot of American romance novels to reinforce my knowledge of the language, and I told Helmi the highlights to whet her appetite. When she asked to borrow them, I conditioned loaning her the books on her underlining and checking every word she didn't understand in the dictionary. Before lending her the next book, I tested her to make sure that she did that with the one she finished."

"Did she?"

"So-so." Helmi rotated her hand. "I always rushed to get to the happy ending." She sighed and looked at Marcel. "I want my happy ending with Tomos."

"I wish I could promise you that, but I can't."

"I know."

When they got to the trucks, William waved him over.

"Give me a moment," Marcel said.

"No problem." William waved hello to Sofia and Helmi. "Take two."

"I need to go." Marcel helped Sofia and her cousin climb up into the back and handed them Jarmo's bag.

"Are you coming back?" Sofia asked.

"Of course. William probably just needs to tell me something. He doesn't need me in the van."

"Okay."

Helmi jumped back down. "I'm going to look for Tomos." She looked up at Sofia. "You can come if you want."

"Nah, I'll wait for the rest of our family to get here. They won't know which truck to board."

Helmi chuckled. "Are you worried about giving Tomos and me some privacy? He's with all his hybrid buddies. We won't have any privacy anyway."

"In that case, I'll come."

42

KIAN

"*H*ere you go, sweetie." Kian handed Allegra a biscuit.

"Dada." She grabbed it in her chubby hand and pushed it into her mouth.

Since she'd started teething, the chewing biscuits had become her favorite, and she demanded them all the time. If anyone dared to offer her a teething toy, she tossed it away with an expression that was part angry and part offended.

"She should eat her cereal," Syssi said.

"Mama," Allegra said around the biscuit.

She'd started saying mama a couple of weeks ago and learned quite quickly that Syssi would give her anything she wanted when she did.

Kian cast Syssi an amused sidelong glance. "I'll try to sneak her a few spoonfuls."

Finally, getting a full night's sleep had done wonders for Kian's mood, and the precious moments he was enjoying with his wife and daughter were all the sweeter after the long hours he'd been away from them.

He'd been stuck with Turner and Onegus in the war room

for what had seemed like an eternity, and they still hadn't finalized their plan.

Kian was starting to think that his idea to transport the Kra-ell on the clan's new cruise ship hadn't been one of his best. That being said, he couldn't think of a viable alternative.

They were operating in the dark, trying to guess what Igor's next move would be, and he didn't like their position. He didn't like that Toven and Mia were planning to remain with the Kra-ell. Hell, he didn't like any of his people being in danger because of the decisions he'd made.

The council supported the move, and so did his mother, but the final decision rested on his shoulders, and it weighed heavily on him.

"Dada." Allegra pointed at the stack of waffles Okidu had put on the table.

He glanced at Syssi. "Can I give her a piece?"

She laughed. "The little manipulator knows who's the weak link. She knew not to ask me."

"I'll give her tiny pieces and follow with the cereal. I played this game with her before, and she knows the rules. She had to eat a spoonful of cereal to get a piece of the waffle."

"Fine." Syssi smiled. "You know that I can't say no to either of you."

Their morning together brought joy to Syssi. A blissful expression of love and contentment was always painted on her face when he was feeding Allegra or playing with her.

Reaching for a waffle, Syssi took a bite and followed it with a sip of her cappuccino. "How are we going to feed the four hundred people on the ship? Cruise ships typically refuel and restock at ports of call along their route, but they might spend a long time at sea. I know that you are planning on them sailing to Greenland, but plans might change in response to Igor's moves."

Kian tore off a small piece and gave it to Allegra. "We are loading the ship up to capacity. It will be carrying both fuel and supplies to last it for weeks. The route we decided on will take much less time, of course, but if we have to throttle up to full speed and sustain it for a duration, the fuel will only last for ten to twelve days. The food is less of an issue. The purebloods subsist on fresh blood, and they bring livestock with them. So that leaves only about three hundred people to feed. The ship can support three times as many passengers and a large service crew to boot, so we have nothing to worry about there."

"That's good." Syssi nibbled on her waffle.

He could sense that something was bothering Syssi, and he'd learned long ago to never dismiss it when she had a bad feeling about something.

"You seem bothered. Are you sensing something I should be aware of?"

As Allegra paused chewing and leveled her intense gaze at her mother, Kian felt the small hairs on the back of his neck tingle. Was she trying to communicate something? Or was she just sensing her mother's unease?

"I am just worried." Syssi let out a breath. "The humans are helpless and untrained, and we have many people on board. What if Turner's assessment proves correct and the ship is attacked? How can we guarantee everyone's safety? Mia is immortal but doesn't have her legs back yet. Can she even swim if the ship sinks?"

Syssi's capacity to always think of the well-being of others was endless. For the umpteenth time, Kian silently blessed the Fates for the boon they had bestowed on him. A boon far greater than what he could have possibly merited, even given his very long life and the many sacrifices he'd made for his people.

Reaching out, he took her hand and kissed it. "We don't

even know if anyone will follow them. Igor might be a powerful compeller, but arranging for a vessel that could threaten a cruise ship at a moment's notice might be a tall order even for him. Nevertheless, Turner's plan accounts for that possibility. Our ship will have a fully armed submarine escorting it. If any serious threat materializes, Turner is confident in the sub's ability to handle it."

"I'm sure he's right. It's just that I'm concerned Igor will come up with something no one is expecting." Syssi took another sip of her coffee.

"Dada," came the demanding reminder that it was time to shift his attention back to the most important person at the table.

Smiling, Kian tore another small piece off the waffle and handed it to Allegra, who grabbed it in her drool-covered little hand and stuffed it in her mouth.

43

TURNER

*T*urner stood in front of the vending machine and looked over the selection of coffees.

Was he in the mood for a regular drip, or did he want a cappuccino?

He was well rested, so the coffee wasn't needed as an energy boost, but he was heading to Kian's office, and they had a phone meeting scheduled with the ship's captain and his top officers in about forty minutes, which might take a while.

After choosing a grande-sized drip, he pulled out his phone and called Kian.

"Good morning. I'm getting coffee and pastries at the vending machines. Do you want me to get you anything else?"

"Good morning, Turner." He could hear Allegra's delightful laughter, which explained Kian's lighter-than-usual tone. "I've just finished breakfast with the family, and I'm not hungry, but I can always use more coffee."

"Should I get coffee for Onegus as well?"

"He's not joining us this morning. I'll let him know if

there are any changes to the plan after our talk with Captain Olsson."

"Good deal. I'll wait for you in the office."

"I'll be there in fifteen minutes." Kian ended the call.

Turner collected his coffee and pressed the button for another one.

The truth was that he enjoyed working with Kian. The missions he was often called to assist with were on a grand scale, challenging, and of great importance to the clan. He also got to spend more time with Bridget when he stayed in the village, and on occasion she helped him with some of the details, and he enjoyed that as well.

Accepting Kian's offer to work for the clan full-time was tempting.

William's technical wizardry and Roni's incredible hacking talent greatly leveraged how sophisticated and elaborate his plans could get. The impressive resources Kian committed to the critical missions were also a bonus. Turner was always mindful of budgeting, and he never splurged on unnecessary luxuries, but rescue missions required serious funds, and cutting corners meant losing lives. He never had to worry about that with Kian.

When safety was on the line, Kian went all out.

But when all was said and done, Turner didn't like answering to anyone. He was a loner who preferred to be the sole and ultimate arbiter when it came to the missions he was running. Working with others was something he could get behind, but not on a daily basis.

He didn't have to wait long for Kian to arrive.

"Good morning." Kian walked into the conference room, heading straight for the coffee.

"Are we doing a video call?" Turner asked.

"Yes." Kian took a sip from the coffee and put the cup down. "I asked Captain Olsson to get his top officers together so that we can give them an update on where we stand and to get a first-hand update from them. It's also a good opportunity to introduce them to Toven." He walked over to the fridge, took out a couple of water bottles, and threw one Turner's way before sitting next to him. "How much do you think we need to share with them?"

Kian wasn't going to like his answer. The guy's main concern was keeping the immortals' existence a secret, and he didn't like to involve humans in their affairs, but in this case, he would have to relent.

"We must give them all the information they need to do their job. Leaders make better choices when they are cognizant of the ramifications of their decisions. I believe that we need to share our suspicions that the ship might be followed and possibly attacked—potentially catastrophically. That means we also need to share information about the submarine we are sending to protect the ship. Naturally, the crew also needs to know about the detour they'll be making to Greenland, the cargo and passengers manifest, and anything else that affects the voyage." Turner glanced at his watch to see how much time they had left before the call.

Surprisingly, Kian didn't shake his head, and his eyes didn't start blazing either. "Let's get Toven on the line. I want him to compel the crew to secrecy."

"They are human," Turner said. "A simple thrall will do."

"I'm not taking chances with that." Kian pulled out his phone and started typing. "Too much is at stake."

The reply from Toven came in a couple of seconds later. "He is available and waiting for the call."

44

TOVEN

"Good evening, captain," Kian said as the guy came on line. "Thank you for making this conference call possible. Joining us are my two colleagues. Victor Turner, who is right here next to me, and Tom Hartford, who is on the other line, and who will be joining you on the ship with the rest of our guests."

The tablet screen was split in two, half taken by Kian and Turner and half by the captain and his top brass. Toven's own face was framed in a small rectangle on the bottom.

He smiled at the captain. "Your reputation precedes you, Captain Olsson."

In the few minutes before the guy had joined the three-way video call, Kian had given Toven a summary of the captain's resume, and it was impressive.

In person, Captain Johan Olsson was an imposing man. Tall and broad, with piercing blue eyes, a full head of white hair, and a beard to match, he fit the image of a Nordic ship captain to a tee.

"Thank you," the captain said in a deep voice that was

pleasantly accented. "Please allow me to introduce my team." He twisted to his right and with a nod of his head acknowledged the officer seated next to him. "This is my executive officer, Lars Lindgren."

"Good morning." Lars dipped his head.

He was a stocky, bald man, seated to the captain's right.

The captain turned to the man sitting to his left. "This is my first officer, Elias Axelsson."

"Good morning, gentlemen." The first officer nodded his greeting.

He had the appearance of a Middle Easterner rather than a Scandinavian. His complexion, hair, and eyes were dark, and there was a calm and confident vitality to him that was reassuring.

The captain pointed at the young officer sitting somewhat apart from the three. "And this is my second officer, Mateo Berg." Olsson pointed to the man sitting on Axelsson's other side.

Berg was the youngest of the four, and he seemed fresh off a navy vessel. He had a military aura about him, and Toven was sure he had served as a naval officer before joining Olsson's crew.

"It's a pleasure to meet you all," Kian said. "Before we continue, I would like Tom to say a few words, and it's important that you listen carefully to what he has to say."

"It is a pleasure to meet you, gentlemen." Toven imbued his voice with strong compulsion. "I would like to stress that you must not share anything of what we are about to discuss here today in any way that could convey meaning or fact with anyone. Not on board the ship and not elsewhere. If you need to communicate any particulars with subordinates on the ship so that tasks can be executed in the best possible way, you will not allude to anything other than the very specific piece of information that is essential for the person to be able to do their job well. Please acknowledge your consent by each raising your right hand straight up."

Given the frowns on all four faces, the crew was puzzled by the odd directive, and as they raised their hands as one, they were visibly startled by their immediate compliance with the command.

"Thank you, Tom," Turner said. "With that out of the way, we can get down to business. The ship should be prepared for close to four hundred passengers and about one hundred and fifty head of livestock. The guests will get their own rooms and meals ready as well as tend to the animals, so there is no need to bring more hands onboard, but someone will need to show the designated leaders where everything is, so they will be able to take over from there."

Lars raised his hand. "We have no physician or nurse on board. Both are required for such a large group of passengers. It's part of the regulations."

"A physician is accompanying the group." Turner lifted a bottle of water and took a quick sip. "We suspect that the ship might be followed at some point of the voyage, possibly by a naval vessel, and it might be fired upon with the intention of disabling it and possibly sinking it. The pursuers' objective is to capture some of the passengers, which they could easily do once all hands abandon the ship and are either in the water or in the lifeboats."

The four men stared at the screen with expressions ranging from 'was that a joke' to 'what the hell is going on here' painted on their faces.

Ignoring their dismayed expressions, Turner pressed on. "Let me assure you that this is only a remote possibility at this point, and we have no concrete intelligence to substantiate it. Nonetheless, we are not taking any chances with the safety and well-being of the passengers, crew, or ship. To that end, we will have a fully armed submarine shadow you all the way from the North Sea to your destination, and it will extend full-force protection against any threats that may materialize during your journey."

Kian signaled Turner to let him interject. "Gentlemen, I know that calling these circumstances odd and unsettling is an understatement. I will, therefore, not hold you bound by your contracts and release any of you who wish to leave. But if any of you wish to do so, I will ask for the resignation right now, so that we have time to plan and adjust accordingly. I have very close friends as well as family among the passengers, and if I doubted our collective ability to deliver them safely to their destination, I would not have authorized this voyage. We have the means and the resources to make this as safe a trip as any other, albeit possibly more memorable. Do any of you wish to resign your commission at this point?"

Kian's interjection was timely and well delivered.

It would have never occurred to Toven to offer the men a way out, but it was a good move despite placing an extraordinary burden on these men's shoulders.

The men exchanged glances and a few sentences in rapid Swedish, and then the captain said, "We are in, but we need to confer with the rest of the crew. I don't expect any of my men to resign, but we need to give them the option."

Kian nodded. "Of course. Please let us know as soon as possible if anyone wishes to leave, as we will need to have Tom speak with them before they disembark. Please also let me know if you need anyone leaving to be replaced or can do without them. Last, I would like to add that given the unique circumstances and the longer duration of the trip, I'm tripling our agreed pay for this voyage for the entire crew."

The captain dipped his head. "I appreciate your generosity, Mr. Kian. But double pay would have sufficed."

Kian smiled. "When you deliver the ship in one piece to its final destination, I'll consider it money well spent."

The captain grinned. "She will be delivered as good as new."

KIAN

ian had a feeling that would be Olsson's answer, and not because the guy was greedy for the triple pay.

The man was a proud, decorated ex-naval captain, and the crew he'd assembled was top-notch. Olsson loved what he did, and he took pride in his work. The triple compensation was meant as an acknowledgment of his skill and dedication, not a bribe to convince him to take on a mission that he otherwise might have declined.

"I have no doubt you will," he told the captain. "I knew I had chosen the right crew for the job."

Beside him, Turner tapped his yellow pad impatiently. "Let's continue with the logistics. The submarine will only start shadowing you at the North Sea because it is moored at the west end of the Baltic. You will not have the armed protection while in the Baltic, but our assessment is that it does not present a meaningful increase in risk because the pursuers will not dare attack there. The Baltic is teeming with ships, and the response time to a distress call from a sinking ship would be fast. They will not have enough time to sink the ship and collect the passengers they are after."

Olsson nodded. "The Baltic is swarming with ships from multiple navies, coast guard vessels, commercial fleets, as well as media helicopters and other onlookers."

Turner continued, "That is why we believe the attackers will not engage until our ship is at least twelve to fifteen hours from land and probably closer to twenty-four."

The captain nodded again. "I agree with your assessment. We should hug the coast until we clear out of the Baltic, and we should follow a zigzagging pattern that is hard to predict while monitoring traffic to see if any vessel is following us."

Turner smiled. "It's a pleasure talking to a professional. That's precisely what we need you to do. In order to give the sub enough time to catch up with you and for you to conserve fuel for the ocean crossing, you will need to keep your speed to fifteen knots. Given the rough waters you will be sailing through this time of year, your slow speed should not be suspicious to anyone following the *Aurora*. Once you clear the Baltic Sea, we need you to remain close to the coast until Bergen, at which point you will head to the Shetlands for a crossing of the North Sea and into the North Atlantic. Your speed at this point will be dictated based on the location of the pursuer, if we identify any, and by the position of the sub, as its max speed is slower than yours."

The captain jotted down the instructions and raised his head. "You still didn't tell us our destination, and how long do you expect we will be out at sea."

Kian leaned in to answer. "At this time, there are two possibilities. We might ask you to sail as originally planned, cross the Panama Canal, stop at Colombia for the armaments we ordered, and continue to Long Beach. The other option is first heading to the southwestern coast of Greenland, which is why we are directing you to the Shetland Islands. This is a big detour, but it might be necessary for the safeguarding of our passengers. We will have a final answer for you by the time you need to plot your course upon leaving the Baltic. In either case, you should carry with you the maximum amount of fuel possible and fill your supply stores to the brim so that our hands are not tied due to fuel or food considerations."

"Understood," the captain said.

"Once you do a full assessment of how long you need to get everything ready and accept the passengers and cargo for an immediate departure, please let me know as we need to get ready accordingly. Does anyone have any questions for us at this time?"

The first officer raised his hand.

"Go ahead, Mr. Axelsson," Kian said.

"I assume that you are all aware that the ship broadcasts its location on an ongoing basis. Anyone can see where we are and what our course is at all times. Why would an attacker need to follow us from the Baltic and chase us halfway around the world when they can simply lie in wait for us anywhere along our route and ambush us that way? The sub following from behind will be useless in that situation."

Turner's lips curled in a rare smile. "A great question, sir. That is why, as soon as you clear the busy shipping lanes and leave the Baltic Sea behind, you will disable your AIS system along with your VHF and become a ghost. In fact, you will only use the equipment we will be bringing onboard for communication, and you will only communicate through us."

The captain and his first officer exchanged looks, and then Olsson turned toward the screen. "Going ghost is unconventional, but I've done it before, and for triple pay, I'm willing to do it again. I can always blame it on a malfunction."

Kian nodded. "You have a lot to do, and little time to do it, so I don't want to keep you any longer than necessary. If there are no more questions, I suggest we get busy. I realize that fueling and supplying the ship will be much more expensive due to the time crunch and the circumstances. Feel free to authorize any expenditures that you deem are necessary that will aid in attaining the mission's objectives."

TOVEN

*W*hile Turner had been explaining the game plan to Captain Olsson and his team, Toven had received a text from Kian, asking if he could call him after the video call was concluded.

Naturally, his answer had been affirmative even though he knew what Kian wanted to discuss, and he needed more time to think about his position.

Toven still didn't have an answer when the call came a few minutes after the video call ended. "Hello again, Kian."

"It was a good meeting. It confirmed my initial assessment of Captain Olsson and all the good things I've heard about him."

Kian's effort at small talk didn't go unnoticed. He also tried to modulate his gruff tone and sound more amicable. Toven appreciated that, especially given the pressure and time crunch the guy had been operating under these past few days.

Nevertheless, he knew why Kian was trying so hard.

"You have chosen wisely," Toven complimented him. "The captain projected all the right vibes."

"Yes, he did." There was a short pause. "I want to thank you for your invaluable help and contribution to this mission. If it wasn't for Mia and you, there was no way we could have pulled this off, and for that you have my gratitude and that of the entire clan, as well as Annani's and the Kraell's."

Although it was clear that this was a preamble to what Kian wanted to get to next, he came across as sincere and earnest.

"I appreciate the sentiment, and I hope to always be here to help the clan. I'm forever in your debt for your unconditional acceptance of my mate, her family, and me into your midst. And as for the mission, it took our collective effort and the hard work of all the teams to make it work. But you know better than most that it is far from complete. It remains to be seen how successful it will prove to be when all is said and done."

Toven was not being self-effacing.

The truth was that others were taking far greater risks and would have died protecting him and his mate, so he truly felt a sense of gratitude.

Modesty aside, though, it was true that no one other than him could have undone Igor's compulsion, and even he had needed Mia's amplification to accomplish that.

Perhaps Annani could have done that on her own, but no one knew how strong of a compeller she was, including Annani herself, and she didn't have as much experience with compulsion as he had.

Besides, she was too important to the clan to risk in any way.

Toven knew that Kian didn't want to risk him either, but his loss wouldn't be as catastrophic for the clan as the loss of their Clan Mother. She was the heart and soul of her people, and without her, they would fall apart.

Kian cleared his throat. "I'm fully aware of the risks ahead, and they are far more serious than what you've had to face until now. That is why I want to ask you and Mia to fly back home from Helsinki with the rest of the group that is not joining the sea voyage. I see no reason to continue exposing Mia and you to more risks. I will feel better knowing that both of you are out of harm's way."

Toven had been expecting that, and he still wasn't clear on what his answer should be.

"Let's think this through together." Unintentionally, Toven assumed a teacher's tone, which some could perceive as condescending, but hopefully, Kian was above such pettiness. "Let's assume that Igor will indeed get a naval vessel to follow the ship, with the intention of firing on it in an attempt to sink her. Is it reasonable to assume that this would be his first and only move, or is it more likely that he will first try to fall back on his compulsion abilities?" He didn't wait for Kian to answer that because he was just thinking out loud. "We know from Jade that he doesn't fight fair. He froze the males of her tribe and slaughtered them where they stood, robbing them of the ability to defend themselves and die honorably in battle. What do you think his most likely first move would be in this case?"

It would be better for Kian to arrive at the conclusion on his own.

"I hate to admit it, but I see your point." Kian sounded resigned. "It should have occurred to me sooner. Igor will first try to compel anyone within hearing range on the ship, and before the disruptor is on, he will try to contact the crew and have them obey his commands. He will start with the bridge, ordering the captain and crew to shut off the engines, drop anchor, and provide access to boarders. I hope that William can come up with a way to install a voice changer on the bridge. But if Igor gets within hearing range, he will attempt to compel the Guardians to drop their weapons, and when that fails because they will be wearing earpieces, he will command his warriors, purebloods and hybrids alike, to attack from within. The Guardians will not stand a chance." Kian's voice carried his growing frustration with the situation. "The only way to prevent it is to keep them chained in their cabins. But that's not a solution either. Eventually, we will have to set them free. We need to make sure that their trail disappears at some point or that Igor is dead. Those are our only two options."

"Since we don't have earpieces for everyone, the only solution is for Mia and me to be onboard. We can counter any compulsion Igor tries to throw at us."

"I don't like it." Kian sounded frustrated. "But I'm grateful for your help. Thank you again, and please give my thanks to Mia as well. I consider you and your mate joining the clan a blessing and a boon. I'm the one who should be grateful, not you."

Toven stifled a chuckle.

Kian wasn't used to thanking anyone so profusely, and he wondered if Syssi had anything to do with it.

"The blessing is mutual, Kian. Besides, in all likelihood we will end up having a grand ol' time in a luxurious cruise liner for a week to ten days on your dime. All in all, it's a good bargain, wouldn't you say?"

Kian chuckled. "It's on the Kra-ell dime, not mine. I will deduct all the expenses from the money we seized from Igor's accounts."

"Perhaps the Fates had a hand in that as well. They didn't want the clan to go bankrupt saving the Kra-ell."

Not that he would have let it happen.

Toven had vast resources, and he'd been sincere when he'd offered to help finance the mission.

His riches meant nothing as long as they sat in gold depositories in Switzerland and elsewhere around the globe.

That being said, he was only willing to support causes where he knew exactly how the money was spent. Human organizations were full of corrupt people. Funneling money there was mostly lining the pockets of the directors, those close to them, and the politicians they needed to bribe with campaign donations.

When helping the clan rescue people or financing the Perfect Match experience for those who couldn't afford but desperately needed it, he knew where every dime went and that none of his fortune was wasted on the undeserving.

That being said, he had no desire to run the show.

Kian was a good and dedicated leader, and Toven had no problem being just a simple clan member. As it was, he felt blessed beyond measure and thanked the Fates daily for his mate, his son, his daughter, his granddaughters, his great-grandson, and their mates. Thanks to them, his zest for life and drive was back.

Toven was finally succeeding in what he'd been miserably failing at for many millennia.

He was making a difference.

47

MARCEL

"*H*op in." William waved at the opened door of the command van.

"Am I supposed to ride with you?" Marcel got in and nodded to Yamanu, Toven, Mia, and Sylvia. "I promised Sofia I would ride with her and her family, so I will have to let her know. She's expecting me back."

William looked disappointed. "I thought we would go over the plan on the way."

"I also need to return to my truck," Yamanu said. "I have to keep shrouding the convoy. Besides, I don't trust anyone else with Valstar." He grinned. "I enjoyed chatting with him on the way here."

Marcel couldn't imagine how Yamanu could shroud a convoy that was twenty trucks long and chat at the same time.

Only fifteen of the trucks contained people with trackers; the rest were filled with livestock, but he needed to shroud them all. A convoy that size passing through Helsinki would raise suspicion. Especially since the trucks were an old

Russian military make that no one in the Western world used.

"What's the matter?" Yamanu asked him. "Your frown indicates that you have something on your mind. Spit it out."

"Don't you need to focus on the shrouding?"

Yamanu leaned back. "I didn't need much focus when we were crossing Karelia because there was no one around, so I could shroud and chat at the same time. But when we drive through Helsinki, it will require my absolute concentration to take ahold of so many minds at once."

That made sense. Marcel's shrouding ability wasn't great, and the more people were around, the less effective it got. The same went for thralling. The most he could do at once were two people.

"Did Valstar tell you anything useful?" William asked.

"Not really." Yamanu flicked his long hair behind his shoulder. "I can't compel him, so he tried to keep his mouth shut, but I needled him into talking."

William let out a breath. "I'll try to make it fast and go over what we need to cover before the convoy is ready to pull out." He glanced toward the back of the venue, where several humans and Kra-ell were trying to herd the sheep and goats toward the trucks. "Smart animals. They know they are not going to have fun."

"I'd say leave them here," Marcel said. "But I don't want the Kra-ell to use the humans for their blood supply."

"Or us," Yamanu said.

"I'm not going." William sat across from Marcel. "Kian convinced me that I would be more useful back in the village, and the truth is that I didn't even try to argue with him. I'm not really needed on the ship, and I miss Kaia. I want to go home. You will have to operate the disruptor on the ship."

"No problem. I know how to work it." Marcel was glad to

have a job to do other than escorting Sofia and her family. "So, what's the plan?"

"I'll have to turn the scrambler off when we pass through the city to get to the port. Yamanu will shroud the convoy, making it look like a regular assortment of cars and vans. Sylvia will disable all the security cameras that we will be passing by, or at least those she can identify, so Igor won't be able to access the feed and see the convoy."

Marcel frowned. "What's the point? He will know where we are heading because of the trackers. I see another issue with this plan. Helsinki is a large metropolis. If Igor can track where we are heading, it will not take him long to identify the port as our destination. How difficult will it be for him to compel the port authorities to disallow anyone from leaving or to send police to board the ship before it casts off or trap us in any number of other ways? I think we should keep killing the signal all the way through the city and the port, and only stop when the ship is ready to cast off and needs open communications with the port authorities. As we arrive at the ship, we will no longer have such a large footprint, and we can modulate the disrupter's bubble to only include a small area. That will allow the port to quickly recover from the momentary loss of communications we cause on our way in."

Yamanu nodded. "Let's bring Kian, Onegus, and Turner into this conversation."

It took all of five minutes to bring the war room up to speed, and the consensus was immediate.

His plan was a go.

"That was a good call," William said after Kian hung up. "The trucks with the animals will back up into the ship's loading docks, and the animals will be transported straight inside. The people will get off and walk in. Naturally, Yamanu will keep shrouding, and Sylvia will take care of the surveillance cameras within line of sight. Port authority and the border agents on duty will all be blind to the fact that we transported passengers and that anyone got on board. All they'll see is cargo being loaded, for which they'll remember checking and approving the bill of lading. The moment everyone is on board, the ship will sail. Everything needs to be done as fast as possible to minimize the time in the port from arrival to casting off. If everything goes according to plan, it should take no more than two hours from the moment we start loading the ship till it can leave. You will need to turn the scrambler off just before the ship sails because communications will have to be restored at that point. Unless Igor is already in Helsinki and somehow guesses our plan and gets his response in motion, he won't be able to stop us in time."

Marcel frowned. "How soon after we sail do I turn the disruptor back on?"

"You'll have to wait until the ship is out of the Baltic Sea and possibly until it reaches the North Sea, but first, you'll have to install a voice changer on the bridge. We can't have Igor contacting the captain and taking over command. I'll reconfigure some of my equipment, but you will have to install it."

"The *Aurora* will hug the coast while it's still in the Baltic," Toven said. "Igor won't dare to do anything when it's so close to shore. Contacting the captain and trying to take over like that would be his best option. I have no doubt that he'll try that."

48

JADE

*A*fter the mandatory hellos to Mia, Sylvia, and everyone else in the van, Jade sat next to the doctor.

Following a full day of rest in the venue, Merlin had asserted that all the injured were doing well enough without him and they no longer needed his supervision.

"Thank you for taking care of our injured and saving Kagra's life," she told him.

Kagra's wounds could have been fatal if Merlin hadn't stitched up her insides. There was only so much that the Kra-ell body could repair, and Kagra's injuries had been too extensive even for her superior healing abilities.

"You're welcome," Merlin said. "She's a trouper."

"She's a Kra-ell warrior." Jade unzipped her jacket. "Are you coming with us on the voyage?"

"I am." He didn't look happy about that. "I'm going to miss my mate and my stepdaughter."

Jade stifled a huff.

Kra-ell didn't form a strong attachment to a singular partner, so going on missions or traveling didn't bother them. Also, they lived in small tribes, so there were many hands to help care for the young and everything else that needed to be done. That was why their way was so much better.

It was a much better system than the gods' and the immortals' exclusive mate bonds.

"All your patients are doing well, so you don't have to come. You can fly back home to your mate and stepdaughter."

His forehead furrowed. "Did nobody tell you I'll be removing the trackers as soon as we board the ship?"

The truth was that she'd forgotten about the trackers. With William scrambling the signals, it hadn't been a concern. Besides, the fact that Sofia had a tracker in her didn't mean that all of them had. Igor might have put it in the girl before he sent her across the ocean on a spying mission.

"I think that only some of us have trackers. Otherwise, why put tracking collars on us? Igor is not the wasteful type. If he had other means to track us by, he wouldn't have spent money on the collars, which needed maintenance and occasional replacements."

Merlin didn't look convinced. "He might have used the collars for intimidation. Also, it's possible that only some of you have the implanted trackers, and he didn't want to explain why some of you had to wear collars and others didn't."

"That actually makes sense." It fit Igor's mode of operation.

He would have done that to avoid questions and speculation.

"How do you think he found your tribe?" Merlin asked.

She'd thought about it after Tom had suggested that the settlers had been implanted with trackers before embarking on the journey to Earth. Still, that hypothesis had a big hole in it.

"I don't think we got them implanted before going into stasis. If all the settlers had trackers in them, Igor would have found all the survivors, but he found only some."

Merlin cast her a sad smile. "The trackers need a live host to transmit. The others are probably dead. It's also possible that some of them malfunctioned after seven thousand years. In fact, I'm surprised that any of them still worked."

He was probably right about the hosts being dead.

The gods made things to last, and since the trackers were inside bodies that were in stasis in protective pods, they could have gone on working forever.

Or not.

She wasn't tech-savvy, and most of what Ragoner had tried to explain to her had gone over her head.

He'd been such a smart male.

Kra-ell didn't get to attend the gods' universities, so all he had known he'd learned on his own. At least the gods hadn't restricted the Kra-ell from accessing their technical knowledge base, so anyone with the brains and the time could teach themselves to build all those marvelous things the gods had used. The hard part had been getting the necessary parts and tooling, some of which were not available for sale to the Kra-ell.

The genetic knowledge was blocked from them in its entirety, though, and Jade couldn't even blame the gods for that. It had been done on the request of the Kra-ell queen, who hadn't wanted her people modified in any way.

She turned to Merlin. "Why didn't you start removing the trackers while we were waiting for the ship to be ready? You could've been done with it by now."

Merlin chuckled. "It's not as easy as pulling out a bad tooth. First, I have to find the tracker, and that takes time. It requires a lot of time when that needs to be done for over three hundred people. Then a small surgery is required to remove the tracker, and even though one is not a big deal, multiplied by three hundred, it is. Still, I would have started on it if I had the right equipment."

"Do you have it on the ship?"

Merlin nodded. "Bridget did the impossible and found us a compact MRI machine. It was delivered and installed in the ship's clinic this afternoon, along with the rest of the medical equipment needed to perform minor operations. I will need the help of your nurse, though."

"Of course. Is Bridget your mate?"

"Bridget is a fellow doctor. My mate's name is Ronja."

"That's a Scandinavian name."

Merlin smiled, his entire face brightening. "It is." He pulled out his phone. "My Ronja is originally from Norway. Let me show you her picture."

Jade glanced at the screen and said what he'd expected her to say. "She's very pretty."

Merlin flicked over to a picture of a young girl with the same blond hair that was nearly white. "That's my step-daughter, Lisa. Well, not officially, since Ronja and I aren't married yet, but we are planning to have the ceremony soon. In fact, we were hoping to get married on the same ship that is picking us up later today, but we applied too late, and all the nights have already been taken. We will have to wait for the next cruise or do it on land."

"That's why Kian purchased the ship and had it remodeled in the first place," Sylvia said. "His sister is getting married on it. He called the ship the *Aurora*, but we all call it the Love Boat."

"'The Love Boat—'" William started singing softly, and then the others joined in, all except for Toven, who regarded them with the same puzzlement as Jade did.

49

YAMANU

*A*s the convoy entered the port, Yamanu had trouble focusing on shrouding it. Mey was waiting for him on the ship, and his mind kept gravitating toward their reunion.

They had only been apart for four days, but it felt much longer. He couldn't wait to hold Mey in his arms, to kiss her soft lips, to hear her laugh at his corny jokes, to hold her hand, to make love to her. But until everyone was off the trucks and the convoy left the port, he had to banish those thoughts and keep shrouding.

The Guardians would thrall the drivers to forget who their passengers and cargo were and where they had picked them up.

Hopefully, Igor couldn't break through a thrall as easily as he broke through compulsion, but Yamanu had a feeling that there was more to Igor than his people knew about.

Letting his thoughts wander to the snippets of conversation he'd had with Valstar on the way was a good way to take his mind off Mey. Those thoughts were not as consuming or emotionally intense, and he could keep the shroud while pondering the enigma that was Igor.

Why had he chosen a Russian name? To hide his true identity?

It wasn't likely that no one had known him on the ship that had brought the Kra-ell to Earth. His pod members must have known. Valstar had claimed that he didn't, but Yamanu was sure that had been a lie. He had to know his boss's Kra-ell name.

The other option was that, like Emmett, Igor was embarrassed about his name. Perhaps he'd been someone's unwanted child.

Yeah, that was probably it.

Given Igor's immense compulsion power, Yamanu suspected that he was a half-breed. Half god and half Kra-ell. If he were, he was a demigod, which meant that he should be much more handsome than the average Kra-ell.

The Kra-ell were good-looking people, but their features lacked the perfection of the gods and the first-generation hybrid offspring of the gods.

When he'd asked Valstar whether Igor was good-looking, the answer had been affirmative, but it hadn't evoked any unusual reaction, and the guy hadn't elaborated, so Yamanu assumed that Valstar didn't know whether Igor was a half-breed.

If Yamanu's suspicion was correct though, it was possible that Igor had thralling ability in addition to the compulsion. Then again, Kra-ell's compulsion had an element of thralling and shrouding in it anyway.

Yamanu tried to remember what Aliya had said about her visits to the village she'd grown up in. Had she shrouded herself, or had she just hidden in the shadows? She'd only gone at night, so maybe it was the latter.

His musings kept his mind occupied throughout the

unloading, but it got more difficult not to think of Mey when he got off the truck. He couldn't go to her yet and had to keep shrouding the convoy until it left the port.

When it was finally done, Yamanu felt like he'd gone through the wringer, but he didn't let the exhaustion slow him down as he rushed into the ship through the cargo bay and took the stairs to the upper decks.

There were way too many of them, and when he finally found his love on the top one, he was out of breath.

"Yamanu!" Mey ran into his arms. "Are you okay?" She leaned back and looked into his eyes. "Why are you panting? Was the shrouding that difficult?"

He grinned. "It was, but only because I couldn't stop thinking about you and about the moment I'd hold you in my arms again." He took her lips in a scorching kiss, ignoring the burn in his lungs.

She broke their kiss first and frowned. "Breathe, my love. You're worrying me. I've never seen you so exhausted after a shroud."

He'd been worse, but he didn't want to tell her that. "It's not the shrouding. This damn ship has way too many decks and too many stairs."

"Why didn't you use the elevator?" Arwel asked.

"There is an elevator?"

Jin laughed. "Don't tell me that you've never been on a cruise ship before."

"The last time I sailed, it was on a sailboat, and it had only one deck and one flight of stairs."

"When was that?" Mey asked.

"A couple of centuries ago. I'm not a fan of boats."

"Then why take this mission?" Arwel asked. "You can still change your mind and go home with Mey. But you have to do it quickly. The captain told us that the *Aurora* is scheduled to leave the port in less than an hour."

"That's good. The sooner we leave, the better. And no, I don't want to take Mey home." He looked into her eyes. "You want to meet your crappy relatives, right?"

She nodded. "But I don't want you to suffer for it."

"I won't. With the help of meditation, I'm sure I can overcome the nausea."

He wasn't sure at all, but he would give it his best shot.

50

TOVEN

*T*he *Aurora* was small, as cruise ships go, with six passenger decks and three hundred and sixty cabins. Compared to the floating cities moored at the Helsinki port she looked tiny, but she was luxuriously appointed, and she was more than enough for what the clan needed. Hopefully, the cargo bay wouldn't be destroyed by the sheep and goats they had brought on board.

They didn't have time for another remodel before the wedding cruise.

As it was, the event would probably have to be postponed, and given that Alena was rapidly approaching full term, it might be a problem.

His future daughter-in-law couldn't care less, but his son didn't want to wait, and neither did Toven. He hadn't had many reasons to celebrate throughout his long life, and the union between his son and Annani's eldest daughter deserved a grand celebration.

"It is a pleasure to meet you in person, Tom." The captain shook Toven's hand, his eyes roaming his face and body.

Toven was used to the reaction and didn't mind the

appraisal. It wasn't sexual, not in Olsson's case, anyway. Humans just needed time to get used to Toven's godly perfection.

He and the captain were about the same height, three inches or so over six feet, but Olsson was stockier. Not that there was an ounce of fat on him. He was just built like a brick wall, and he was groomed to perfection, with his white beard and mustache neatly trimmed and his full head of hair swept back in an elegant style. The only indications that the man was in his late fifties were the laugh lines around his eyes and frown lines on his forehead, as well as the white hair that in his youth had probably been blond.

"I'm sorry," the captain shook his head, "but I don't know your last name, or I would have addressed you properly."

Toven shook his hand firmly. "It's Hartford, but Tom is fine, and the pleasure is all mine, Captain." He put his hand on Mia's shoulder. "This is my fiancée, Mia."

The captain leaned down to offer her his hand. "Welcome aboard the *Aurora*, Miss Mia."

"Thank you, Captain Olsson."

Toven proceeded to introduce Yamanu, Phinas, Merlin, and Marcel as representatives of the passengers. When he got to Jade and Kagra, he wondered what Yamanu was shrouding them as. Olsson's eyes widened momentarily, so Yamanu was probably making them look exceptionally good.

Not that either of them was lacking in any way, but their alien looks would have been too shocking for the captain and his men, and they didn't have time to thrall everyone who needed thralling. The pilot was about to board the ship in mere minutes to get her out of port.

"Welcome aboard, ladies." Olsson shook each of their hands and then turned to Toven. "I'm needed on the bridge. Our first assistant engineer, Mr. Mikael Hedlund, will show Doctor Merlin the clinic, and our chief electrician, Mr.

Peter Dahlberg, will show the rest of you where everything is."

"Thank you, Captain."

"I'll come along." Marcel followed the captain, holding a box with William's makeshift voice changer. "I need to check out your communication equipment."

Marcel must have used a thrall because the captain didn't object.

The disrupter was down in the cargo bay, but since they couldn't use it yet anyway, it could stay there until it was needed.

"Do you want to join us on the bridge as well, Mr. Hartford?" the captain asked.

"Not right now. I'm curious to see the rest of the vessel, and please, call me Tom."

The pilot was about to come on board, and Toven didn't want the guy to see that there were passengers on the ship. "Remember what we discussed. The *Aurora* has no passengers. Marcel is part of your crew."

The captain nodded and turned on his heel.

As the engineer left with Merlin, the chief electrician smiled nervously. "Forgive me, but I've never given a ship tour before, so I'm not very good at it, but I'm the only one who is not needed right now."

"That's okay, Mr. Dahlberg." Toven gave him a reassuring smile. "As I said before, we are an informal bunch. We don't need you to show us the cabins or the entertainment areas. We can explore the ship on our own. We only need you to show us where we can get linen and toiletries for the cabins, where we can launder our stuff, where the food is stored, the kitchen, etc. After this first tour, we won't bother you again."

"It's no bother." Dahlberg glanced at Mia's wheelchair. "We need to use the elevator. Follow me."

Marcel's finger hovered over the row of buttons as they

entered the spacious elevator. "Which level are the animals stored at?"

"The cargo bay." Dahlberg entered a code on the keypad, and the elevator lurched down. "As the owner requested, we sectioned off part of the bay for the animals. We also got separate crates of feed for the sheep and the goats." He smiled. "I grew up on a farm, so I know that sheep and goats have different nutritional needs. They have plenty of both over there. I just wonder why you are taking them to Greenland."

"These are a special breed," Marcel said.

"Oh, I see." Dahlberg nodded. "This is their breeding season, and gestation is five months. Does or ewes bred in the fall will usually kid or lamb in the spring of the next year. Luckily for you, I knew it was not good to mix the herds during mating season, so I divided the cargo bay into two sections, one for the goats and one for the sheep. The bucks and rams get very aggressive during this time, and a ram can easily kill a buck."

"We wouldn't want that," Kagra said. "We are very fond of these animals. You might say that our lives depend on them."

PHINAS

*P*hinas held his breath as their group exited the elevator at the cargo bay. Sofia, her father, and several other humans were tending to the animals. As Dahlberg walked over to show them where everything was, Phinas sidled up to Jade.

"Do they taste good?"

She eyed him from the corner of her eye. "They are not bad, but I prefer the blood of wild animals. It tastes much better."

That shouldn't have excited him, but everything about the Kra-ell leader affected him.

"Which ones are your favorites?"

The corner of her lips kicked up in a lopsided grin. "Those that provide a challenge. I don't like easy prey."

He leaned to whisper in her ear. "Should I play hard to get, then? Do you want me to run so you can give chase?"

She lifted her hand and put a finger on his lips. "Save it for later. We are not alone."

They stood apart from the others, with the bleating of the

sheep and goats providing enough background noise to prevent the others from hearing them.

Tonight, he and Jade would resume their sexual training, and he was going to demonstrate what he'd planned to show her the day before.

Yamanu put his hand on Dahlberg's shoulder. "I'm eager to join my mate in our cabin, so the quicker you can complete the tour, the better."

"We will take our leave," Toven said. "I will escort Mia to our cabin, and I'll come down again to get the linens and other necessities."

Mia looked tired, which was not surprising given all that she'd been through lately and the fact that her body was working on regrowing lost limbs.

It was a painful process, and Phinas didn't know how she could handle the pain so well. Evidently, females had a much higher pain tolerance than males.

"Don't worry about it," Kagra said. "I'll get you what you need." She winked at Mia. "We owe you much more than room service."

"Thank you." Mia smiled gratefully. "I appreciate it."

When the two headed toward the elevators, Dahlberg motioned for the rest of them to follow him. "Let's use the stairs. The desalination equipment and waste management are just one level down. I know it's not something you will use, but it's fascinating to see." He glanced at Yamanu, who was emitting impatient vibes. "If that's okay with you."

"Make it quick," the Guardian said.

"I will." The chief electrician opened the door to a staircase and started down the utilitarian stairs. "All modern cruise ships use desalination to turn seawater into drinking water. Pumps on the hull suck the water from the ocean and transfer it to the desalination equipment." He opened the door at the lower deck and ushered them inside.

The clan used desalination equipment to provide water to the village, so Phinas was familiar with how it looked, but Jade eyed the enormous block of equipment with wide eyes.

"How does it take the salt out of the water?" she asked.

"This one uses reverse osmosis." Dahlberg patted the side of the block. "A pump pressurizes the seawater and pushes it through a semi-permeable membrane. Most dissolved salts and organic compounds, including bacteria and suspended solids, can't pass through. What comes out on the other side is mostly clean water. The next step is to mineralize and disinfect it using chlorination, ozonation, silver-ion treatment, and UV radiation. The process is completed with filtration and, finally, heating up the water. Only then can it be used as drinking water." He kept walking and pointed to large water tanks. "This is where the water is stored. From here, it is distributed throughout the ship."

"Fascinating," Yamanu bit out. "Can we get to the food area now? I'm hungry, and I want to know where I can get something to eat."

"Of course." Dahlberg looked disappointed at Yamanu's lack of interest. "The food storage area and the kitchen are two levels up. Would you like to use the elevator or the stairs?"

"The stairs," the Guardian said. "How much food do you have stored?"

"We have enough provisions that should last four hundred passengers two weeks."

As the chief electrician led them up the stairs, Phinas took position behind Jade so he could watch her ass.

Sensing his eyes on her, she exaggerated the sway of her hips, encased in a pair of low-hanging fatigues secured with a wide belt. Her extremely narrow waist was not as prominent in the loose black Henley she was wearing, but he could still trace the contours of her graceful spine through the fabric.

"The *Aurora* has four cold storage rooms," Dahlberg said. "Currently, they contain about eighteen hundred pounds of chicken, seven hundred pounds of fish, five hundred pounds of hamburger meat, and one thousand pounds of hot dogs. That's just the meat."

That was a lot of food, and since the purebloods and some of the hybrids didn't need to eat any of that, they could probably spend a month at sea if needed. The question was whether they had enough fuel.

"How long before the ship needs to refuel?" Phinas asked the chief electrician.

"If we cruise at a moderate speed, we can probably go for nearly a month before we need to refuel, but if we need to speed up, we will go through the reserves much faster." Dahlberg opened the door to another storage room and motioned for them to follow. "Despite the reserves, the protocol is to refuel at every port we stop at so we never run low."

"Got it." Phinas stayed close to Jade as her eyes roamed the contents of the room.

It was stocked with hundreds of wooden crates with a variety of alcoholic beverages. They were stacked one on top of the other and secured with metal bands.

"Four thousand bottles of beer," Dahlberg said. "One thousand bottles of wine and seven hundred bottles of assorted spirits."

Yamanu grinned. "Is there a chance you can hook me up with a few whiskey bottles?"

"It's all yours." The chief electrician waved his hand at the crates. "Just secure the crates after you take what you need. This is a ship, and everything that's not tied down moves."

"Aye, aye, sir." Yamanu clapped the guy on his back. "I'm going to take a few bottles right now."

JADE

"Where does the waste go?" Kagra asked after they finished touring the kitchen.

Jade couldn't care less about the food prep areas or the waste processing, but Phinas had seemed very interested in the kitchen tour, which made her wonder if he liked to cook.

Not that she could ever sample what he made, but she was curious.

Fascinated was a better word.

Phinas affected her in unexpected ways. She'd told him that he'd done fine, and he'd taken it as an insult, but the truth was that she couldn't put into words what she'd experienced with him. She'd climaxed from him penetrating her with his fingers, which had never happened to her.

Heck, she'd even licked his shaft and had enjoyed doing so. Another first for her.

The chief electrician cast a cautious look at Yamanu. "Do you want me to take you where it's done?"

"No," Yamanu answered categorically.

Holding two bottles of whiskey under one arm and two

bottles of wine under the other, the Guardian seemed impatient to deliver them to his mate and his other companions.

Jade had only seen them in passing, but she'd noticed that the two ladies were of Chinese descent and strikingly beautiful by human standards.

Kagra hadn't been happy to see that Yamanu had a gorgeous mate who he was obviously in love with, but she hadn't been overly disappointed either. Her interest in Yamanu had been nothing but curiosity, which had been sparked by Jade's liaison with Phinas.

Her second had always been a competitive female.

Yamanu nudged Peter Dahlberg with his elbow. "You can tell us all about it while you show us where the linen and the laundry are, and then I'm out of here. After that, if any of the others want to see where the poop goes, you are more than welcome to show them."

"Understood." Peter headed down the corridor. "Housekeeping is on the same level as the kitchens and the food storage."

After showing them the laundry machines, Dahlberg led them through rooms full of housekeeping supplies, and as they each loaded up a cart with what they needed, he talked.

"The ship can't just dump sewage into the ocean, and it has to have a wastewater treatment plant on board. The black water is treated in several steps, mechanically and chemically. First, the coarse stuff gets filtered out, then it goes through biological purification, with microorganisms decomposing the organic matter, and lastly, it runs through filters with extremely fine sieves that sort out all microorganisms. The final step is nitrogen and phosphorus reduction. After that, it can be disposed of into the sea or ocean water, but only if the ship is at least twelve nautical miles from land."

Frowning, Kagra pushed the cart in front of her. "But what do you do with all the stuff filtered out of the water?"

"That's an excellent question." Peter grinned, happy that at least one person was interested in the subject that seemed to fascinate him. "The by-products are dehydrated and dried in a centrifuge, then burned in an incinerator. Once the ship docks, the ashes are disposed of with the remaining waste."

"You mean the garbage?" Kagra asked. "Where we come from, we used to burn it. We need to know what to do with it on the ship."

Most of the waste in the compound had been produced by the humans and the hybrids who needed cooked food. They didn't use a lot of paper or plastic products, and most of the organic stuff had been turned into compost for the vegetable gardens.

Then again, Jade hadn't been involved in any of that, so maybe she was wrong about what was done with the leftovers.

"Food waste can be shredded and thrown overboard if the ship is at least three nautical miles away from land," Peter explained. "Cardboard, metals, and plastics should be collected and brought over to the hydraulic garbage compressor. Glass needs to be fed to the crushing machine and stored in bags. Non-recyclable garbage is burned in incinerators and turned to ash."

"I'm familiar with the process," Yamanu said. "That's what we do with garbage where I come from." He put the bottles in his cart, added a few toiletries, and turned to Jade. "I would like to invite you to our cabin later tonight. My mate and her sister are eager to meet you."

Jade stifled a groan. She had more things to do than she had time, and at some point, she wanted to relax with one of the bottles of fine vodka she'd seen in the liqueur storage room and perhaps invite Phinas over.

She had yet to choose a cabin, and hopefully there were enough left so she could have one to herself and wouldn't have to share with Kagra.

"After we leave the port, I need to deal with my people." She let out a breath. "Except for Valstar and his buddies, all the others need to be released and shown where everything is. I don't know when I will be done."

Yamanu nodded. "Then let's do that tomorrow. Maybe we can meet at the top deck for a swim in the pool."

Peter cleared his throat. "The pool isn't filled with water, but it can be arranged. It will take time, though."

"Don't worry about it." Yamanu clapped him on the back. "We will figure it out on our own. You can go back to your electrical engineering duties." He turned to Jade and Kagra. "Unless the ladies have more questions for you?"

They needed Yamanu to keep shrouding them, and he needed to go.

"We don't," Jade said. "Thank you for the tour, Mr. Dahlberg."

"You are most welcome." He dipped his head.

53

PHINAS

*A*fter Jade had declined Yamanu's invitation, Phinas decided it wasn't a good idea to suggest that they meet for drinks in his cabin as he'd planned.

The cabin that he still needed to secure.

He'd put Dandor in charge of allocating rooms to his men, but he hadn't had time to check out the accommodations before meeting with the captain.

"I wonder what the cabins look like." He fell in step with Jade and Kagra, the three of them pushing their loaded carts toward the elevators.

"I hope they are fancy," Kagra said. "I've never been on a cruise ship."

"Neither have I," Jade said. "But I've stayed in nice hotels back in the day when I still traveled for business." She winced. "I also had nice luggage instead of a pillowcase to put my things in."

Phinas regretted not paying more attention to what Aliya had told them about Jade. Now that he thought back to their conversations, he remembered Aliya mentioning the animated movies that Jade had brought for the kids from her travels.

Aliya had also talked about the stories Jade liked to tell the children. He couldn't imagine the hard warrior enjoying doing that. But there was still a lot he didn't know about her, which wasn't surprising, given their short time together. She was always busy with one thing or another, and she'd ridden in the command van that he hadn't been invited into.

Even Merlin had ridden in the van when his patients no longer needed him, and it rankled that Phinas had been left out.

He and his men had volunteered their help, so the least Phinas had expected was to be included in the decision-making.

Kalugal had expected the same, but Kian hadn't invited him to the war room either. After all this time, the clan still regarded them as outsiders.

"Where did you travel to?" he asked Jade as they waited for the elevator.

"I've been all over the world." She had a wistful expression on her beautiful face. "Singapore, South Korea, most of Europe, the United States, Canada, Brazil, Venezuela, and many more. It was mostly for business, but I have to admit that I also did it because I enjoyed it."

"You never took me along," Kagra grumbled.

Jade put a hand on her shoulder. "You were the only one I could trust to hold the fort in my absence."

"I know. But I wish I had seen more of the world. Maybe it would have made captivity easier."

"It made it harder." Jade pressed her lips into a tight line. "I knew what I was missing out on."

As the elevator doors opened and the three of them squeezed in together with their carts, Jade looked at the panel. "Any idea which deck we are on?"

Kagra shook her head. "The Guardians will know."

"Hold the door open while I check." Phinas stepped out and called Dandor. "I'm heading up. Which deck are we on?"

"We are on the fifth deck. I put you in the best cabin at the bow. In ship speak, that's the front. You have a very nice view."

"Thank you. What about the Kra-ell? Which deck are they on?"

"The Guardians put them on decks three and four. I think the purebloods are on the fourth, and the hybrids are on the third. The humans are on decks one and two."

"Who is on deck six?"

"Toven and the Guardians."

"Of course they are." Phinas grimaced. "They think they are at the top of our food chain." He pressed the button for deck four. "Although to be fair, it's their ship. Please arrange for the men to go down in groups and collect what they need. I'll unload my cart and take you and the first group to show you where everything is. After that, you can show the others."

"Yes, boss."

As Phinas stepped inside and the door closed behind him, Jade cast Kagra a reproachful look. "You should have stayed to help the Guardians organize our people."

"They didn't want my help. I've told you that."

"You should have insisted."

As the door opened, Kagra pushed her cart out, but Jade didn't follow. Instead, she lodged her cart in the door to prevent it from closing. "If it's not too late when I'm done with my duties, I'll come to check out your cabin."

Phinas's heart leaped...

Leaped? What was he, a human teenager?

"It will not be too late for me. I'll be delighted to show you my cabin no matter what time it is. What would you like to drink? Other than blood, that is."

"Vodka with cranberry juice." She pushed her cart out.

Phinas was still smiling long after the elevator door closed and the cabin lurched up.

When he got out of the elevator on deck five, Dandor was waiting for him and took over pushing the cart. "Let me show you your cabin." He sounded excited.

"Aren't they all the same?"

"Most of them are, except for this one, which is why I reserved it for you. It's bigger, and it has a huge balcony. All the cabins have a living room, a bar, and two-bedroom suites. They are very nicely done, but they are small in scale. Nevertheless, I think even Kalugal would approve."

Phinas chuckled. "I wouldn't be sure of that. Kalugal likes everything he owns to be on a grand scale. It would be a luxury yacht if he ever got a boat."

54

KIAN

"They are out of the port," Roni announced as Kian answered the phone.

He already knew that, but Roni was showing off that he could track the *Aurora* in real time. He'd hacked into the navy's system monitoring marine activity and could see her and every vessel surrounding her.

Once Marcel reactivated the scrambler, they would lose the ability to track the ship, but so would everyone else. Thanks to their own satellite network, which William's scrambler was programmed to let through, they could still communicate through their phones and tablets.

"Congratulations, Roni. Thanks for letting me know, and keep me updated if you spot any suspicious activity around the ship."

"Will do, boss." The kid ended the call.

It was too early to determine if any vessel was following the *Aurora*, but Roni might spot something.

"Let's call Yamanu and Toven," Turner said. "If they have nothing of concern to report, I'll take a break to check on a few things in my office."

Kian tilted his head. "I thought you didn't have any pending jobs at the moment."

"I didn't a few days ago, but my office had a couple of inquiries I need to look into."

"Please don't take on any new jobs until this is over. I need you and your international connections."

It seemed as if Turner knew every private operator in every corner of the world. Whenever Kian needed to hire human teams to assist in missions, he was the guy to turn to.

That was the official version.

The unofficial one was that Turner was good at what he did, and neither Onegus nor Kian could match his level of expertise.

"Don't worry," Turner said. "I'm enjoying running this operation too much to let go before seeing it to its happy ending."

That had been a polite way to say that he wouldn't leave a critical mission like this in the hands of amateurs, and as much as it rankled to admit, he was right.

Onegus and Kian might have centuries of experience, but they had never been trained in modern warfare, they didn't have connections to former special operations personnel or their foreign equivalents, and they lacked Turner's computer-like brain.

That being said, even Turner hadn't always thought of all the angles, and several brains working on the same problem were better than one.

"Appreciated." Kian glanced at his watch and calculated the time difference before placing the call.

It was ten o'clock at night in Finland.

"Hello, boss," Yamanu answered.

"How are things going over there?"

"Couldn't be better. The cabin is great, and Mey loves it.

She's soaking in the Jacuzzi tub and waiting for me to join her."

Yamanu sounded happy, which Kian was glad about, but he still didn't like that Mey and Jin had joined the cruise.

"What about the Kra-ell?"

"Valstar and the rest of Igor's original group are under guard, and Toven has compelled the hell out of them. They don't dare go to the bathroom without asking permission. We released the rest of the purebloods and hybrids, but we are watching them. Toven's compulsion should prevent them from doing anything they shouldn't, but I prefer to keep an eye on them."

"How is their morale?" Kian asked.

"Some are excited, and others look anxious, but all of them are putting on a brave face. They are trained not to show emotions, but they can't hide from Arwel. He says they don't project much, though, and he has to get close to get a read on them."

"I'm not surprised," Turner said. "Did Arwel sense any anger?"

"Naturally, Valstar and the rest of Igor's circle are angry and anxious. They know that their days are numbered."

"We can't just execute them," Kian said. "Don't let Jade do that either. Everyone deserves a fair trial and a chance to defend themselves."

"Didn't Toven promise Jade Valstar's head?" Yamanu asked.

"Yeah, he did, but only after we caught Igor, and he didn't promise her the heads of the others."

"Got it. Anything else I need to fill you in on?"

There was plenty more, but Kian didn't want to keep the Guardian while his mate waited for him to join her in the Jacuzzi.

"I can get Toven to do that. Have a good night."

"I will. Good day to you."

After ending the call, Kian placed another to Toven.

"Hello, Kian," Toven answered. "We left the port."

"I know. Roni is tracking the ship. How did the meeting with the captain go?"

"As expected, he followed our instructions to the letter, and his crew is doing what we asked as well. After the initial tour, they know to stay out of our way. By the way, the cabin Mia and I are staying in is beautifully done."

Kian smiled even though it wasn't a video call. "Thank you. I had Ingrid design the decor, but I haven't seen the finished product yet. How is the craftsmanship?"

"Excellent."

"I pulled it out of the shipyard before they could do the final detailing, so I assume that not everything is spotless."

Toven chuckled. "Mia says it's as clean as any hotel room we've stayed at, but I don't know if she means it as a compliment." He paused. "She says it is."

"How come I can't hear her?"

"She's out on the balcony, wrapped in a floor-length puffer jacket, a hat, a scarf, and gloves. It's freezing at night, but she enjoys the fresh air."

"What about the food situation? Who is handling the cooking?"

"Sofia's aunts are organizing shifts," Toven said. "We are invited to a midnight feast."

"That's great. I spoke to Yamanu before I called you. He said the Guardians released all the Kra-ell except for Valstar and those remaining from Igor's original crew. It would be a good idea to continue their interrogation tomorrow."

"It is, and I will do that," Toven said. "Merlin is all set up in the clinic and ready to receive his first patients. Who do you want him to start with?"

"It doesn't really matter because we need to check everyone. I assume that all the pureblooded females he captured have trackers in them, so maybe it's a good idea to start with them. Those who were born in the compound probably don't, but who knows."

"It will be interesting to see," Toven said. "If the trackers are from the home planet, they must have been implanted by the gods. According to Jade, the Kra-ell didn't have access to such sophisticated technology. But if that's the case, I wonder where Igor got the one he implanted in Sofia. I doubt their escape pods had equipment that was not necessary for keeping them alive."

"My thoughts exactly," Kian said. "He either took it out of himself, those he trusted, those he killed, or all of the above. I'm waiting for William to return and take apart the one we have to see if it's alien technology. I wouldn't be surprised if he finds a microscopic inscription saying that it was made in China."

JADE

"Who do you want to get checked first?" Kagra asked. "Max said it doesn't matter, and it's up to us."

"Who is Max?"

"A handsome Guardian with a charming smile."

Her second had shifted her focus to a new immortal.

Jade's lips twisted in an involuntary smile. "I see that you found a new candidate to experiment with."

"Maybe." Kagra put her hand on her hip. "We shall see. I haven't asked him if he has been taken yet. So, who goes first?"

"Drova, Morgada, Tomos, and Helmi." Jade started down the corridor, and Kagra fell in step with her. "I'll get Drova and Morgada. You get Tomos and Helmi."

"Why those four?"

"They each represent a different group. Morgada is from our tribe, and I also know her from before we boarded the gods' ship, but she doesn't remember being implanted either.

"Drova is a pureblood who was born in the compound, Tomos is a hybrid, and Helmi is a human who didn't get to study at a university, so there was no reason to implant her, but I want to double-check. Finding out which of them has a tracker will give me valuable insight."

"Why not me?" Kagra asked. "I'm a pureblood who was born on Earth."

"I need you to organize our people, including the humans. I'll get checked first to show them it's not a big deal, and Helmi will go next. We can safely leave the humans for last if she doesn't have a tracker."

"It doesn't really matter." Kagra stopped in front of Morgada and Drova's cabin. "We need to check every person. As long as even one tracker remains, Igor can find us, and Max told me that they can't activate the scrambler until the ship leaves the Baltic Sea."

"The sooner the trackers are out, the better. I don't know how long it takes, but I assume about half an hour to an hour per person. That means between one hundred and fifty hours to three hundred and twenty, and that's with Merlin not taking any breaks, which he can't do. He needs to sleep from time to time."

"Maybe he can teach someone how to do that? How complicated can it be to scan a body for a tracker?"

"I don't know." Jade put her hand on the door handle. "I'll know more after the initial group is scanned. I hope we can do that faster, or we will not get them out before reaching Greenland."

Kagra tilted her head. "Is that where we are going?"

"It's just a stop on the way, and I hope that we catch Igor before we get to the North Sea and can turn around without ever reaching Greenland. That would be the perfect solution and the one I pray for. If we don't catch him, we will sail to Greenland, and from there, they will take us somewhere else. They haven't decided where that would be yet."

"Tell Tom to take us somewhere warm. The jungles of

South America would be ideal for us. Plenty of game to hunt and places to hide."

Jade had no desire to live in a jungle. If she had her pick, she would choose a location that was not too far from a major metropolis like her old compound near Beijing. She was a traditionalist in many things, but not when it came to technology.

The Kra-ell had been left in the dust by the gods not only because they'd been tricked into servitude but also because of a much earlier decision.

They'd chosen to cling to their way of life and had looked down their noses at the gods for turning away from nature and trusting their future to genetic manipulation and technology.

That decision had doomed them.

Jade was against tampering with nature and making dramatic genetic changes, but she was all for technology and the conveniences and advantages it offered. It was possible to live traditionally and be technologically advanced at the same time.

"Let's hope we catch him and that he didn't destroy the compound just so we can never take it back. Without Igor, the place is perfect. It's easy to defend, has great hunting grounds, but is still driving distance away from two major cities." Jade tried the door, but it was locked from the inside.

Kagra's lips twisted in a grimace. "I don't want to go back there. You and I got used to the closet-sized rooms and considered them a luxury because others had to share communal spaces, but that's not how I want to live. Just look at this place." She waved a hand around. "This ship's cabins are the nicest rooms I've ever stayed in. Even Igor and Valstar didn't have luxurious accommodations like this."

Their quarters in the old compound in China were much nicer than what Igor had provided them with, but Jade had to admit that they had been spartan compared to the luxury of the ship cabins.

"I would like to have that too, and with the money Tom's people retook from Igor, we can make improvements. But it's not as important as getting our freedom back and being able to protect ourselves. I pray to the Mother that we catch him without him recapturing us. I'd rather die than go back to living under his thumb. And as decent as Tom appears, I don't want to live under his or Kian's thumb either."

SOFIA

"I stink." Sofia pulled out of Marcel's arms. "I need a shower."

Helping her father with the animals had been fun. It reminded her of many happy childhood days with him while he tended to the herd.

Even as a young girl, the irony hadn't been lost on her. Most of the time, the herd was in its enclosure, eating hay. But from time to time her father and the other shepherds took the herd to graze in the hunting grounds, and they always headed out with at least one Kra-ell pureblood to guard the animals against predators.

The Kra-ell were the strongest, most dangerous of the predators roaming the hunting grounds, but at the same time, they were the best protection for the herd. The other predators feared them. The Kra-ell didn't kill the animals they fed from, but if a predator dared to attack, they would kill to protect the herd.

"You don't stink." Marcel took her hand. "You smell like sheep and goats."

She crinkled her nose. "I love animals, but I don't like the smell. I hope Helmi got towels and bedding for us." She looked up at him. "I don't even know which cabin we are in. Can you call one of your Guardian buddies and ask?"

"They are not monitoring the human decks. But why would you want to share a cabin with Helmi? You should stay with me."

Her mood lifted in an instant. "Can I? I thought that only Guardians were allowed on deck five."

Sofia had hoped she could stay in the same cabin with Marcel, but he'd been in the meeting with the captain, and she'd been helping her father with the animals, and there had been no one to ask.

"I'm not a Guardian, and I'm staying on deck five. Yamanu and Arwel's mates are also staying with them. They took the two cabins next to Mia and Toven's grand suite."

"Did you get to see it?"

He shook his head. "I was told that each deck has two large cabins and the rest are the same size. Each suite has two bedrooms, though. Even the regular-sized ones."

Sofia was willing to bet that the cabins on the upper decks were fancier than the cabins the humans had been given, but that was fine. The ship belonged to the immortals, the Kra-ell needed to be guarded, and the humans were the least important.

"I can't wait to see your cabin, but let's find Helmi first. I need to tell her that I'm staying with you. Did you ask if it was okay for Tomos to share her cabin?"

Marcel shrugged. "Since the Kra-ell were set free, I figured it wasn't necessary. Tomos can go wherever he wants."

"Isn't he guarded?"

"Toven compelled all of them to behave, so it's not really necessary, but I'm sure Yamanu organized the Guardians to patrol the ship."

She tugged on his hand, guiding him toward the elevators. "Helmi will be so happy to hear that Tomos can stay with her. I hope her mother doesn't have a problem with that."

Marcel halted, pulling her to a stop. "Will your father mind that you're staying with me? I don't want to upset him."

Sofia snorted. "What I told you about my unreasonable father was a made-up story, remember? I've been an adult for a long time, and my father knows that I'm not a virgin."

"There is a difference between knowing hypothetically and having it shoved in his face."

"It's okay." She leaned into Marcel and kissed him on the lips. "You are my fiancé, and he knows that we are working on making me immortal."

Marcel arched a brow. "Are we?"

They'd been using condoms to prevent her from entering transition while her family had been in danger, but now that they were on their way to the village, they could start. They even had a clan doctor with a fully equipped clinic on board, so there was no reason to wait—except for Igor sinking the ship.

"We are." She smiled. "My family is safe. We have a doctor and a clinic, so why wait?"

"We are not out of the woods yet. Igor might try to sink the ship, and I don't want you to be in the middle of transitioning in case that happens. I'm just as anxious as you are for us to start the process, but it would be irresponsible to do it now."

JADE

"*D*o I have to go?" Drova stared at the television. "Do you know that they have all the latest movies?"

Her daughter didn't seem troubled by the prospect of her father catching them or the possibility that they would catch him and end his life. She was enamored with the luxurious cabin, the big-screen television, and all the mindless entertainment she could consume.

Perhaps she was numbing her pain.

After hearing from Morgada more about their tribe's history and what had been lost and stolen, Drova might be distracting herself from dark thoughts by watching silly movies.

Jade had asked to put Drova in the same cabin as Morgada for a reason.

She'd already told the girl about their tribe and what Igor had done to their males, but that was just the tip of the iceberg, and Drova probably had a lot of questions. If she heard them from Jade, she would question whether her mother had put a spin on them to make herself look good, but she would believe Morgada.

Not everything the female would tell her about Jade would be positive, but that would make her stories more believable.

"The movie will still be there when you come back." Jade imbued her tone with command. "Let's go."

"Fine." Drova pushed to her feet and stretched her arms over her head. "I'm so tired. Why do I need to see the doctor tonight? I'm not injured."

"That's not why you need to see the doctor. Tom's people found a tracker implanted in Sofia. All of us probably have one, and I want you to be among the first to get it removed."

Drova's hand lifted to her throat. "Why would we have implanted trackers? We had collars. Sofia lived outside the compound and didn't have a collar. That's why she had an implant."

"That's logical." Jade opened the door. "But then we need to ask ourselves how Igor found our tribe and the others. Trackers that were implanted in the original settlers before would explain that."

"But I was born on Earth."

"That's why you are one of the first to go through the scanner. I chose one representative from each group. Original purebloods, purebloods that were born on Earth, hybrids, and humans that didn't get to leave the compound."

Drova nodded. "Makes sense."

"I'm glad you finally agree."

Her daughter was so much like a human teenager. When Jade had been her age, she'd already been a warrior, training to get a spot on the queen's guard. She never would have dared to talk back or question anything her mother had said.

She'd raised her sons the same way, but she'd been more lenient with Drova, and not by choice. Igor hadn't allowed her to train their daughter for a future position as a Kra-ell leader. He hadn't expected Drova to do anything other than breed and produce strong grandchildren for him.

When they got to the clinic, Helmi and Tomos were already there, and given their solemn expressions, Kagra or Merlin had told them about the trackers. They had brought pillowcases stuffed with all of their belongings so Merlin could put them through the scanner as well.

Jade hadn't brought her things, but she planned on doing so after laundering her clothes.

"The doctor stepped out for a moment," Kagra said. "Who do you want to go first?"

"I'll go." Jade gave Helmi a reassuring smile. "It's a simple procedure. You have nothing to fear."

"I know. Sofia told me."

"Then I assume that all the humans know about the trackers."

Helmi nodded.

"Good. It will save us time explaining."

"Hello." Merlin strode into the clinic. "I grabbed a quick bite." He smiled at Helmi. "Your mother and aunt and several others, whose names I've already forgotten, are cooking a feast in the kitchen. The nurse is with them, so I will start with the scanning first. I don't think she'll be in any shape to assist me with the removal tonight. After the midnight meal, she'll need to go to sleep."

"Perhaps scanning everyone first is a better plan," Jade said. "You can make notes where the trackers are and remove them after all the scanning is done."

The doctor shook his head. "I need the precise location. I will probably need to scan all of you again before I cut the trackers out, but at least I'll know where to look, so I won't have to waste time scanning your entire body again."

"It is what it is." Jade let out a breath. "You can start with me."

"Yes, ma'am." He opened the door to the other room where the machine was.

Even without having any medical knowledge, she had no trouble identifying the donut-shaped contraption with the bench sticking out of it. "I assume that I need to lie down on this." She pointed.

Lifting his hand, he stopped her from taking another step. "First, you need to remove anything made of metal and put it on the chair over there. The device has a powerful magnet inside of it."

Nodding, Jade sat on the chair and removed her boots. Then she unstrapped the sword belt and the knives and put them under the chair. Her spiked bracelets were next.

Merlin eyed her arsenal with an amused expression. "Who did you plan to use all that on?"

"My enemies." She padded to the platform on her socked feet. "What if trackers are hidden in my weapons. If they can't go into the device, how are you going to scan them?"

"How precious are they to you?"

"I don't have an emotional attachment to them. If I can get good replacements, I have no problem throwing the old stuff overboard."

"Good." He gave her a once-over. "Are you sure that is all? Some ladies wear bras with underwire. If you have one of those on, I need you to take it off."

"Do I look like someone who wears a bra? What would I need it for?"

Merlin's eyes never strayed from hers. "My beautiful mate is generously blessed. Since turning immortal, she doesn't need bras, but she wears them anyway. It's always better to make sure."

"I don't."

"Very well. Close your eyes, think happy thoughts, and don't move until I tell you."

"Yes, doctor."

As Jade closed her eyes, she was surprised that she didn't need to frantically search for something happy to think about. Memories of the previous night with Phinas eased her tense muscles, made her heart feel lighter, and brought a smile to her lips. The languid feeling wasn't brought about by the memory of the pleasure he'd given her or the pleasure she'd given back, although that had been very satisfying. It was caused by the memories of their conversation, his silly self-deprecating comments, his humor, and the way he'd regarded her.

When Phinas looked at her, he didn't see a fearsome leader or a female to be conquered or impregnated. He saw the person inside.

He saw her, and he liked what he saw.

PHINAS

on't you want to stay for the desserts?" Dandor asked as Phinas pushed to his feet and picked up his plate.

"I'm stuffed. But save a piece of cake for me."

"Sure thing, boss. Do you want me to bring it to your cabin?"

"No need. I'll come to yours."

Jade had said she would come to his cabin when she was done with her duties, and Phinas hoped that was still the plan. Dandor wouldn't be too upset if he didn't show up.

Dandor grinned. "We can share a glass of whiskey and watch a game. You can choose any game played over the last five years. I took a couple of bottles from the storage room to my cabin. I checked what they have on their servers, and it's the same as in the village."

"I'll take a rain check." Phinas walked to the dirty dishes bin and put his plate and utensils in.

The humans who had prepared the meal seemed happy to do that, but they probably needed help cleaning up after, and he wanted to offer his men's services.

Striding into the kitchen, he found Sofia's aunt and walked over to her.

His Russian was so-so, but he could manage enough to ask if they needed help.

"Hello, *menya zovut* Phinas." He offered her his hand.

"Isla." She shook it, then turned around and waved over at a girl who looked no older than thirteen.

After the older woman spoke to her in rapid Finnish, the girl nodded and turned to him. "My mom asks if you enjoyed dinner."

Apparently, Isla had determined by his accent that his Russian wasn't good enough.

"Very much. I want to thank her and everyone else who pitched in to prepare this excellent meal." He rubbed his stomach. "It has been a long time since I ate so well."

He hadn't lied. Atzil was an okay cook, but he lacked imagination, and they had been eating the same dishes for years. The alternative was to eat in restaurants or learn how to cook himself, but Phinas didn't like doing either. His repertoire was limited to throwing a frozen pizza into the oven, and he barely even managed that. It either came out undercooked or burned.

Usually, he ate lunch at one of the eateries near Kalugal's office building downtown, and dinner was a sandwich from the café.

Isla smiled, and when the girl translated, her smile grew even wider.

"My mom says she's delighted and appreciates that you came to thank her."

He dipped his head. "I also came to offer the help of my men with the cleanup."

When the girl translated, Isla looked shocked by his offer, and her answer in rapid Finnish took an entire minute.

The girl nodded and turned to him. "My mom says that

no help is needed. She and the others are grateful for the help you have provided so far and all the help you will provide in the future. She says that cooking, serving, and cleaning after the meal is the least they can do. They will also take care of the laundry and anything else that needs to be done."

Up until now, he hadn't been sure that the humans appreciated being uprooted. On the voyage through Karelia they'd looked scared, not to mention hungry. There hadn't been time to pack provisions, and all they had on the fourteen-hour journey were the field rations that the clan had brought with them.

"I'm grateful for the offer, but we will take care of the laundry ourselves. The meals, though, will be greatly appreciated. None of us are good in the kitchen."

When the girl translated, Isla bobbed her head and smiled.

"What's your name?" Phinas asked her.

"Lana."

"Nice to meet you, Lana." He offered the girl his hand. "I'm Phinas. If you or your mother or any of the others need help with anything, come find me. I'm on deck five in the first cabin at the front of the ship. Or you can tell any of the Guardians that you are looking for me, and they will let me know."

"Thank you." She pulled her hand out of his grasp. "Do you know where we are going?"

He didn't know whether the humans had been told that they were sailing to Greenland. Besides, their final destination hadn't been decided yet, so he couldn't tell her.

"Maybe you are not going anywhere. If we catch Igor, you can go back to the compound, and those who don't want to can ask to be taken somewhere else."

As Lana translated, Isla nodded and then said something back.

"My mom says they haven't decided what they want to do either. They all want to stay together and don't even mind co-existing with the Kra-ell if they'll get paid for their services, but they don't want to make babies for them. They want to be free to choose who they want to have babies with."

Phinas's fangs twitched as he thought about how terrible it must have been for the women who'd been forced to breed with the Kra-ell to produce hybrids for them.

"Tell your mom that I will personally make sure that this kind of exploitation will never be sanctioned again. I can't guarantee that every male will behave, but I can guarantee that anyone who does that will be severely punished."

"Thank you," Lana said quietly.

59

JADE

*T*he results of the scan were interesting, and as Jade made her way to the fifth deck, she wasn't sure whether it was a reason for celebration or not, but she was excited about sharing the discovery with Phinas.

She took the stairs instead of using the elevator to avoid meeting anyone on her way up and to give herself a few moments to think.

Usually, Kagra was the one with whom she shared everything. On some level, Jade felt as if she was betraying her second by preferring to talk with a male who she'd just met and who wasn't even a Kra-ell. But there was something about Phinas that put her at ease, that made her feel less burdened.

She couldn't put her finger on what it was.

Was it his sarcastic, self-deprecating humor? Or was it that he was an outsider who was also a leader of his people and understood the difficulties she faced?

Or maybe she didn't need to put on a mask with him. She didn't have to front being invincible, untouchable, and above it all. He wasn't one of her subordinates she needed to keep at arm's length.

Most likely, it was all of the above.

No guards were posted on the fifth deck, which indicated that the Guardians put a lot of faith in Tom's compulsion and didn't expect any trouble from the Kra-ell they had freed.

Phinas's cabin was at the front of the ship, which was the nicest cabin on each deck and probably identical to hers. It was such a waste for a single person to occupy such a space, but she appreciated the privacy and didn't want to share the cabin with Kagra or Drova. Her second was too talkative, and Drova would have driven her insane with the television being on all the time.

Jade knocked on the door and waited for Phinas to invite her in, and when he didn't answer, she knocked again, this time louder.

He either wasn't in his cabin or had fallen asleep.

It was after one o'clock at night, so the second option was more likely, but in either case it was disappointing.

Turning around, she started down the corridor and was about to go down the stairs when the elevator door opened, and Phinas walked out. He had a bottle of vodka in one hand and a bottle of cranberry juice in the other.

"I've got what you asked for." He didn't smile, and he sounded as if getting the vodka and juice had been a chore.

"If you're tired, we can do this another time."

"I need to talk to you." He passed by her and kept on walking toward his cabin, expecting her to follow.

What the hell was his problem?

Jade followed more out of curiosity than wanting to be with him. She had no patience with moody males or females, no matter which species.

He opened the door, walked to the sitting area, and put the bottles on the coffee table. "Please, take a seat." He pulled two glasses out of his pockets. "I hope you don't mind." He showed her that they were clean. "I can wash them if it bothers you that I carried them in my pockets."

"That doesn't bother me. What bothers me is your unpleasant mood. I came here to relax, so unless you can shake it off, we should postpone this for another time."

Phinas put the glasses next to the bottles. "I need to talk to you." He opened the vodka, poured it into the two glasses, followed with the cranberry juice, and handed her one of them. "Cheers."

Given his mood, they had no reason to be cheerful. "To catching Igor." She clinked her glass with his and took a long swig. "What do you want to talk about?"

"The humans. No more enforced breeding. If you get to lead them again, you'll have to establish new rules of conduct."

That was what was bothering him in the middle of the night?

"Who told you that the breeding was forced on the humans? Igor is evil, and he's a murderer, but rape was not sanctioned in his compound."

He let out a breath. "Maybe it's a cultural difference that you don't understand, but as a female coerced into breeding with the murderer of her people, you should. If a female feels she has no choice and has to accept the male's advance, that's rape. And if the roles are reversed and the male has no choice but to serve the female, it's also considered rape."

60

PHINAS

*T*he irony wasn't lost on Phinas.

As a former member of the Devout Order of Mortdh Brotherhood, followers of the biggest misogynist to have ever walked the Earth, he had no business lecturing a female about what was consensual sex and what was rape.

But perhaps his past gave him a better insight than most.

Holding the glass between her thumb and forefinger, she eyed him from under lowered lashes. "According to your definition, the entire Kra-ell society perpetrates rape. On the home planet, when a female invited a male to her bed, he felt obligated to accept the invitation because refusing was considered a great offense. Would you consider that coercion?"

He wasn't sure.

There had been times he'd succumbed to a female's advances even when he would have preferred another because he hadn't wanted to hurt her feelings. He could've walked away, and the only consequence would have been a guilty conscience. But he hadn't had to do it.

"I guess it depends on the consequences to the male. What

would he suffer other than the anger of the female he scorned?"

She snorted. "He would be shunned by all the other females of his tribe and would never get invited to their beds again. His only choice would be to find another tribe to join, but the chances of that would be slim. The only way he could find a new tribe was if that tribe had lost too many males and needed to replenish its ranks."

"Then it's rape. He has no choice but to accept or live the rest of his life as a hermit."

She lifted her glass in a salute and took a long sip. "That's our culture. You can't apply human standards to Kra-ell society. It doesn't work."

"But it could if you weren't so set in your ways. Your society won't fall apart if the males can politely decline and still get invited by other females."

"Perhaps." She crossed her legs. "It worked fine for hundreds of thousands of years. You have to understand that our society has different values. The tribe was the ultimate entity, not the individual. The females were expected to produce offspring whether they enjoyed motherhood or not. They didn't have options either. We all had to do our share, and everyone knew what their duties were."

Phinas shook his head. "I can't argue with you about how the Kra-ell on your planet should lead their lives, but you are on Earth now, you coexist with humans, and they don't appreciate being coerced to breed with purebloods to produce hybrids. That has to stop."

"Why is it so important to you?"

He briefly closed his eyes. "It's not something that I like to talk about. I didn't choose the circumstances of my birth or the society I grew up in, so I shouldn't feel shamed by it, but I am." He let out a breath. "My mother was forced to breed with humans to produce immortal warriors for our leader.

Her life was miserable, and yet she did everything she could to give me and my sisters and brothers as much love as she was allowed. It was a very long time ago, many centuries before I joined the clan, but I never forgot what she suffered and what my sisters had to endure. I couldn't help them back then, and my only option to escape that life was to run away. But I'm no longer forced to live in a society that does that to women, and I'm in a position to make a difference for others."

Jade nodded. "I understand. We all want to do better than our parents. What brought it about tonight, though?"

"I spoke to one of the human females in the kitchen." It would be better if he didn't mention Isla by name. Jade might retaliate against her for opening her mouth. "She said that most humans wouldn't mind returning to the compound and serving the Kra-ell if they were paid decent wages, but only if the enforced breeding stopped. They want none of that. I promised her I would ensure it would never be sanctioned again. If a male disobeyed the rules, he would be severely punished."

Jade glared at him. "It wasn't your promise to make."

"Yes, it was. Kian would demand no less, and if you think he will let you continue running things as they were before, you are gravely mistaken. Do you know what the clan's biggest humanitarian effort is?"

"I didn't know that they had any."

"They save victims of trafficking. If you don't know what that is, it's essentially the kidnapping or manipulating of young women to accompany the traffickers and then forcing them into sex slavery. They also take men and boys, but to a much lesser degree. The clan raids the slavers, frees the victims, and rehabilitates them."

"Are you involved in that?"

Phinas deflated. "I'm not, but I would be if the position

was open to me and if I wasn't Kalugal's second-in-command."

"Why isn't the position open to you?"

"It's complicated. Kalugal joined the clan, but more as an affiliate than a member. We live in the same place, but we have our own section, and we don't work on the same things. In case of an attack, though, we will join forces to defend our people."

Her foot swinging back and forth, Jade took another sip from her drink. "Who are you expecting to attack you?"

Had he told her too much?

Yamanu hadn't given him instructions on what was okay to tell Jade and what wasn't, but Phinas saw no harm in telling her about the thousands of immortals Navuh commanded. She needed to know that her Igor was small fry compared to the might of the Brotherhood.

61

JADE

"Who are you expecting to attack you?" Jade regarded Phinas from under lowered lashes, pretending that she wasn't anxious to hear his answer.

She hadn't come to his cabin to pump him for information, but if he was volunteering, she wasn't going to say no.

Her intention had been to relax with a drink, tell him about the trackers, and finish the night in his bed. Perhaps even stay until morning if it didn't feel too weird.

Jade had never spent an entire night with a male, had never felt like it was something that she wanted to try out, and she probably wouldn't enjoy it, but it was liberating to be free of the Kra-ell rules of engagement between the genders and try new things.

For better or worse, Phinas wasn't Kra-ell, and he didn't have the same expectations from her.

But things weren't working out the way she'd planned, and out of the blue, Phinas was criticizing the Kra-ell's way of life and demanding changes as if he was entitled to dictate what she should or shouldn't do with her people.

"My former so-called brothers." Phinas lifted the nearly

full glass and emptied it down his throat. "Do you want another one?"

"Please." She handed him hers.

"The clan's immortals are not the only descendants of the gods." He poured vodka into the two glasses and followed up with the cranberry juice. "There is another faction that is much less benevolent. It was founded by a rogue god who pissed on the gods' matriarchal traditions, much like Igor pissed on yours.

"Like you and Igor, his descendants believe that humans should serve their betters, and they want dominion over humanity."

Jade didn't appreciate being lumped together in the same category as Igor. "I don't think that humans should serve us, and I didn't think that back when I was in charge either. We needed their services, and I compensated them for that. A hundred-some years ago in China, providing them with lodging, clothing, and food was considered adequate compensation."

He arched a brow. "Including bearing hybrid children for you? Even the Chinese regime wouldn't have sanctioned that."

Obviously, Phinas didn't know much about China, or he wouldn't have said that.

"You'd be surprised what they sanctioned, but that's a subject for a different time. Please continue."

"Navuh, the son of that rogue god, formed the Brother-hood and a breeding program to provide him with as many immortal warriors as possible. He inherited a few female Dormants from his father, and he prevented them from transitioning by pairing them only with human males. That way, they could bear many more dormant children. If he had let them turn immortal, their fertility would have significantly dropped. The breeding program continues to this day. The boys are induced at puberty, turn immortal, and become warriors. The girls are not turned, and they are forced to continue breeding like their mothers. In time, his army grew to over twenty thousand strong. That's where I grew up, and it wasn't a good place. Females were considered good only for serving males and breeding, and human lives were worth very little."

"What happened to the rogue god? Navuh's father?"

"He attacked the assembly of gods with what we believe was a nuclear weapon, killing nearly all of them and perishing alongside them. No one knows the precise details of what happened because there was no one left alive to tell the story. The entire region was destroyed, and every living thing in a radius of about five hundred miles died."

"At least it was contained. When did that happen?"

"About five thousand years ago."

Two thousand years after their ship had left their home planet, which meant that the incidents were not connected. Their journey was supposed to take a couple of centuries, and no one could have foreseen that they would arrive after the gods were no more.

"Tom survived, and he told me that there were others. How many gods are still around?"

Phinas hesitated. "Three that we know of. They were outside the five-hundred-mile radius. Tom will need to compel you to keep this a secret, and I'm pretty sure that I will be reprimanded for telling you too much."

"Who am I going to tell?" She took a sip from her drink. "How did you escape the son of the rogue god?"

"Navuh is a powerful compeller, perhaps on par with Igor, so even though I was uncomfortable following the orders I was given, I didn't have a choice. Then one day, Kalugal approached me and started a conversation. He was a young commander, but he was Navuh's son, so I was cautious, but I soon discovered we saw eye to eye. He asked for me to be transferred to his unit, releasing me from his father's compulsion. He kept it a secret that he was nearly as strong a compeller as his father. He couldn't command as many minds at once, but he was just as strong one on one." He rubbed a hand over his jaw. "Which makes me think that Navuh is not as strong as Igor. Kalugal couldn't remove the compulsion from Sofia. Then again, he tried to do it over the phone, which is probably not as effective as doing it face to face."

This was all fascinating information but pretty useless to her. Navuh and his followers were not going to help her catch Igor, and given the size of their force, it would be best that they never found out about her and her people.

Nevertheless, Jade wanted to learn more about the new potential threat.

"Did Kalugal fear his father?"

Phinas nodded. "Navuh had many sons, or so we believed. Kalugal feared his father would kill him if he discovered that he had competition. During World War Two, Kalugal got us stationed in Japan. When the Americans dropped a nuclear bomb on Nagasaki and Hiroshima, he used the opportunity to run away with his unit. We were presumed dead."

"Good plan. How did he know that the Americans would drop the bombs?"

"He didn't. He just took advantage of the situation."

Kalugal sounded like a smart and resourceful male, and she would love to meet him and have a conversation with him and with Kian. Those hybrid children of the gods were more interesting than their full-blooded predecessors, and from what she'd heard and witnessed so far, the immortals were not as full of themselves as the gods.

62

PHINAS

*W*hy was he telling Jade about his sordid past? He was supposed to woo her, seduce her, not push her away with sob stories.

"Enough about me." Phinas finished what was left in his glass and poured himself another. "Do you want me to top yours up?"

"Please." She handed him the glass. "Alcohol has only a moderate effect on us. For some reason, we get lightheaded and talk too much when we take human painkillers. I wish I could research the reason for that."

Kagra had said that she felt drunk after taking the painkillers, and she'd become more talkative, but he'd assumed that it was the relief from pain.

"You should ask Merlin. He usually does more research than doctoring."

"I will do that. Speaking of Merlin, he scanned me, Drova, Morgada, Helmi, and Tomos, and the results were very interesting."

Phinas was glad of the change of subject. They hadn't reached an agreement regarding the human females, but he could bring that up another time. Then again, he needed to ensure that the Kra-ell males didn't coerce the human females during the voyage. He'd given Isla his word, and he intended to keep it.

"Was there a reason for choosing these particular people for the first round of scans?"

"There was, and Merlin confirmed my suspicions. Only Morgada and I have tiny trackers like the one that your other doctor took out of Sofia. Tomos and Drova had larger trackers that Merlin said were common and easy to get, and Helmi had none. It confirmed my suspicion that Morgada and I were implanted before boarding the ship. The trackers in Drova and Tomos were obtained on Earth, and Helmi didn't get one because she never left the compound. I bet that other than the students, none of the other humans have trackers. Igor didn't deem them important enough. The other good news is that all four were in the same place on the body. Merlin said it would significantly shorten the time it would take him to scan for them because he knows where to look."

Phinas wasn't sure that was smart. "He needs to conduct a thorough scan on everyone in case there is more than one tracker. If I were a paranoid guy like Igor, I would have implanted everyone in the same way and then hidden additional trackers in random individuals to throw my enemies off."

"You're right. It's precisely the kind of thing Igor would do, and it's bad news for us. Merlin might not be able to take all the trackers out before we leave the Baltic Sea."

"Perhaps that's a good thing. As long as Igor is following us, we have a good chance of catching him."

Jade sighed. "I hope you are right. Everything would be so much simpler if we eliminated him."

"Well, not necessarily. We still didn't solve the issue of

coercing human females. I gave my word that it would stop. Promise me that you will have a talk with your people about it. The Kra-ell and the humans should sit together, talk it out, and agree on what is acceptable and what is not."

Jade chuckled. "Do you want to lead the discussion?"

"Sure. But I don't speak Russian or Finnish, and many of your people don't speak English."

"I'll translate for you. After all, you gave your word, not me, so you should give the talk."

Tricky female.

"Fine. I will feel like a fish out of water, but I'm not the type of guy who is afraid of a challenge."

"I guessed as much about you." She leaned over and took his hand. "Out of all the females you could've pursued, I'm probably the most challenging." She tilted her head. "Or maybe you enjoy the exotic and the different?"

"There is some of that."

"Or maybe you like tall, skinny brunettes. What's your type?"

He should tell her about Aliya before someone else mentioned his brief courtship of the girl, and Jade reached the wrong conclusion.

"You are very much my type. I like strong females who know what they want and how they want it." He took another sip from his drink. "For a short while, I was fascinated by Aliya—your former tribe member. She's incredibly strong, smart, and resourceful, and she is also honorable and hard-working, but there were two things she lacked, which were maturity and experience. You have those in spades."

Jade narrowed her eyes at him. "Why are you telling me about her? It's not my business who you had sex with, and it's not your business to inquire about my partners."

Did she think that he was telling her about Aliya as a way to ask her about her past lovers?

He'd already learned all he wanted to know from Kagra.

Jade had never gotten attached to any particular male, and she'd treated the males of her tribe as friends with benefits. Friends wasn't the right word either, but co-workers with benefits didn't sound any better.

"I told you about Aliya so you wouldn't hear it from someone else. I never had sex with her. I was interested in her for a while, and then I got to know her better and realized that she was just a kid. Vrog was a much better choice for her, and she reached the same conclusion."

"Did Aliya pick up several males to breed with? Or is she exclusive with Vrog?"

How she'd said it sounded like exclusivity was a bad word.

Phinas really didn't like Jade's attitudes toward sex. They weren't animals, and sex was about pleasure and intimacy, not just about breeding.

"They are exclusive. They love each other."

Jade shook her head. "Hybrids are too much like humans. Love is an illusion. Devotion, friendship, and loyalty are real because they're earned. The concept of unconditional love with a breeding partner is absurd. It's nothing but lust in a pretty wrapping."

63

JADE

*A*s the word lust left Jade's mouth, something shifted between them, the tension sending a bolt of awareness through her.

She wanted Phinas, but after all his talk about rape and coercion, perhaps it was best to let him make the first move.

His nostrils flared, and his brown eyes turned amber. "What are you thinking about?"

"You."

He narrowed his eyes at her. "What about me?"

"You're confusing me with all this talk about love and exclusivity. Do you want me?"

The glow in his eyes intensified. "You know I do."

"So maybe you should stop talking and start doing." She took her glass and leaned back against the sinfully plush couch pillows.

He arched a brow. "What do you want me to do?"

"Use your imagination." She pretended nonchalance, sipping her cranberry vodka and watching him from under lowered lashes.

"I want to get you naked. Do I have your permission?"

Was he still under the influence of his talk about coercion? Would he ask her permission for every move from now on?

Where was the excitement in that?

"Go ahead." She waved a hand.

"Thank you."

"So polite." She sipped on her drink.

"I'm trying." Sliding off the couch, he turned around, sat on the coffee table, grabbed hold of her boot, and pulled it off.

When a dagger clunked to the floor, he arched a brow. "Do you have more of those on you?"

"You'll have to find out. I suggest caution. I keep my daggers sharp." She leisurely lifted the glass to her lips and took another sip.

"I'll keep that in mind." He lifted her other foot, pulled the top of the boot as far as it would go, and peeked inside. "No daggers here." He pulled it off and tossed it aside.

Her socks were next, and as she wiggled her toes, he watched them with fascination, and the glow in his amber eyes intensified. "You have such elegant toes."

She didn't know that toes could be elegant, but it sounded like a compliment. "Thank you."

"You're welcome. I wasn't sure how you would take it. I'm glad that you considered it a compliment."

Was she wrong to assume that it was?

"What else could it have meant? Am I wrong to think that elegance is a good thing?

"It is, but different cultures have different attitudes toward beauty. Perhaps the Kra-ell consider hobbit feet sexy."

As Jade snorted out a laugh, she was glad that she'd already swallowed the sip of vodka she'd taken, or she would've sprayed him with it.

"I don't think that even hobbits find other hobbit feet sexy. What with all those thick, hairy toes."

His lips curling in a smile, he patted the pockets of her cargo pants. "I wasn't sure you'd get the reference." He pulled out a dagger from one of the pockets. "Why are you carrying so many daggers on you?"

"Where would I put them? The pillowcase?"

"Good point." He leaned over her and unbuckled her belt. "What did you do with the sword?" He curled his fingers under the band and pulled without bothering with the zipper.

"I put it under the bed in my cabin." She lifted her bottom to let him tug them down past her hips.

The moment he exposed her panties, his nostrils flared again, and he closed his eyes as he inhaled. "You smell divine."

She chuckled. "Since the Kra-ell were supposedly created with the help of the gods' genes, I'm part god, and I should smell like one."

He opened his eyes and smiled. "That's not what I meant."

"I know." She took another sip from her vodka. "I'm curious about that godly sexual prowess you boasted about."

"Not godly. Immortal, and it's coming up."

"Same difference."

He pressed a kiss to her mound over her panties, took another sniff, and leaned up. "Lift your arms for me."

"I can't. I'm holding my drink."

He snatched it from her hand and put it on the coffee table. "Lift your arms."

A part of her bristled at the command, but another part, the lazy one enjoying their playfulness, purred like a kitten.

She did as he asked, and his breath caught as he pulled her Henley shirt over her head. "I didn't expect such a nice surprise. No bra."

Her nipples pebbled under his intense gaze. "Why would I wear one?"

"To protect these ripe berries from the cold." He cupped both with his warm palms. "Alternatively, you can hire my services. I will walk behind you and warm them for you." He lifted one palm and closed his lips around the hard peak.

Stifling a moan, she threaded her fingers through his hair. "It would be very awkward to walk around like that, but it would speak of your devotion to me."

He let go of her nipple and lifted his eyes to hers. "Do you want my devotion? Or are you only interested in my body?"

"I'm interested in the whole package, and I shouldn't be."

"Why not?"

"Why not indeed?" She leaned and reached for his shirt. "Lift your arms."

PHINAS

*A*s Phinas lifted his arms, he wondered if Jade had been holding on to the glass for so long to keep herself from taking over.

He couldn't give her the fight for dominance her kind found so exciting or maybe even needed to get going, but he wished he could.

No, that wasn't true.

A little pretend wrestling could be fun, but he wouldn't have enjoyed scratching, biting, and a real fight. He'd never used his superior strength to subdue a woman, and it didn't appeal to him, even if it turned her on.

Perhaps this was a foolish attempt on both their parts, and despite the mutual attraction, they were sexually incompatible.

It would be a shame since his attraction to her went beyond the physical. Surprisingly, he enjoyed her company more than anyone else's, and that was saying a lot.

Kalugal and Rufsur were like brothers to him, but the truth was that he often felt like the third wheel in their bromance. Still, he would give his life for either of them, and he would also die defending the rest of the men and the clan.

His brothers by blood were a different story. He wouldn't lift a finger to save any of them. If his poor mother could hear him, she would turn in her grave, but she didn't know what monsters they had grown up to be.

Fortunately for her, she hadn't seen them after they'd turned thirteen and had been taken away from the Dormants' enclosure.

She would have been horrified.

As Phinas's shirt hit the floor and Jade put her hands on his chest, the past receded to where it should have stayed, a dark corner of his mind that he didn't visit often.

"You have a beautiful body." She ran her hands down his chest, stopping short of his belt and moving to his arms. "I love how bulky you are."

He chuckled. "Muscular is a better term. Bulky usually means fat."

A smile lifted one corner of her mouth. "Is that one more of those cultural differences you were referring to? Perhaps we should stop talking and let our bodies do it for us. They speak a universal language, and they don't care about our different cultures."

Phinas wished that was true.

"Does it bother you that you are stronger than me?" he asked.

Her hands stilled. "I thought it would, but it doesn't. I'm learning a new way to be intimate with a male. Who knows? Maybe I'll like the gentle style better. The Mother knows I've struggled and fought enough. I long for tranquility."

It was a beautiful sentiment but probably unattainable for Jade.

He doubted she was capable of being tranquil. With the rage simmering just below the surface, and the pain and grief still ravaging her soul, she probably could only find tranquility in her final place of rest.

Phinas could understand that better than most.

Despite how easy and peaceful his life was since running away with Kalugal and the rest of their platoon, he was never at ease, never tranquil, and he suspected that was true for all of them.

They had killed, and there was no coming back from that, no matter the circumstances. Every life he'd taken had cost him a piece of his soul.

Plastering a smile on his face, he looked into Jade's expressive eyes. "Naturally, I hope you'll enjoy this more than anything you've experienced before."

"I admire your confidence. If I do enjoy this, though, don't tell anyone. This is an experiment, and I'm not supposed to enjoy it."

Phinas hoped Jade was just teasing, but he suspected she'd spoken the truth and thought of him as a novelty she wanted to try.

If he didn't care for her, it wouldn't have bothered him, but he did, and he wanted her to be interested in him as a person and not an immortal body to take on a test run.

Then again, hadn't that been precisely what he had promised her? To show her how immortals made love?

"Who would I tell?" he echoed her words.

"Who, indeed." She leaned toward him and kissed him with surprising tenderness.

He let her explore his mouth at her leisure for long moments, but when her long tongue wrapped around his fang, his arousal kicked up a notch, and his patience ran out.

With a groan, he leaned away, wrapped his arms around her narrow waist, and lifted her off the couch. "Tonight, I want to make love to you on a comfortable mattress."

As he shifted her weight so one arm was around her waist

and the other under her knees, she wound her arm around his neck. "I will always remember that wood bench fondly. It was our first time."

He groaned. "Please erase it from your memory." He carried her to the bedroom and put her down on the bed. "That one doesn't count. Tonight, is our first real time."

"If you say so." She stretched her arms over her head. "Show me that prowess."

Kicking his boots off, he pushed his fatigues down along with the undershorts and prowled over to her.

"So amiable," he teased as he got on top of her, letting her bear his weight. "So beautiful." He lowered his head slowly and kissed her.

JADE

*P*hinas's body felt good on top of hers, but Jade's instincts screamed for her to flip them around and pin him down.

That was what she would have done with a Kra-ell male, and if he was strong enough, he wouldn't have let her pin him down for long, and she would have been back under him in a split second. The game would have continued until they both got either exhausted by the struggle, madly turned on, or both.

It couldn't work with Phinas, though. If she pinned him down, he wouldn't be able to get free, and that would be the end of the game. He would feel humiliated, and his arousal would deflate. That was what had happened to the Kra-ell males she'd invited to her bed who couldn't overpower her.

Fighting the instinct, she forced herself to remain still and just experience the pleasure of the closeness.

Closeness.

She hadn't felt that with any male she'd been with.

Kra-ell sex was intense and furious—instinct driven. It didn't leave space for feelings or even thoughts.

The realization that this was more than just sex hit her like a bolt of lightning and disturbed her down to her core.

Phinas's alienness allowed her to transcend convention and regard him as more than a contributor of sperm for conception. She liked him and enjoyed his company, which she'd only experienced before with a handful of Kra-ell females.

To be honest, she'd always considered Kra-ell males inferior, and therefore not worthy of her friendship. She'd cared for the males of her tribe and enjoyed playing sex games with them, but they'd never been her friends.

Phinas was a descendant of the gods and a leader of his men, which made him her equal.

Letting go of her mouth, he lifted his head and looked into her eyes. "Are you with me? You don't seem like you are into this."

"I am more than I should be." She lowered her arms and folded them over his muscular back. "I like you, Phinas. I consider you a friend."

He frowned. "A friend with benefits, I hope."

Jade shook her head. "You don't know what this means to me. It's normal for me to seek the benefits part with a male. It's not normal for me to befriend one. I can only do that because I consider you my equal."

Frowning, he looked at her for a long moment before nodding. "I think I get it. This is one of those cultural differences we will need to work on." He dipped his head and kissed her softly. "Not right now, though. Stop thinking and just let yourself feel."

As he slid down her body and took her nipple in his mouth, sucking on it gently, Jade threaded her fingers in his short hair and closed her eyes.

He spent a few more moments giving equal attention to

her other stiff peak. Then he slid further down her body until he was facing her center.

She'd heard about the strange human mating custom of orally pleasuring each other, but since it wasn't conducive to conception, it wasn't something she or the males she'd been with ever tried.

Lodging his broad shoulders between her spread thighs, he lifted her legs. He positioned them over his shoulders, further exposing her to his heated gaze.

She lifted on her forearms, fascinated by what he was about to do.

It was a strange sensation to be gazed upon down there, but it wasn't unpleasant. It sent a zing of pleasure through her that was all about anticipation.

"Ever since I smelled the sweet scent of your desire, I wanted to taste you."

She chuckled. "I doubt there is anything sweet about me."

"Even a prickly pear is sweet on the inside." He lowered his head, and his breath on her sensitive flesh felt like a prelude to pleasure.

She was about to be kissed there for the first time, and her core thrummed with excitement.

He didn't kiss her, though. Instead, he turned his head and dragged his lips along her inner thigh, his fangs scraping the soft skin and adding a touch of danger to his ministrations.

As more moisture gathered in response to his teasing, Phinas inhaled deeply and closed his eyes. "Paradise. That's what you smell like."

He flicked his tongue over her lower lips, and when he flattened it and dragged it upward to where she was the most sensitive, her hips arched off the bed, and as he closed his lips over that nubbin of pleasure, she cried out.

He sucked softly at first and then harder, and when it

became too much, he let go and thrust that talented tongue of his inside of her.

Her fingers threaded into his hair, but despite the haze of pleasure, she still had enough presence of mind to let go before she tore out fistfuls of his hair, repaying him with pain for the pleasure he was giving her.

Unable to hold still, Jade arched up, taking more of his tongue inside of her, and as he growled his approval, the vibrations threatened to send her over the edge.

Phinas alternated between thrusting his tongue into her, flicking it over that nubbin, and lapping at her juices while making sounds that belonged to a beast.

When his fangs scraped over her soft flesh, the implied threat snapped the coil inside of her, and she climaxed with a shout.

PHINAS

*I*t was a thing of beauty to watch Jade fall apart, and Phinas had a feeling that she'd never been pleasured like that before.

He loved being the first to introduce her to the pleasures of the tongue, and he hoped there would be many more opportunities for a repeat performance.

Sucking and licking until her tremors subsided, Phinas wrung every last drop of pleasure out of her, and when the last of them rocked through her, he kissed her petals one more time, put her limp legs down, and came over her.

"Hello, gorgeous." He kissed her, his tongue finding her wicked one and wrapping around it.

She kissed him back, her hands roving over his back gently, almost lovingly.

Where was the ferocious Kra-ell leader who he'd feared would scratch him, bite him? Not that he would mind a bite or two as long as she didn't suck him dry.

In fact, he was looking forward to experiencing it. He wanted her to drink from him.

Would his immortal blood taste good to her?

Would it provide her with more vitality than the blood of animals?

How much would she take?

Would he be able to stop her if she took too much?

As trepidation ignited his arousal, Phinas wondered what was wrong with him. That shouldn't be a turn-on. Besides, he trusted Jade despite barely knowing her.

Above all, she was honorable and would never break his trust if she could help it.

She kissed him back, and as he dragged his shaft through her wetness, the scent of her arousal intensified, and as he eased into her, he found her surprisingly tight for a female who had given birth three times.

He regarded her with concern, searching her face for discomfort, but all he saw in her expression was bliss.

In no time, her sheath stretched to accommodate his girth, and as he seated himself fully inside of her, he had the absurd notion that he had finally found his home.

Resting his forehead against hers, he began to move, rocking into her gently at first, then a little faster when she curled her arms around his neck and lifted her lips to his for a kiss.

Did the Kra-ell enjoy kissing? Or was that a first for her as well?

She seemed to know what she was doing, so maybe it wasn't, but then it didn't require much practice or even imagination to know how to kiss.

As she lifted her hips to meet him halfway, he banded his arms around her slim frame and alternated between shallow, short thrusts and longer, deeper ones. Jade kept the rhythm with him, adjusting to his tempo in perfect harmony.

She was right.

Their bodies knew all the steps to this intimate dance, and their cultural differences didn't matter.

They moved together, faster and faster, their sweat-slicked bodies locked in a tight embrace as if neither of them ever wanted to let go, and as the tension inside of him tightened, he licked her neck and struck with his fangs.

Jade cried out, but not in pain, and as her tight sheath spasmed around his shaft, he erupted inside of her and kept coming for what seemed like forever.

When he stopped shuddering, he retracted his fangs, licked the puncture wounds closed, and lifted his head to look at her.

Her eyes were closed, and her lips were curved up in a relaxed smile he'd never seen on her beautiful face before. The hardness was gone, and she looked almost soft.

"Jade?" he whispered.

She didn't answer, and when he gently pulled out of her, she still didn't move or open her eyes.

She hadn't blacked out the other time, but maybe she had now. He'd pumped her with more venom than he'd ever dared to release into a female, even the few immortals whose beds he'd been invited to.

Worry tightening his chest, he stilled and listened to her heart. Finding the beat strong and steady, he released a relieved breath.

He wouldn't have wanted to harm any female with an excess of venom, but especially Jade.

Over the few days he'd known her, she'd become dear to him.

He cared about her.

After cleaning himself in the bathroom, he brought a couple of washcloths and cleaned her as best he could. With that done, he climbed in bed, pulled the blanket over them, and wrapped his arms around her.

"Goodnight, sweetheart." He kissed her forehead and chuckled softly.

If Jade were awake, he wouldn't have dared call her that. The prickly leader didn't want anyone to know that she was sweet on the inside, and she would have taken that as an offense.

YAMANU

*A*lthough the day was cold—check that, the day was freezing—Yamanu leaned against the railing outside the bridge with a big smile plastered on his face.

There should be a law against having so much fun and getting paid for it.

His reunion with Mey had been spectacular. Well, since they were technically still reuniting, it still was.

The ship was much nicer than he'd imagined, and the cabin he and Mey were staying in was fancier than any hotel suite he'd ever stayed in, and he'd been to some nice ones.

The midnight feast the humans had put together for them last night had been the icing on the cake. It had been a long time since he had eaten that well.

Mey and he prepared their meals at home, but neither of them was any good at it. Not that he would ever say that to Mey. She fancied herself a good cook.

Callie's restaurant was amazing, but the waiting line was insane, and it wasn't the same as home-cooked.

As a helicopter passed by a mile or so off the starboard side, Yamanu's happy grin turned into a frown. As instructed, they were keeping close to shore, but no one had considered an air attack. Igor wouldn't send fighter jets to attack them. That would draw too much attention, but he could send a helicopter with a few commandos and a rocket launcher.

Stepping into the bridge, he tapped Olsson's shoulder. "Captain, can I have a word, please?"

Nodding, the captain followed him back outside and closed the hatch behind him.

"Is there a problem?"

"There might be," Yamanu said. "Our working assumption is that the *Aurora* will be followed by an armed vessel, possibly a Russian cruiser, and that we would not be in danger until we are too far from land for the rescuers responding to our distress signal to get to us before the aggressor is done plucking the passengers he is after out of the water."

A short nod from Olsson was an acknowledgment and a signal for him to continue.

"I am not trying to second-guess Kian and Turner, but this close to shore, it wouldn't take much for anyone to put together a band of mercenaries, and either land them on the ship's helipad or have them rappel down on board and attempt to take over the ship. In fact, they could have another helicopter providing cover for them, shooting at the defenders." Yamanu paused and looked questioningly at the captain.

Olsson considered his answer for a spell. "You are correct. As per the instructions we were given, the *Aurora* is only about ten miles offshore. A helicopter taking off from a nearby location could reach us within fifteen to twenty minutes, leaving enough fuel to execute an operation like that and fly back." The captain gestured in the direction of the coast and then pointed ahead to where the ship was heading. "But as they would be uninvited guests, we can make things very difficult for them." The captain's tone and posture hinted at a harnessed excitement at the prospect of such an altercation.

The guy must miss his military days.

"How would you make it difficult for them?" Yamanu asked.

"For a helicopter to land on the helipad, they need us to keep our heading and speed constant, which we obviously won't do. They also need to use their ILS, i.e. Instrument Landing System. If your guy activates the scrambler, they won't be able to use it, and most of their avionics will also be rendered useless. To your concern about a helicopter landing on the ship, I believe we can rule that out."

Yamanu could practically hear the but coming up.

"Having said that, unless the signal scrambler's footprint is larger than I think, it won't be enough to prevent a couple of helicopters from approaching us to weapons' range and launching a shoulder-fired missile directly at the bridge, something that will effectively disable the *Aurora*."

This was not a scenario that Yamanu had considered, and he was certain that neither had Kian or Turner.

"I need to contact my boss and let him know."

Olsson lifted a hand to stop him. "Before you do, I need you to know that our radar will be able to pick up any approaching boat, ship, or aircraft. If they don't identify themselves well in advance, we will know that we are dealing with foes. That should give us a few minutes to take defensive action, which may be all we need."

It was good to know that the bridge would have a forewarning, but if a missile could be launched at the bridge, that wouldn't do them much good.

"If they fire missiles at the ship, what would be their maximum range?"

"For a shoulder-launched missile, it is no more than one kilometer."

"That doesn't sound like much. Are you sure?"

"I'm unaware of any weapons that can be used from a helicopter and have an effective range exceeding that." The captain tilted his head. "Can your scrambler cover a radius of one kilometer around the ship?"

Yamanu nodded. "That is still within its range, so if we identify a threat, we can activate it and render the aircraft's avionics and targeting equipment useless."

"Precisely." The captain offered him a nod.

Yamanu ran his hand over his clean-shaven jaw. "I want to play it safe. I will post armed guards here and on the decks below around the clock, and I will have the device with a trained man on the bridge around the clock so it can be readily activated on a moment's notice."

If the circumstances surrounding this trip were not so extraordinary and unusual, Captain Olsson would have never allowed anyone to presume to do anything aboard his ship without his approval. Given the tightening of the man's lips, Yamanu realized that he should have phrased it as a request and not a statement.

There was no reason to antagonize the man.

"If that meets with your approval, captain."

The tightness eased, and Olsson nodded. "Very well. Make it so."

"Thank you, captain." Yamanu offered Olsson his hand. "It's a pleasure working with you."

"The pleasure is all mine."

KIAN

"Good thinking. Keep me updated." Onegus ended the call and turned to Kian and Turner. "I'm surprised that none of us had considered an aerial attack."

"I did," Turner said. "But I dismissed it given how congested the Baltic Sea is and how narrow. The response from shore would be immediate."

Kian opened his water bottle and took a sip. "What will happen if he takes out the bridge?"

Despite Turner's assertion that he'd thought about the possibility of an attack from above, Kian was pretty sure he hadn't. Yamanu's observation and the captain's response had caught them all off guard.

None of them, including Turner, had considered the possibility of Igor trying to take over the ship by blowing up the bridge.

"When the ship signals distress, military jets from the country closest to it will respond within minutes. He's not going to risk that."

"I disagree," Onegus said. "He doesn't care if they blow up

the helicopter and its crew. The military jets will destroy the threat and turn around. Until the rescue ships arrive, he can board the ship from another vessel and take over."

Turner smiled victoriously. "Which means that he would have to follow the ship with a naval vessel, which is what we have been discussing all along. It doesn't make sense for him to deploy a helicopter and a ship. He will want to attract as little attention as possible, and he will not attack while the *Aurora* is in the Baltic and staying close to shore."

"I agree." Kian pulled out his phone. "I wonder if Roni has picked up on any vessel following them."

The guy had spent all day hacking into a naval tracking system and working on some program that he claimed would help them to identify a pursuer among the hundreds of vessels crowding the Baltic Sea.

"We are in the war room," he said when Roni answered. "Are you ready to show us what you've been working on?"

"I'll be there in a couple of minutes. I stopped at the café to grab a cup of coffee and a sandwich. Anyone want anything?"

Kian lifted his gaze in an unspoken question to Turner and Onegus, who shook their heads. "We are all good. Thanks. See you here."

"Do you know what he's been working on?" Onegus asked.

"He said he'll explain when he gets here. He said he's designing a program to do the tracking for us."

Several minutes passed until Roni walked in with a cup of coffee in one hand, a paper bag in the other, and a laptop tucked under his arm.

"Good evening, gentlemen." He sat at the conference table, opened his laptop, and turned it toward them so they could see it. "Take a look at the screen. There are literally hundreds of vessels sharing the same shipping lanes in the

Baltic right now. Many are heading into or out of existing ports. While most travel up and down the length of the Baltic, a considerable number are crisscrossing it from shore to shore. We are dealing with ferries, ships from several navies in all sizes, fishing boats, yachts, and of course, commercial traffic of goods and commodities."

As Roni paused to take a sip of his coffee, Kian observed the dots in an array of colors filling the entire screen and wondered how they could identify their pursuer in such dense traffic.

"I hacked into NATO's naval surveillance system," Roni said as he unwrapped his sandwich. "So the screen is also showing the whereabouts and movements of naval ships. The civilian systems tracking sea traffic don't show that." Taking a bite of his sandwich, Roni touched the screen and highlighted one of the dots. "This is the *Aurora*. As you can see, there is a huge number of ships that could potentially be our pursuer. When the *Aurora* starts her zigzagging pattern, the number of potentials will naturally decrease, and at some point, only a single vessel will be left that's clearly following her odd course. That will be our pursuer."

Leaning back, Kian looked at the screen. "You can't watch the screen around the clock. You need to assign people to keep watch in shifts and alert us as soon as the pursuer is identified. As soon as we have confirmation, we will need to alert Captain Olsson and our people on the ship as well."

Roni smiled smugly. "Way ahead of you, boss. I wrote an algorithm that monitors the data and continuously eliminates from view any ship that is clearly not a suspect based on its course, heading, and speed over time. It is set up to notify me when only ten possible targets are left and from then on, whenever one more is eliminated. Given the vast number of ships, I don't think we'll have identification by morning, meaning their evening. I estimate that we will need at least another full day before the algorithm narrows the field of possible pursuers down to only ten and then between five to ten hours to narrow it to a single vessel. This will greatly depend on Olsson's heading and course changes at the time."

Smiling, Turner shook his head. "Good work, Roni. I should have thought of that, but given that I don't know much about programming, I probably couldn't have."

Basking in the compliment, Roni squared his shoulders. "Thank you. But with me around, you don't need to know anything about programming."

Onegus cast Turner a glance full of mock horror. "Look what you've done. He was full of himself before. Now he'll get too big for his emperor chair."

When Turner arched a brow, Kian explained, "He's referring to Roni's enormous chair in the lab."

Despite how closely Turner had often worked with them, he'd never visited the lab.

Kian clapped Roni on the back. "I want to know when the count is down to ten, and from that point on, unless it's in the middle of the night, bring the laptop with you and join us here."

"You've got it, boss."

JADE

*J*ade woke up in Phinas's arms, calmer and more relaxed than she'd ever felt. Not even as a little girl in her mother's tribe had she felt so safe and cared for.

It was an illusion, a remnant from the euphoric trip Phinas had sent her on, but she wasn't ready to strap herself to the tether of reality yet.

She'd actually managed to sever the tether for once and soar carefree and happy over the clouds. Were the alien landscapes she'd passed over real? Was it another dimension that was only accessible through a venom trip?

The aliens had been friendly, waving and smiling as she passed them by. Did they know who she was?

Maybe what she'd seen were the fields of the brave, and the males waving at her had been her sons? The aliens didn't look like them, but then who said that the soul retained the same shape on the other side?

Perhaps the venom had opened a portal in her brain that allowed her a glimpse of what lay beyond the veil.

As the thought ushered another wave of tranquility and

contentment, Jade snuggled closer into Phinas's solid chest and circled her arms around his substantial bulk.

"Muscularity," she murmured. "Not bulkiness."

He opened his eyes and smiled at her. "What are you mumbling under your breath?"

"Nothing important." She kissed his jaw and closed her eyes. "I'm not ready to get up. I feel too good to face the day."

She'd never spent the night with a male, but Phinas's venom had knocked her out, so she could use that as an excuse for enjoying the warmth and connection for a little longer.

Evidently, the venom of an immortal male was much more potent than that of the Kra-ell, and she was still light-headed and a little drunk from it. But what was really price-less was the incredible sense of well-being.

Phinas's venom was a miracle drug.

Jade wished hers had a similar effect on him, but so far, she had refrained from biting Phinas. Like goddesses, immortal females didn't have fangs and venom, so he wasn't used to that and might find it emasculating. It was probably difficult enough for him to deal with her superior strength.

He smoothed his finger over her forehead. "Why are you frowning? You looked so blissed out only moments ago."

"It's nothing." She turned around and presented him with her ass. "Let's go back to sleep."

As his erection prodded her bottom, he groaned, and she smiled.

"Do you think I can sleep like this?" He rubbed himself against her. "You have the most spectacular ass." His hand cupped her breast. "Am I bothering you?"

"Not at all." She covered his hand with hers. "I've never spent the night with a male. They knew they had to leave as soon as we were done."

A breath left him in a whoosh. "This is my cabin, but if

you are uncomfortable, I can leave. There is another bedroom."

"I don't want you to leave." She pushed her bottom into his hard length. "I like this. But if anyone asks, it's the venom's fault."

He chuckled. "Who is going to ask?"

"Kagra."

"Tell her to mind her own business."

"That's exactly what I'll do." Jade turned around and cupped Phinas's stubble-covered cheeks. "Kiss me again."

He smiled. "Do you like it when I kiss you?"

"If I didn't like it, I wouldn't have asked for it, now would I?"

"No, ma'am, you wouldn't."

COMING UP NEXT
The Children of the Gods Book 69
DARK ALLIANCE
Turbulent Waters

To read the first 3 chapters JOIN the VIP club at
ITLUCAS.COM —To find out what's included in your free
membership flip to the last page.

When a dangerous foe turns the tables on the clan, complicating the Kra-ell rescue operation in unforeseeable ways, Kian and his crew bet all on a brilliant misdirection.

On board the Aurora, Phinas and Jade brace for battle while enjoying a few stolen moments of passion.

Drawn to the woman he sees behind the aloof leader, Phinas realizes that what has started as a calculated political move has evolved into a deepening sense of companionship.

Jade finds reprieve in Phinas's arms, but duty and tradition make it difficult for her to accept that what she feels for him is more than just gratitude and desire.

After all, the Kra-ell don't believe in love.

Dear reader,

Thank you for reading the Children of the Gods.

As an independent author, I rely on your support to spread the word. So if you enjoyed the story, please share your experience with others, and if it isn't too much trouble, I would greatly appreciate a brief review on Amazon.

Love & happy reading,

Isabell

Also by I. T. Lucas

PERFECT MATCH
VAMPIRE'S CONSORT
KING'S CHOSEN
CAPTAIN'S CONQUEST

THE CHILDREN OF THE GODS SERIES SETS

BOOKS 1-3: DARK STRANGER TRILOGY—INCLUDES A BONUS SHORT STORY: **THE FATES TAKE A VACATION**
BOOKS 4-6: DARK ENEMY TRILOGY —INCLUDES A BONUS SHORT STORY—**THE FATES' POST-WEDDING CELEBRATION**
BOOKS 7-10: DARK WARRIOR TETRALOGY
BOOKS 11-13: DARK GUARDIAN TRILOGY
BOOKS 14-16: DARK ANGEL TRILOGY
BOOKS 17-19: DARK OPERATIVE TRILOGY
BOOKS 20-22: DARK SURVIVOR TRILOGY
BOOKS 23-25: DARK WIDOW TRILOGY
BOOKS 26-28: DARK DREAM TRILOGY
BOOKS 29-31: DARK PRINCE TRILOGY
BOOKS 32-34: DARK QUEEN TRILOGY
BOOKS 35-37: DARK SPY TRILOGY
BOOKS 38-40: DARK OVERLORD TRILOGY
BOOKS 41-43: DARK CHOICES TRILOGY
BOOKS 44-46: DARK SECRETS TRILOGY
BOOKS 47-49: DARK HAVEN TRILOGY
BOOKS 50-52: DARK POWER TRILOGY
BOOKS 53-55: DARK MEMORIES TRILOGY
BOOKS 56-58: DARK HUNTER TRILOGY
BOOKS 59-61:DARK GOD TRILOGY
BOOKS 62-64: DARK WHISPERS TRILOGY

MEGA SETS
INCLUDE CHARACTER LISTS

THE CHILDREN OF THE GODS: BOOKS 1-6
THE CHILDREN OF THE GODS: BOOKS 6.5-10

TRY THE CHILDREN OF THE GODS SERIES ON AUDIBLE
2 FREE audiobooks with your new Audible subscription!

FOR EXCLUSIVE PEEKS AT UPCOMING RELEASES & A FREE COMPANION BOOK

JOIN MY *VIP CLUB* AND GAIN ACCESS TO THE VIP PORTAL AT
ITLUCAS.COM
(http://eepurl.com/blMTpD)

INCLUDED IN YOUR FREE MEMBERSHIP:

- **FREE** CHILDREN OF THE GODS COMPANION BOOK 1 (INCLUDES PART 1 OF GODDESS'S CHOICE)
- **FREE** NARRATION OF GODDESS'S CHOICE—BOOK 1 IN THE CHILDREN OF THE GODS ORIGINS SERIES.
- PREVIEW CHAPTERS OF UPCOMING RELEASES.
- AND OTHER EXCLUSIVE CONTENT OFFERED ONLY TO MY VIPS.

If you're already a subscriber, you'll receive a download link for my next book's preview chapters in the new release announcement email. If you are not getting my emails, your provider is sending them to your junk folder, and you are missing out on **important updates, side characters' portraits, additional content, and other goodies.** To fix that, add isabell@itlucas.com to your email contacts or your email VIP list.

Made in the USA
Middletown, DE
28 March 2023